Looking for Love

ROSIE HARRIS

arrow books

Published by Arrow Books in 2004

5 7 9 10 8 6

First published in the United Kingdom in 2003 by
William Heinemann

Arrow Books
The Random House Group Limited
20 Vauxhall Bridge Road, London, SW1V 2SA

Addresses for companies within The Random House Group Limited
can be found at: www.randomhouse.co.uk/offices.htm

The Random House Group Limited Reg. No. 954009

www.randomhouse.co.uk

A CIP catalogue record for this book
is available from the British Library

The Random House Group Limited supports The Forest Stewardship
Council (FSC®), the leading international forest certification organisation.
Our books carrying the FSC label are printed on FSC® certified paper.
FSC is the only forest certification scheme endorsed by the leading
environmental organisations, including Greenpeace. Our
paper procurement policy can be found at
www.randomhouse.co.uk/environment

ISBN 9780099460374

Typeset by Deltatype Ltd, Birkenhead, Merseyside
Printed and bound in Great Britain by Clays Ltd, St Ives PLC

Chapter One

Abbie Martin knew she ought to be in bed and asleep, but tomorrow, Sunday, would be the 18th July 1926, and it would be her eleventh birthday, and she couldn't sleep for worrying about whether or not she would be getting the wooden hoop she'd set her heart on. If she didn't get one this year then she'd be too old to have one at all.

Her friend Sandra Lewis, who lived in the same street, had a lovely red hoop, and Abbie had begged her mammy to buy her a blue one. Then, when they played together, they wouldn't have to take it in turns to share Sandra's. They'd be able to run races or bowl them along side by side and pretend they were riding bikes or that they were sitting alongside one another in a posh motor car.

'You can think yourself lucky if you get a new pair of shoes for your birthday,' her mammy had said caustically. 'We've not got money to waste on rubbish like hoops. It's all right for Sandra, her dad's in regular work and so is her mam.'

'I wish my dad would come home,' Abbie murmured wistfully.

'What dad?' Ellen Martin snapped. 'You never even knew the bugger. One look at you and he was off! He skedaddled when you were only a couple of days old. He said he was off to join the

1

Army and that was the last any of us ever heard of him.'

'Father Patrick said he still might come back one day, if we all pray hard enough,' Abbie said, her lower lip trembling.

'Shurrup with your daft talk!' Ellen's mouth tightened and the wrinkles around her dull brown eyes increased. 'He's gone for good, and after all this time I wouldn't even give him house room if he came home and stood on the doorstep and begged me to take him in.'

Abbie looked at her mother, wide-eyed. How could she say that, she wondered. If her dad ever did come back then she was sure her mammy would be happy again. She might even kiss and cuddle Abbie like Sandra's mammy cuddled Sandra. And if her dad came back she was sure he would take her on his knee and kiss her and tell her how much he loved her, because that was what Sandra's dad was always doing; it was what dads did.

Abbie's dad would buy her a hoop, too, even though she was almost too old for such a plaything, she was sure of that. Hoops and tops and dolls were really only for little kids. When she went back to school in September it would be skipping-ropes, roller skates if you were lucky enough to be able to afford them, and swopping cigarette cards and comics.

Abbie was so desperate to have her own hoop that she'd even plucked up the courage to ask Billy, her eldest brother, who was twenty-six and worked down at the Docks helping to unload cargo from the boats, if he'd buy her one. He'd not even bothered to reply, simply cuffed her around the ears, told her to grow up, and then shoved her out of the back door into the dark jowler, which separated their house in Bostock Street from the houses in Kew Street, with the toe of his boot.

Only her other brother Sam, who was almost three years older than her and would be fourteen next January, seemed to understand how much she wanted a blue hoop. Even though he had started working on Saturdays as a delivery boy for the ironmonger in Scotland Road, he still hadn't got enough money saved up to buy her one.

'It will soon be the school holidays and I'll be working every day in August, so if you don't get a hoop for your birthday then I might be able to manage to buy you one – if Mam doesn't take all my money off me,' he promised.

Abbie moved away from the window the moment she saw her brother Billy and her mother come staggering down the street, their arms linked as they swayed drunkenly from side to side.

They were an odd-looking couple. Billy was short and as skinny as a beanpole, while her mammy was twice his size. They looked alike, though, because they both had lank brown hair that was so thin that in places you could see the shiny pink of their scalps through it. Sam had the same colour hair as them, but his was as thick as a brush, and short and shiny.

Abbie's own hair was quite different. It was jet black, very thick and very straight with a heavy fringe. When it grew too long her mammy used to stick a pudding basin on her head and then chop off any hair sticking out beneath the rim.

In the twilight, with her broad shoulders, stout legs, muscular arms, and a greasy old cap on her head the same as Billy's, her mammy looked like a big strong man. She drank like a man, too, Abbie thought with a shudder.

Every Friday night, as soon as they were paid, both her mammy and Billy went drinking, trailing from one pub to the next in Scotland Road and Great Homer Street until closing time. And they were back in the pubs again on Saturday night, if there was any money left after they'd been to the pawnshop to get their Sunday-best clothes out.

On Sunday they went to Mass if they'd sobered up enough. Her mammy would be dressed up in her best brown coat, brown felt cloche hat and brown lace-up shoes, whatever the weather, and Billy would be wearing his shiny navy suit with a white shirt and spotted red tie.

They'd all be on their knees, praying for their souls, and her mammy and Billy kowtowing to Father Patrick by slipping a shiny bright tanner into the collection plate, even if there was nothing at home for Sunday dinner. And her mammy always lit a penny candle to the memory of her daughter, Audrey, who'd been a year younger than Billy, but who'd been dead now for about eleven years.

By the following Wednesday all their finery would be back in Solly Greenberg's pawnshop. Abbie's mammy needed the money to buy some scrag-end of mutton from Bank's meat shop, and some potatoes, onions and carrots from the market, to make a pot of scouse that had to last them all until payday came round again.

On payday they always redeemed their clothes, ready for Sunday, and then started all over again.

Abbie couldn't understand why Billy didn't find himself a girlfriend and get married instead of going out drinking with their mam all the time. She'd talked about it to her friend Sandra.

'He's like Michael Ryan,' Sandra told her solemnly. 'He's about the same age as your Billy and he doesn't have a girlfriend either.'

'But he doesn't go out drinking with his mam, does he!'

'No, he goes drinking on his own or with his dad whenever Paddy Ryan's ship is in dock.' Sandra giggled, 'I think Michael Ryan's ever so handsome, don't you?'

Abbie shrugged. 'He's old, like our Billy,' she said dismissively.

'Your Sam isn't old, though,' Sandra grinned.

Abbie didn't answer. Sam was special, and she didn't want to talk about him or share her thoughts about him with anyone.

If it had been anyone else but Sam she would have been happy to talk about him, and tease Sandra about having a crush on him, but not when it was Sam. She wanted to keep him all to herself. He was the only person who really loved her, who cuddled her and comforted her when she was lonely or sad.

Sandra was her very best friend and Sam's pal, Peter Ryan, was a good friend as well. She liked it when the four of them played together, but they didn't understand her or love her like Sam did.

Although it was very late it still wasn't properly dark, and the July night was so warm that the poky little back-bedroom in the small terraced house in Bostock Street was stuffy and airless.

Knowing her mother would be home at any minute, Abbie quickly got ready for bed. She removed her flowered cotton skirt and the shrunken jumper that had once belonged to her brother Sam, and put them over the bedrail. Gingerly, she took off the rubber-soled plimsolls that had also been his until he'd outgrown them. His big toe had gone right through the canvas upper leaving a frayed jagged hole, and sometimes her big toenail caught on it and made her yelp with pain. She had no socks and the plimsolls chafed her ankles because they were too big, and her heels felt sore where they had been rubbed raw.

She still felt hot and sticky, even though she was wearing only her grubby cotton knickers as she scrambled into bed. She pulled the grimy sheet up over her head to try and shut out the sound of raucous voices, as her mammy and Billy came into the house and stumbled into the table in the living room, knocking over a couple of chairs. They'd been out drinking all evening and spent enough money on beer and cigarettes to buy a dozen hoops, she thought sadly.

Abbie trembled as the noise from downstairs became louder, and she burrowed deeper into the bed, but it was no good, she couldn't shut out the racket they were making and she knew it would go on for another hour at least. At present they were only singing and joking, but any moment now they would start argy-bargying with each other, and that's when one or both of them could turn nasty.

Her mammy had a terrible temper when she was riled, and if she came upstairs and found Abbie still awake, even though it was her birthday the next day, she'd still wallop her. Yet how could she sleep when they were kicking up such a din, she thought peevishly.

Sneaking out of bed, she padded across the bare boards to the door. 'Sam, Sam, are you still awake?' she called in a sibilant whisper. 'Can I come in your bed with you?'

'You know you can't! What would happen if our Billy found you in here? Stay in your own bed and curl up and go to sleep before they come upstairs and find you still awake, Abbie,' Sam called back from the room along the passage.

'I can't sleep, Sam!' A sob shook her voice. 'I'm so frightened.'

She knew she was lucky to have a bedroom all to herself, even if it wasn't much bigger than a cupboard. It was at the back of the house, a tiny room built over the scullery, and she felt cut off from the two main bedrooms. She heard Sam's bed-springs creak and the next minute he was padding along the landing towards her room.

'You'd better get back into bed before they come upstairs,' he warned again.

7

'Will you stay with me then? Please, Sam,' she pleaded.

'For a few minutes, but only if you promise to go to sleep.'

'If you cuddle me, then perhaps I might be able to,' she agreed plaintively.

'You'll get me into trouble if Mam or Billy catch me in here so hurry up and go to sleep,' he murmured as he climbed into her bed.

'I will try, Sam.' Abbie's huge blue eyes filled with tears and her mouth trembled as she snuggled into him. 'No one else but you loves me or ever cuddles me.'

He curled up beside her on the narrow iron bedstead, whispering words of comfort as the noise from downstairs became even louder. One minute their mother and Billy were singing at the top of their voices, the next they were viciously cursing each other.

Sam had intended to slip out of Abbie's bed and creep back into his own room before Billy came up to bed, but he was so tired that even though he didn't mean to do so, he dozed off. The next thing he knew, Billy was in the room, hauling him out of the bed by the scruff of his neck and booting him along the passage to the bedroom they shared.

'I've told you before, you little bugger, about running in to that little bitch every time she whimpers. Encourage her, you do. She's always whingeing or whining about something,' he snarled as he stumbled after Sam into their own room.

'You and Mam woke her up with all the noise

8

you were making when you came home and she was frightened,' Sam protested.

'Don't you bloody well answer me back!' Picking up the boot he had just taken off, Billy hurled it in Sam's direction.

Sam ducked and the heavy steel-tipped boot smashed into the window, and there was the sound of breaking glass.

'Now look what you've done, you stupid sod!' Billy grunted.

'What the hell's going on?' Ellen Martin stumbled into the room. Her eyes were bleary, her hair was straggling round her face and there were beer stains down the front of her red cotton blouse and black skirt. 'Was that glass breaking?'

'It's this silly young bugger's fault,' Billy muttered, making a grab at Sam and missing.

'You broke the window when you threw your boot at me,' Sam argued.

Ellen glared at Sam. 'I don't care whose fault it is, you can sodding well mend it and pay for the glass. That will take care of most of the money you earn during your school holiday,' she told him sharply.

'Oh, come on Mam, that's not fair . . .'

'Any more lip and you'll feel my hand round your face,' Billy growled menacingly.

'Shut up, the pair of you,' Ellen bellowed. 'I've had a skinful and I've got a head on me like a bucket, and I need some kip.'

Reeling drunkenly she made her way to her own bedroom at the front of the house, slamming the door shut with such force that the whole place shook.

Belching and reeking of beer, Billy collapsed on the bed fully dressed and still wearing one boot. In a befuddled, drunken stupor he began snoring noisily almost at once.

Sam could hear Abbie sobbing and started to creep out of the room to make sure she was all right, but Billy suddenly snorted violently and sat up. Sam kept perfectly still, clinging on to the edge of the bed as far away from Billy as possible, holding his breath, waiting for him to pass out again.

As soon as he did, Sam made his way back into his sister's bedroom. 'Ssh!' he warned as her sobbing grew louder. 'If Mam hears you then you'll be in for a hiding. Now go to sleep or you won't be able to get up in time for Mass in the morning, and then you'll be in even more trouble.'

Abbie's eleventh birthday started out as one of the most miserable days of her life.

She woke early, dying to find out if her mammy had bought her a hoop after all, but when it was time for Abbie to leave for church, Ellen was still in bed, sleeping off her excesses from the night before.

Abbie didn't know what to do. She couldn't possibly wait until she came home again, so she crept into her mother's bedroom to see if she could waken her. Gently, she kissed her mother's raddled face.

Ellen's hand came up and slapped at her as if

swatting away a fly or a bedbug. Her bleary eyes opened and she stared angrily at Abbie.

'For Christ's sake, Abbie, get off me, let me be,' she screeched as Abbie tried to kiss her again.

Roughly, Ellen freed herself from the two skinny arms that had crept round her neck, and she forcibly pushed Abbie away.

'Can I come in your bed for a quick cuddle, Mammy?' Abbie pleaded. 'It is my birthday, so can I have a cuddle?' she asked again, hopefully.

'Cuddle? At your age! Bugger off and leave me to get some shuteye before I belt you one.'

'It's my birthday, Mammy,' Abbie repeated forlornly. 'You haven't even given me a kiss!'

She stood by the side of the bed, shifting uneasily from one foot to the other, knowing it was dangerous to ask, but she simply had to know. 'Mammy, did you get me a hoop for my birthday?' she asked in a tiny voice that was little more than a whisper.

'Hoop! No, I didn't get you a bloody hoop, I've already told you I haven't money to waste on rubbish.'

'So you got me new shoes, did you? Can I wear them to church?'

'Shoes? I haven't bought you any new shoes, I haven't bought you any bloody thing. Now clear off and leave me in peace.'

Abbie fought to keep back her tears as she called for Sandra so that they could walk to church together as usual. She wished Sandra didn't know it was her birthday, she wished no one in the world knew, then she wouldn't have to explain

11

that her own mammy wasn't giving her any sort of present at all.

Sandra, dressed in a pale blue dress, white socks and black shoes, and with a blue bow in her shining fair hair, was jumping up and down on her doorstep impatiently as Abbie approached. 'Come on, run,' she shouted, 'or we won't have time to look at your present.'

'I haven't got a present,' Abbie muttered, and the tears she had been struggling so hard to hold in check began to slowly trickle from the corner of her eyes and channel their way down her thin cheeks.

'Yes you have,' Sandra giggled, her pretty face wreathed in smiles. She grabbed hold of Abbie's hand and dragged her over the doorstep and into the living room.

It was a light, airy room, where everything was shiny and smelled of lavender furniture-polish. The walls were painted cream and there were flowered curtains and matching cushion covers. There was a vase of artificial roses in the middle of a highly polished table. At each end of the mantelpiece were two white china dogs, and in between them was a big mirror.

'Here,' Sandra grabbed a huge, thin package wrapped up in gaudy paper that was propped up against the wall. 'Happy birthday,' she said as she passed it to Abbie. 'Go on then, open it!' Sandra giggled, her grey eyes sparkling with excitement.

It was such pretty paper that Abbie tried to take it off as carefully as she could, so as not to tear it, but Sandra was impatient for her to see inside the parcel and grabbed one end of the paper and ripped it from top to bottom.

'There!' she exclaimed.

Abbie stared, too choked to speak as she gazed at the wonderful bright-blue hoop. It was exactly what she had set her heart on owning. She couldn't believe her eyes.

'You do like it, don't you?' Sandra asked anxiously. 'Your mam hasn't bought you one as well, has she?'

'It's wonderful,' Abbie breathed, her blue eyes shining, a smile splitting her thin face almost in two. 'It's exactly what I dreamed of having. The best present in the world!'

'Your Sam told me that your mammy was buying you a pair of new shoes,' Sandra commented. 'Why aren't you wearing them?'

The light went out of Abbie's face for a moment. 'Well, she didn't do that either,' she muttered.

'So what did she buy you?'

Abbie didn't answer, simply shook her head.

'You two had better get a move on or you'll be late for church,' Mrs Lewis told them briskly. 'I'll stand your new blue hoop alongside Sandra's red one, Abbie, until you come back.'

Abbie hesitated. Now that she had the hoop in her hands she didn't want to let go of it, in case it was all a dream and it vanished into thin air.

'Come on, Abbie, it will be quite safe with me.'

Reluctantly, Abbie passed it over to Mrs Lewis, but not before she had run her hand all the way round its smooth, shining edge.

Then, on impulse, she flung her arms around

13

Sandra's mother's neck and kissed her fervently on her soft plump cheek.

'Happy birthday, Abbie!' Mo Lewis returned her hug and kissed her on the brow.

Her birthday was going to be special after all, Abbie thought happily, as she and Sandra set off for St Anthony's.

There was more to come. Sam bought her a bar of milk chocolate which she shared out with him, Sandra and Peter Ryan. Peter's mother gave her a bright blue bag, which had a long strap so that she could wear it like a satchel. Inside it was a white handkerchief trimmed with lace with an 'A' embroidered in blue silk in one corner, and a little mirror, and a blue comb.

By the time she went back to her own home, eager to show off all her birthday presents, her mother and Billy were already back from late Mass.

'Put all that rubbish up into your room and help our Sam lay the table,' her mother told her sharply. 'I stuck a chicken in the oven before I went to Mass, seeing as it's your birthday, and it's probably cooked by now.'

Abbie's heart lifted. Her mammy did love her after all, she thought happily, as she cleared away the dirty crockery, the overflowing ashtray and the empty beer bottles.

From a dismal beginning, her eleventh birthday had become the happiest day of her life, Abbie reflected when she went to bed that night, her new blue hoop leaning against the wall where she could reach out and touch it.

Chapter Two

Abbie and Sandra spent every moment they could after school each night playing outside with their hoops. The long July evenings meant that it was often well after nine o'clock before they went home to bed.

Peter often joined them and they'd try and keep up with him, trundling their hoops as he rode up and down Bostock Street on his bike. Abbie, because she was thinner and taller than Sandra, usually managed to do so. When they reached the corner they would wait until Sandra, puffing and panting, her short plump legs aching with the effort, caught them up.

Mo Lewis came out into the road occasionally to make sure they were all right. Sometimes she brought them a jam butty each, or a piece of her home-made seed cake, which Abbie loved but Sandra wouldn't eat because the caraway seeds stuck in her teeth. Maggie Ryan would often join her for a gossip and she never came empty-handed either. She usually brought them some biscuits or a wedge of Wet Nelly.

Sam, too, would join them after he'd finished making deliveries in the Scotland Road area, riding up and down Bostock Street on his delivery bike and circling around them, wobbling like crazy because the big metal basket fastened to the front of his bike made turning in tight circles difficult.

Life had never seemed so wonderful, even though her mammy was forever scolding her. And when school broke up towards the end of July, Abbie looked forward to spending even more time playing out with Sandra and the others.

She was in tears when her mother told her that now the school holidays had started she would be taking Abbie along to work with her each day.

'Why do I have to come with you?' she asked sulkily.

'Our Sam will be working and he won't be able to keep an eye out for you, that's why.'

'I'll be all right on my own. I'll be playing with Sandra and Peter, and Mrs Lewis or Mrs Ryan will give me a butty if I'm hungry.'

'You can stop scrounging off those two,' Ellen Martin said. 'I've told you before to find someone else to play with. We don't want charity off the likes of them!'

'It's not charity,' Abbie protested. 'And if you think it is then let me bring them back home for a scoff, and that will pay them back.'

'Feed that horde! You must be out of your mind. Takes me every penny I earn to put food on the table for my own lot, without feeding the rest of the street,' Ellen snapped. 'You'll come with me, starting Monday morning. You're big enough to give me a hand so let's not hear any more about it.'

Abbie resented having to accompany her

mother to work. Ellen was employed as a cotton picker, and worked along with a dozen other women in one of the huge sheds on the dockside. Their job was to hack open the great canvas-wrapped bales that had been damaged and tease out the cotton inside them into usable strands again.

The damage that was caused by the salt water, whether because of storms or because the bales had accidentally fallen into the sea, was considerable. The cotton, which had already been packed in as tightly as possible, turned into a solid cake once the salt water impregnated it.

When they'd ripped away the outer canvas they then had to hack out the contents using a sharp, curved knife like a cutlass. One slip and there were cut hands and nicked fingers.

Each wedge they hacked out had then to be torn apart into strands, until it was once more as soft and downy as when it had been first picked from the bushes in southern America.

It was back-breaking work and their hands at the end of the day were raw, their fingertips sore and their nails torn and often bleeding.

Abbie found it was so hot and dusty inside the warehouse sheds that she could hardly breathe. Her mother, like the rest of the women, wore a heavy long black skirt to protect her legs against the roughness of the bales, and an old blouse or shirt. When the weather was cold or wet they each wore a thick black shawl that they could pull up over their heads if necessary. Most of them also wore a man's cap to keep the dust and the flying downy fragments from the teased cotton out of their hair.

Abbie had always considered her mammy to be a big woman, but some of the others who worked there were taller and broader and even stronger than her mammy. One woman, Abbie saw to her amazement, could move the huge bales, which were as big as the kitchen table at home, on her own.

They all made it clear right from the start that they didn't like Abbie being there.

'The sort of things we talk about while we work aren't for a little kid's ears,' one grumbled.

'She's no little kid, Ruby Stacey, she's eleven years old, so you can keep your big gob shut,' Ellen told her.

'Doesn't bloody well look it. Skinny as a rabbit, arms and legs like sticks. Ever tried feeding her?'

'She gets her share!' Ellen scowled.

'Wouldn't like to see the rest of your lot then,' Ruby Stacey retorted. 'No wonder your old man buggered off! Probably went to look for a square meal.'

The other women sniggered and Abbie felt her cheeks burning with shame.

Ellen glowered, but said no more. Ruby Stacey was a florid-faced aggressive woman, much bigger than her, and from the murmurs around her the other women seemed to be siding with Ruby.

Ellen wasn't prepared to let such taunts slide by, though. She waited her time, watching Ruby like a hawk, determined to have her revenge.

At midday, when work stopped, they all sat on

the floor with their backs propped up against the cotton bales, to eat the chip butties or lumps of Wet Nelly they'd brought with them, and it was then Ellen saw her chance.

Ruby Stacey had pulled off her big clumping boots to give her aching feet an airing. Tucked into the top of the thick woollen socks she was wearing was a small wad of something wrapped in newspaper. As she got up to go and relieve herself in the bucket that stood screened off by a piece of canvas in a corner of the shed, the wad dropped to the ground with a dull thud as she walked past Ellen.

Swiftly, Ellen stuck out her leg and flicked her long black skirt so that it covered the package. She waited to see if anyone else had noticed, but no one seemed to have done so. Carefully, she leaned forward as if scratching her leg, and slid the wad into the palm of her hand, and then, still appearing to be scratching herself, hid it away in the front of her blouse.

She saw Abbie was watching her open-mouthed, her blue eyes saucer wide, and gave her a warning frown that she was to say nothing.

Ruby returned, collected up her bits and pieces and went back to work. Ellen did likewise. The moment she got Abbie on her own she turned on her fiercely.

'Now, you keep your mouth shut and say nothing to no one about what you saw, you understand!' she warned.

'Was there money in that newspaper . . .?'

'I've told you! One word and I'll tan your

19

backside, and that's just for starters. You've seen nothing! Understand? Now get outside and take a breather in the fresh air and think about what I've told you,' Ellen continued, pushing her towards the open doors.

A heat haze shrouded Liverpool. Across the Mersey, which was as smooth as a millpond, Abbie could see, to the left, Cammell Laird's shipyard at Birkenhead, black smoke pouring from its chimneys. Away to her right, though, was the holiday coastline of Seacombe, Egremont, and New Brighton, and she wished she could be there instead of having to go back inside the hot, dusty cotton shed for the rest of the afternoon.

'What you going to do with that money, Mammy?' she asked as they left work and began to make their way home up Water Street and Dale Street towards Scotland Road.

'What money?'

'The money that woman dropped!'

'The heat in that shed has addled your brains. I know nothing about any money.'

'You picked it up. I saw you.'

'You want to watch your tongue, saying things like that!' her mother warned her. 'Keep your trap shut about what goes on in the shed, and about anything you hear, do you understand?'

Abbie nodded, but it worried her. What would Father Patrick say when her mammy confessed to him that she'd picked the money up and kept it. He'd think she was a thief. He couldn't tell the police, of course, because everything you told Father Patrick when you went to confession was strictly between you and him and God. He'd know, though!

It was such a big secret that she had to tell someone. She mustn't tell Sandra in case she told her mother, and her mother told her dad and then they told the police. There was only one person she could tell, and that was Sam.

The minute they'd finished their meal, Ellen shooed Abbie and Sam out to play. 'Billy and me's got a bit of business to see to, so we might not be here when you get back. Put yourselves to bed and no larking about, mind.'

'Where are you going, Mammy?'

'Out!'

Abbie felt uneasy. She was sure it had something to do with the money her mammy had picked up off the warehouse floor earlier that day. She was longing to confide in Sam, but her mother's threats stopped her. She'd had a pasting from her mammy before, and well remembered how her mammy's heavy-handed slaps had left her bruised for days afterwards.

She couldn't put it out of her mind, though, and she came in from playing with Sandra early, complaining she didn't feel well.

'What you got then, a bellyache?' Sam asked.

She shook her head.

'You haven't fallen out with each other at last, have you?' Sam grinned. 'Like a pair of Siamese twins, you two. See one, see the other.'

'It's nothing like that.'

'So what's bothering you?'

'I got things to think about, that's all. I'm going to bed.'

Abbie found it was impossible to sleep. She sat by the window, staring out, watching people come and go until it grew so dark and she became so cold that she was shivering.

She'd undressed and crept under the covers when she heard her mammy and Billy coming down the street, singing drunkenly at the top of their voices. Immediately she knew what sort of business they'd had in mind.

'Have you heard those two?' Sam said, coming into her room. 'It's only the beginning of the week! Where have they found the money to go boozing?'

Abbie bit her lip. Should she tell him? She was bursting to do so. Could she trust him to say nothing. She was sure she could.

'Mammy picked up some money in the warehouse today, that's where they got the beer money from,' she said in a dramatic whisper.

'Picked it up? What do you mean? Some sort of bonus?'

Abbie gave a hysterical giggle. 'No, she stole it, stupid. You mustn't tell anyone you know, or that I told you,' she added quickly. 'She said she'd skelp me if I told on her.'

Sam stared at her, his brown eyes widening in disbelief. 'So whose money was it, and how did she come to steal it?'

In hurried whispers Abbie told him all about the wad of newspaper-wrapped money falling out of Ruby Stacey's sock, and her mother picking it up and saying nothing.

'Silly cow! Everyone down the Docks knows that Ruby Stacey will fight anyone. She beats her old man to a pulp when he steps out of line. She'll make mincemeat out of Mam if she finds out.'

'You won't tell, though, will you?' Abbie pleaded.

Before Sam could answer, the bedroom door burst open and Billy stood there staring at them. He lurched into the room, holding on to the doorpost for support.

'I'm fed up with telling you about coming in here and pandering to that little bitch,' he snarled. Seizing Sam by his mop of thick hair he began shaking him.

'Leave off, you're scalping me,' Sam growled as he tried to struggle free. 'I only came in because the noise you and Mam were making woke Abbie up and she was frightened.'

'Frightened! I'll tan her backside in a minute if she doesn't shut up and get to sleep, and then she'll have something to be frightened about. So will you if I take my belt off to you.'

As she heard them arguing, Abbie cowered down in bed and stuffed a corner of the pillow into her mouth so that Billy wouldn't hear her crying.

When her mother came stumping up the stairs, Abbie hoped she was coming to see if she was all right. She wanted the chance to tell her mammy to keep out of Ruby Stacey's way because she didn't want her to get hurt.

A moment later she heard her mother slam her

bedroom door shut, and she felt completely rejected.

She knew Sam wouldn't be able to come back to her room so she pulled the bedclothes over her head and sobbed herself to sleep.

Chapter Three

Abbie sensed there was going to be trouble from the moment she woke up the next morning. Billy didn't even put in an appearance before Abbie and her Mam left for work, and her mother, still hungover from her binge the night before, said she felt too ill to walk from Scotland Road to the dockside. They took a penny ride on one of the Green Goddesses, but as the tram swayed violently from side to side Ellen had a hard job not to throw up, and they had to get off at the top of Water Street and walk the rest of the way.

Abbie felt ashamed to be seen with her mother as she lurched from one side to the other, belching loudly and bumping into people if they got in her way.

'Do you think you should go back home, Mammy?' she asked worriedly, when Ellen was violently sick as they approached the grim-looking five-storey warehouse.

'Keep your trap shut. When I want your advice I'll ask for it,' Ellen muttered, wiping her mouth with the back of her hand. 'I'll be all right now I've brought that lot up.'

In Abbie's opinion she was far from being all right. She followed her mother into the ground floor of the warehouse. She hated it in there. The

air was thick with dust, and the enormous spiders'
webs that hung from the ceiling were coated with
fibres and hung like grey clouds above her head.
As usual she started sneezing. Quick, dry sneezes
in such rapid succession that they brought tears to
her eyes and left her choking and gasping for
breath.

'Pinch your nose between your thumb and
finger, chooks,' one of the women told her. 'That'll
stop you sneezing, luv.'

She did as she was told, hurrying after her
mother who was scuffling along sending up
clouds of dust from the cotton-strewn floor as she
weaved her way unsteadily between the massive
bales.

'What happened to you this morning then, Mrs
Martin?' Polly Hicks, the forewoman, demanded
as she eyed Ellen up and down. 'Overslept? Or
were you too bloody drunk to get up?'

Ellen belched loudly, but didn't answer.

When they reached the bale assigned to her,
Ellen slithered to the ground, rested her back
against it and closed her eyes.

'I've already docked you an hour for being late,'
Polly Hicks rasped. 'If you sit there a moment
longer then I'll stop another hour out of your
wages.'

Ellen opened her eyes, ran her hand over her
face, and struggled to her feet. Picking up the
cotton-hook lying on top of the bale, she slashed
away savagely at the canvas covering.

'You'd do better if you cut off the steel bands

first, wouldn't you?' Polly Hicks muttered scathingly. She handed Ellen a pair of heavy shears and watched, frowning, as Ellen tried to use them.

'Give them here, you daft cow.'

Snatching the shears back, Polly Hicks deftly cut through the steel bands that held the bale intact.

'Now get on with it!' she snapped as she walked away.

It took Ellen several more minutes to open up the bale enough to reach the tightly packed, water-soaked cotton inside, then she sank down on the floor again, completely exhausted. Leaning against the bale she dropped her head on to her knees.

'You make a start on it,' she muttered, pushing the vicious looking cotton-knife towards Abbie.

Abbie looked at the sharp, curved blade and shook her head. 'I can't, Mammy. I don't know how to use this knife.'

'Take hold of it and hack out as many wads as you can. You know how to tease it out with your fingers until it's like cotton wool. You've seen me do it, now get on with it.'

Abbie tried, but the cotton was rock hard and the sharp knife simply skittered over the surface. She did her best at digging the point in and then twisting it to try and free even a small wedge, but she hadn't the strength in her small hands to do even that.

Abbie made another attempt, tears of frustration trickling down her cheeks. She stabbed wildly at the bale. The knife spun out of her hand and, rebounding from the iron-hard surface, landed point down on her bare knee drawing a thin trickle of blood. Abbie screamed in fright.

'Give it here!' A scrawny woman who had been watching her antics snatched the knife from her hands and slashed out a dozen wedges. 'There you are, luv, pick those up off the floor and start teasing 'em out. That should keep you going for a while. Perhaps your mam'll be feeling more herself by the time you've done that and then she can take over again.'

'Not her! By the looks of things she was on the booze again last night and she's had a skinful!' Ruby Stacey snarled. 'Beginning of the week, too, so I wonder where the drunken bitch got her money from?'

The women paused in what they were doing and an expectant hush fell on the warehouse. One or two of them nudged each other and grinned, as if they knew there was a row brewing and they were looking forward to whatever happened next.

Ruby Stacey looked round at all the expectant faces and smiled grimly, then she strode across the warehouse and stood, arms akimbo, in front of Ellen. 'I suppose yer didn't pick a nice little wad of money up off the floor by any chance, did you, missus? Four nice, bright, shiny florins wrapped up in old newspaper?'

Ellen groaned, but didn't look up.

Ruby's boot went out and made contact with Ellen's chin. 'I'm speaking to you!'

'Lemme be, can't you, I'm not feeling so good,' Ellen moaned.

'I bet you're bloody not! That was my week's

wages. That was to keep me, me old man and me four kids in grub this week! And you stole it, yer thieving bitch.'

Ellen pushed the woman's boot out of her face. 'I didn't steal yer rotten money,' she muttered.

'You bloody well did! Lulu over there saw you. She saw me drop it, and then she spotted you picking it up and sticking it down the front of yer dress. Too frightened of you to open her gob, the silly bitch. Any decent body would have handed it back to me.'

Abbie held her breath, scared of what was going to happen next. She wanted to run and fetch Polly Hicks, the forewoman, who had gone across to the office about something, but her legs felt like lead and she was rooted to the spot.

'So what you goin' to do about it then, missus?' Ruby thrust one of her large hands under Ellen's chin, forcing her head back so that she had to look up. 'Well, do I get my ackers back or not?'

'I haven't got yer money!'

Ruby Stacey gave a mirthless laugh. 'No, you probably haven't got it now, judging by the looks of yer!' Her hand closed threateningly into a fist.

Ellen screamed with pain as it made contact with the side of her face. Abbie rushed to her side and put her thin little arms around her mother's neck protectively. 'You get away from my mammy, you're nothing but a great big bully,' she stormed, her blue eyes flashing with anger as she stared up at Ruby Stacey.

'Nice try, kiddo, but this is between grown-ups,' Ruby said contemptuously. She grabbed hold of

Abbie and, picking her up with one hand, swung her feet off the ground then dumped her on top of the nearest cotton bale. 'Stay there or you might get hurt as well,' she warned. 'Your mam's got no right bringing you here with her. The Gaffer would do his nut if he knew.'

She turned back to Ellen who was nursing her bruised face. 'Well?' she barked, dragging her unceremoniously to her feet. 'What have you got to say for yerself?'

Ellen tried to wriggle free, but Ruby's grasp became even tighter, shaking her as if she was a rag doll. Ellen lashed out with her feet and caught the other woman a resounding blow on her shin with the toe of her boot.

'Want to play rough, do you?' Ruby snarled.

She released her hold on Ellen without warning and Ellen landed in a heap at her feet amidst a cloud of dust.

Ruby regarded her scornfully. 'Now give me my money or get up and fight,' she ordered.

'How can I?' White-faced and shaking, Ellen stared belligerently at her opponent. Normally she knew Ruby wouldn't want to fight her because they were much the same size as each other, but Ruby knew how groggy Ellen was feeling at the moment.

'For the last time, are you going to give me my money back, or am I going to beat it out of you?'

'I told you, I haven't got your money,' Ellen muttered sullenly.

'Better find it, then, hadn't you!'

The other women left their bales and congregated round in a semicircle, watching with avid interest. Ruby had a reputation as a fighter and most of them had felt the power of her fist at some time, and they were keyed up to see what the outcome of the altercation would be.

With a grunt like a Samoan wrestler, Ruby pitched into Ellen. She punched her, butted and kicked her until Ellen was almost senseless.

Crouched on top of one of the bales, Abbie was witness to all that was happening. As Ruby raised one of her big muscular arms to take another swipe, Abbie was sure the woman was going to kill her mother.

Ruby finally stopped, leaving Ellen lying on the floor in a pool of blood and vomit.

Abbie's heart was pounding with fear as she tried to climb down to see if she could help her mother. Ruby heard her move and swung round and barked at her to stay where she was.

In the second that Ruby's attention was diverted, Ellen managed to get up off the floor and snatch up the sharp, curved cotton-knife that Abbie had been using.

As she brandished the knife with the intention of stabbing her opponent, a warning scream from one of the onlookers alerted Ruby. Despite her massive size she twisted away, so that instead of the knife plunging into her chest it was deflected and sliced through her sleeve into her upper arm.

With a scream of rage Ruby jumped on Ellen, tearing her clothes almost off her back. Blood from Ruby's arm pumped out over the pair of them, soaking their clothes and running into a pool on the floor.

The noise and screams could be heard outside the warehouse, alerting the Gaffer who came storming into the shed, shouting at the top of his voice and demanding to know what was happening. Like mice, the onlookers scurried back to their bales and pretended to be working.

'What the hell's going on,' he raged. He gawped at Ruby. 'You're bleeding like a stuck pig, woman! Someone call the scuffers and an ambulance!' he yelled over his shoulder as he turned back to Ruby to apply pressure to her arm, to try and stop the blood that continued to pump out at an alarming rate.

As he spotted Ellen leaning exhaustedly against a bale he called to the forewoman to come and look after Ruby.

'You two bitches been fighting?' He hauled Ellen to her feet. 'You were the one who used the bloody knife on her, weren't you? That'll have to be reported to the scuffers, you know that, don't you?'

'And while you're at it, tell them that she stole my week's money,' Ruby added weakly. 'Lulu's a witness.'

Ellen was trembling and frightened, but she refused to get in the same ambulance as Ruby Stacey.

Since, apart from torn clothes, bruises and a cut lip, she didn't seem to be hurt too badly, the Gaffer shrugged and told her she'd better get off home once the police had finished with her.

'And take your kid with you, and don't ever bring her back here again. Understand! I've warned you before about it. This is no place for youngsters and it will be no place for you if you cause another brawl.'

'It wasn't my bloody fault, the woman's mad,' Ellen defended.

'You'd be mad an' all if someone pinched your money and you knew that you and your kids would have to go hungry all week,' one of the women muttered angrily.

The Gaffer wheeled round angrily. 'I don't want to hear any more about it, so shut your mouth,' he raged. 'Get back to work, or the lot of you will find yourselves with no money for grub at the end of the week. I'll sack the whole bunch of you if there is any more trouble.'

Chapter Four

It was two days before Ellen Martin was out of pain sufficiently to face going to work. Her mood and her temper became worse every time she thought about the money she was losing from her pay packet.

On the Friday morning she dragged herself out of bed, knowing that if she didn't make the effort to go in then she'd get no money at all. As it was there would only be her wages for Monday to come.

'Make sure you don't get into any mischief, Abbie,' she scowled as she stood in the doorway, ready to leave, but still debating whether to go or stay at home.

'I won't have time. I'll be too busy doing all the chores you've told me to do,' Abbie told her sulkily.

'Mind you do the lot, and do them properly or I'll tan your backside when I get home,' her mother snapped peevishly.

'Couldn't I do some of them today and the rest tomorrow?' Abbie pleaded.

'You do them all today, my girl! Now don't forget you're to donkey-stone that front step first, it hasn't been done in months. After that, scrub the kitchen floor and then tidy up the bedrooms. And mind you get the whole lot finished before you go off out to play,' Ellen Martin repeated. 'Go on then, get the apron on and get started. I've left the pumice stone for the step out ready.'

Pulling a face, Abbie tied the piece of canvas sacking that her mother used as an apron around her middle. It was far too big so she had to double it over. The moment the door slammed shut behind her mother she whipped it off, dropped it in a heap on the floor, and shot out of the back door straight round to the Lewis's house to see if Sandra was up.

Mrs Lewis, wearing a flowered pinafore over her dress, answered the door. 'Sandra's still having her breakfast, luv. Did you want to come in and talk to her?'

Abbie nodded hopefully.

'Come on then, ducks. Go and sit at the table with her and I'll make you a jam butty.'

'Me mammy's gone back to work,' she told Sandra as she pulled out a chair. 'She's left me an awful lot of jobs to do, though, probably take me all day before I can get out to play. What are you going to be doing?'

Sandra shrugged. 'I'm not sure. Shall we do something together?'

'Like what?'

'Ssh!' Sandra held a finger to her lips. 'It's a secret!'

'Why?'

'Because I think my mam would stop me if she knew.'

'Go on then, tell me.'

35

'Wait till she's brought in your butty.'

'There you are, luv!' Mrs Lewis handed Abbie a plate with a doorstep of bread oozing with strawberry jam. 'Get that down you.'

'So what are we going to do, then?' Abbie asked, her mouth full.

'We could go round all the posh shops in town,' Sandra told her.

'Why go into town? There's plenty of shops in Scotland Road we can look at, and even more on Great Homer Street, and they're only at the bottom of our street.'

'The shops there are bigger and better than the scrubby little ones here,' Sandra sniffed.

'So, what difference does that make? We haven't got any money to spend, have we!'

'We can take a look. Could be fun.'

Abbie took another large bite and contemplated the idea while she chewed. 'We'd have to walk there, we've no money for the tram.'

'So? It's a nice day and it's not all that far.'

''Tis when you're coming home.'

'Do you want to come with me or not?' Sandra said, slightly miffed by Abbie's lack of enthusiasm.

'Yes, of course I do, but I have all the jobs me mammy told me to do first.'

'I'll help you with those. We'll finish them this morning and then we'll have all afternoon to go into town. My mam goes to work at one o'clock, and I'll tell her that I want to play with you instead of going with her. I'll ask her to leave us some sarnies.'

Abbie looked doubtful, but the thought of Sandra helping her with all the cleaning jobs that she'd been told to do persuaded her that perhaps it wasn't such a bad idea after all.

'I'll do the front step and you can scrub the kitchen floor,' Sandra said bossily when they got back to Abbie's house, 'then we'll do upstairs together.'

Abbie shook her head. 'That's no good! I'll have to be the one who does the step. If someone sees you doing it they're bound to tell my mammy that you were cleaning our step.'

'So? What does that matter?'

Abbie pursed her lips. 'She told *me* to do it, so she'd probably leather me for letting you come in, as well as for getting you to do it. You know what she's like. She hates me to bring anyone home because it's always in such a mess here.'

Sandra gave an exaggerated shrug. 'Orright! I'll do the kitchen floor and you do the step, then.'

It was nearly midday before they finished.

'I'm whacked,' Sandra exclaimed dramatically, throwing herself down on to Abbie's bed.

'Me, too!' Abbie flopped down beside her. 'Shall we leave walking into town until another day?'

Sandra sat bolt upright, a heavy frown marring her pretty round face, her grey eyes stormy.

'You're a cheat, Abbie Martin. You promised to come with me if I helped you with your cleaning. I don't have to scrub floors or even tidy around at home and my house always looks much better than yours. Your place is a tip, and your brother Billy's room is like a pigsty, with the cigarette ends all over the floor and beer bottles under the bed.'

'It's Sam's bedroom as well,' Abbie reminded her.

'It's not his fault he has to share with your Billy. I know it's not Sam who makes it a mess like that,' Sandra defended. 'His clothes were all hung up on nails, and your Billy's were in a heap on the floor.'

Sandra climbed off the bed. 'Are you coming into town with me or not? If you're not then you can't have any of the sarnies me mam left for us.'

A rumble of hunger in her stomach decided Abbie. ''Course I am, I was only teasing,' she grinned.

'I'm going to put on a clean dress,' Sandra announced the moment they'd finished eating the potted meat sandwiches that Mo Lewis had left on the kitchen table. She regarded Abbie critically. 'You'd better borrow something of mine because there's doormen on the big posh shops and they'll never let us in with you looking like that.'

Sandra was plumper than Abbie, and Abbie was much taller, so Sandra's clothes looked completely different on Abbie than they did on Sandra. She loaned Abbie a blue dress that had a white Peter Pan collar and white trims on the puff sleeves, and she decided to wear a green one with white daisies printed all over it.

'I'm not wearing your shoes, they're all too tight, I wouldn't be able to walk all that way in them,' Abbie told her.

'You can't go in those old plimsolls with your big toe sticking through the top.'

'I haven't got any others.'

Sandra chewed on her lip for a moment, trying to decide what to do. 'I know!' she said at last, 'wear your plimsolls to walk in and take a pair of my shoes to put on when we get there!'

Even though the sun was very hot there was a cooling breeze coming off the Mersey, and, revived by the sandwiches, the journey didn't seem nearly as far as Abbie had thought it would be. They sang the latest songs, 'Yes, We Have No Bananas', and 'Red, Red Robin', at the top of their voices as they walked along.

When they reached Dale Street they cut through Crosshall Street and into Whitechapel, and within minutes they were in Church Street and feasting their eyes on the wonderful window displays.

'We'll go into C&A's in Church Street first,' Sandra said, taking charge. 'You'll have to change your shoes first, though.'

She waited impatiently as Abbie sat down at the entrance to a shop doorway and removed the offending plimsolls and put them into the canvas bag that had held Sandra's sandals.

'They're pinching something chronic,' Abbie moaned as she stood up and took a few tentative steps.

'That'll soon ease off,' Sandra told her. 'They only feel tight because you've had those great, wide boy's plimsolls on,' she added dismissively. 'Hurry up.' Impatiently she led the way into C&A's and Abbie hobbled after her.

Inside, the store was very busy. The two girls roamed from one floor to the next, looking at all the dresses and blouses and coats hanging on the rails.

'This is nothing but clothes,' Sandra said. 'We'll go further up Church Street to Bunney's. They do everything.'

It had been busy in C&A's, but Bunney's was absolutely packed. Men, women and children of all ages surged around the busy department store. Sandra took charge. 'Come on,' she ordered. 'I've been here before with my mother, I know where everything is.'

She headed straight for the toy department and they spent a glorious half an hour looking at all the dolls and wonderful toys that were on display, and wishing they could afford to buy them.

'We don't want to look at any clothes again, we saw all we wanted to in the last shop,' Abbie said, as they left the toy department and made their way down the wide marble staircase.

'Well, not clothes, perhaps, but you'll love the department where they sell scarves and necklaces and ribbons and hair slides,' Sandra told her.

Several times they found themselves separated. The crowd was so dense that Abbie felt a sense of panic in case they couldn't find each other again. Sandra didn't seem to mind a bit. She was in her element, her eyes were shining and she was smiling happily.

'I love going round shops, don't you?' she said gleefully.

'My mammy never has time to do things like this. She says there's no point if you haven't got any money to spend.'

'You're enjoying it today, though, aren't you?' Sandra frowned.

Abbie smiled weakly. 'Yes, but I'm afraid of losing you and not being able to find my way home,' she confessed.

Sandra laughed. 'We'd better hold hands then, hadn't we, at least until we get out of here.'

They were still holding hands when they found the haberdashery section. It was an Aladdin's cave of delights. They tried on hair-bands, held slides up to their hair to see which colour or design looked best, and even tried wrapping scarves round their necks and pirouetting in front of the cheval mirror.

'And what exactly do you two think you are playing at?'

The stern authoritative voice startled them. In his chocolate-brown uniform piped with cream braid the shop-walker was a very forbidding figure.

'We're only looking,' Sandra said boldly.

'You're doing a little bit more than looking,' he boomed. 'I've been watching the two of you, you've been picking things up and putting them down for the last ten minutes. Are you intending to buy anything?' he asked, looking directly at Abbie.

Blood rushed to her face. 'I ... I haven't any money, sir,' she blurted.

'Just as I thought! Right, then I think the pair of you had better come this way to the Manager's office and he can call a policeman and we'll see what he has to say!'

'Leave off!' Angrily, Sandra shook away the detaining hand he placed on her shoulder. 'We ain't done anything wrong. We're simply looking!'

'Looking? We've already established you were doing more than looking, young lady. We'll leave it for the police to decide, shall we?'

Despite her struggles his grip on Sandra's arm tightened, and with his other hand he took Abbie by the shoulder and began to march the two of them towards the door.

'Abbie . . . Abbie Martin? Is it you? And Sandra Lewis! What in the world is going on?'

The shop-walker stopped as Maggie Ryan approached them, a look of bewilderment on her face.

He paused uncertainly. 'You know these young girls, madam?'

'Yes, I know them both, for goodness' sake. What is it they are supposed to have done, and why are you marching them off like that?'

'I've been watching them for some time. They've been behaving in a highly suspicious manner, picking things up and trying them on.'

Maggie smiled broadly, her blue eyes sparkling. 'Well, don't we all do that when we come into a shop like this? There's so many lovely things on display that most of us would buy up the whole lot if we had the money to do so.'

'That's the point, madam! These two girls haven't any money.'

'So? Don't they call it window shopping?' She gave a warm friendly laugh. 'I know they're doing it inside the store, but it's the same thing really, isn't it? When I need a new pair of shoes I often pop in the week beforehand to see what you have on offer, and I sometimes try on half a dozen pairs before I can decide exactly what I want. I don't buy them right then, I check out how much they are going to cost me and then come back later in the week, or sometimes it's the following week, whenever it is I've got the money together.'

He looked uncomfortable, charmed by her friendly smile and the Irish lilt in her voice. 'Yes, madam, but that is somewhat different.'

'It is?' Maggie looked at him in surprise. 'Now why do you say that?'

'Well, madam, you are a grown-up, and understandably you are budgeting for your next purchase.'

'Quite right! And these young girls are doing the same. Their mams will be proud of them when I tell them. It's a lesson a girl can't learn too soon in life. In a few years' time they'll be married and have to plan their budget and their spending so that their families don't end up in debt.'

'Yes, madam, but . . .'

'I'm sure you're a busy man and we've taken up quite enough of your time with all our chattering,' Maggie Ryan told him with a broad smile. 'If it's all right with you I'll see these two home before their mams start worrying and think they've got lost.'

She divided her bags of shopping between Abbie and Sandra, then possessively took each of them by the arm and smilingly escorted them out of the store before the shop-walker could make any further protest.

Once they were back out in Church Street and well away from Bunney's, Maggie Ryan stopped, reclaimed her shopping from the girls, and drew a deep breath.

'Whew! Do you realise you almost got your-selves done for pilfering?' she asked them.

'It wasn't our fault, Mrs Ryan, honestly,' Abbie told her. 'We were only looking!'

'And trying things on! You never want to do that unless you intend to buy something.'

'It's her fault,' Sandra muttered sulkily. 'When he asked us if we intended buying, she told him she had no money.'

'Well, it was the truth!' Abbie retorted.

'You mean you haven't even got your tram fare home?'

Abbie shook her head. 'We walked.'

'And we'd better start walking home now,' Sandra said. 'My mam comes home around five and she'll wonder where I am. She knows I'm playing with Abbie, but she said I had to be home and have the table laid by the time she got in.'

'Well, you won't manage to do that if you walk,' Maggie Ryan told her. 'It's after half-four now. Here,' she began to pick up the bags she'd rested on the pavement, 'give me a hand with these and I'll pay for your tram fares.'

Chapter Five

'You're not going to say anything to your mam about what happened today, are you?' Sandra asked anxiously, after they had carried Mrs Ryan's bags as far as her door and were hurrying home along Bostock Street.

Abbie shook her head emphatically. 'I might tell Sam, but I won't be telling my mammy. She'd only wallop me if I did. She'd say I shouldn't have been there in the first place and that I was daft to get caught pinching something.'

'We weren't pinching anything,' Sandra said huffily. 'We was only looking.'

'We more or less got accused of pinching, though, didn't we, so we might just as well have been,' Abbie said resentfully. 'That man was a right pig!'

'Yeah, but it all turned out all right in the end, didn't it,' Sandra giggled. 'Good job Mrs Ryan spotted us and saw we were in trouble.'

'She was ever so kind, wasn't she,' Abbie agreed. 'I like her a lot. She's always nice to me.'

'You mean you like Peter Ryan a lot, don't you,' Sandra said craftily.

Abbie's face turned bright red. 'He's nice, too,' she admitted.

'More than nice! Come on, I've seen the way you keep looking for him when we're playing out.'

'So! You're always looking for our Sam!' Abbie retorted crossly.

When she saw that Sandra didn't look at all pleased at being teased, Abbie quickly changed the subject. 'You coming into my place so that I can take your dress and stuff off and give them back to you?'

Sandra shook her head. 'No, my mam will be home by now. Bring them round later on, after tea, but don't let my mam see you with them, though.'

'Why not? She knows I borrow your clothes sometimes.'

'Yes, but if she sees you in my blue and white dress then she's bound to ask why you needed it, because she knows I don't lend you my best dresses just to play out in the street.' She paused, looking thoughtful. 'I don't think you should tell your Sam anything about what happened today.'

'Why don't you want him to know?'

Sandra shrugged. 'No reason, but it's probably best if no one except us knows anything about it.'

'Mrs Ryan does.'

'She won't tell. She wouldn't want to get you into trouble with your mam. She knows the sort of ruction your mam would kick up if she did hear about what happened.'

Abbie looked startled, but said nothing. Sandra was right, she thought, as she made her own way home. Mrs Ryan was especially nice to her. She always made her welcome whenever Abbie called there or she saw her talking to Peter, and it had been kind of her to speak up for them in Bunney's.

She shivered as she thought what might have happened if the shop-walker had taken them to the Manager's office and called the police. It would have been their word against his, and she knew which one the police would listen to.

She was relieved to find that she was the first one home. She changed out of Sandra's dress and put her own shabby clothes back on. She rolled up the dress and the shoes which Sandra had lent her into a bundle, and hid it under her bed. She'd find a way of smuggling them out and taking them back to Sandra when she went out to play later on in the evening.

The fire was almost out, so she raked out the ash from the bottom and then made it up with more coal, and then put the kettle on the gas ring so that it would be boiling when her mammy came in.

She looked in the larder to see what she could find for their meal, but apart from half a loaf, a dish with a lump of margarine in it, and two sausages lying in a pool of yellow fat, there seemed to be nothing. Perhaps her mammy would bring some fish and chips for their tea, she thought hopefully.

Sam arrived home first, whistling cheerfully, a big smile on his face when he saw her.

'Where d'you get the money from for a ride on the Green Goddess this afternoon, then?' he asked. He walked over to the kitchen sink and turned on the cold water tap, and tipped his head underneath it to get a drink, letting it run over his face to cool himself down.

'Seeing things now, are you,' Abbie grinned, as she passed him the threadbare towel that hung from a hook behind the kitchen door so that he could dry himself.

'I saw you and Sandra getting off the tram. So where'd you been, kiddo? Both of you were all dressed up. And why were you both helping Mrs Ryan to carry her shopping home?'

Abbie hesitated, remembering what Sandra had said about not telling anyone, not even Sam, about what had happened, and then decided to tell Sam as much as she felt he needed to know.

He liked Sandra a lot so he wasn't likely to squeal on them if she said Sandra didn't want her mam to know they'd walked into town. It couldn't possibly hurt to tell him that they'd bumped into Mrs Ryan in town and she'd paid for them to come home with her on the tram. There was no need to tell him about what happened in Bunney's, she reasoned.

'You won't say anything, Sam? Not to Mammy or anyone else, promise,' she begged, after she'd explained.

'Your secret's safe with me, kiddo,' he grinned. 'You both must be daft, though, walking all that way just to look into shop windows on a scorching hot day like this.'

'It was a killer, I can tell you,' she smiled. 'I was dead whacked walking all that way, because Mammy had said I had to scrub the kitchen floor

48

and clean the front step and tidy the bedrooms before I could go out. Not fair, really, you boys get away with it, you're never asked to do any housework.'

'I have to go all the way to the cooperage in Bridgewater Street to collect the leftover scraps from the barrels, and I always bring in the coal. I usually have to clean out the grate and re-lay the fire when it goes out,' he reminded her.

'Yeah, but earlier on in the week when Mammy wasn't feeling well I had to do almost everything. She even had me doing the washing, and that made my arms and legs ache, as well as my back, because we haven't even got a dolly tub like other people. It's not fair! Our Billy doesn't help out at all around the house.'

'I don't remember our Billy ever having to do deliveries after school, or work all through his summer holidays, either,' Sam told her.

'Lucky dog!'

'No he wasn't, not really. I'd sooner be delivering things than be penned up in reform school like our Billy was for a couple of years.'

'Didn't do him much good, did it,' Abbie observed. 'He's still a layabout.'

Sam nodded in agreement. 'Work and booze, that's all he's interested in. Anyway, what's for tea? I want to be off out early, got things to do and people to see.'

'Where are you going?'

Before Sam could answer, their mother and Billy arrived home.

'I expected you to have a cuppa brewed and

waiting for me when I got in,' Ellen grumbled irritably, as she flopped down into a chair and looked round the room in a disgruntled manner. Her ribs were still hurting and after a long day at work she wanted to vent her anger on someone.

'The kettle is boiling, Mammy, and I've laid the table,' Abbie told her quickly. 'I didn't know what to start getting ready for tea because there's nothing in the larder.'

Ellen's scowl deepened. 'Sam, run down to the fish shop for a couple of bits of fish and three-penny worth of chips.'

'How many pieces of fish?'

'Better make it three, I suppose. You and Abbie can have a piece between you.'

'Orright.' He began whistling cheerfully, then stopped and held out his hand, 'Where's the money then, Mam?'

Ellen regarded him angrily. 'I haven't got any bleeding money. Been off sick for almost a week. You've got money! It's Friday so you got paid today, didn't you? You buy them.'

'But, Mam . . .' He gave her a pleading look, but, seeing the anger on her face, turned away. It was quite true, he had been paid, but it was only a pittance. If he bought fish and chips for them all then he'd only have about a shilling left, which meant he'd have nothing to spend for the rest of the week.

Billy had been paid as well, he thought resentfully. Billy might only be a casual labourer down at the docks, but he earned a man's wage, not a couple of shillings like he did as a delivery boy, so why couldn't Billy be the one to pay out?

He was about to explain this to his mam, but as he turned round to do so, he saw Billy watching him. There was a calculating look in his brother's small dark eyes, and a cynical sneer on his mouth. Sam decided to keep quiet. If he said anything and it started an argument, it wouldn't only be his mother he'd have to deal with, but Billy as well.

As Billy exhaled a cloud of acrid smoke, Sam felt the familiar sickening drop in his belly as he avoided Billy's eyes. He decided that the best thing he could do was to leave things as they were, and get out of the house before Billy asked him to bring back some fags as well as fish and chips. If that happened then all his money would be gone, and if he refused then Billy would probably hammer him and take his money from him.

By the time he got back, Abbie had plates ready, bread cut and the tea already made and brewing.

The thought that it was his money that had bought the fish and chips, which Billy was wolfing down, spoiled the meal for Sam. As soon as he'd finished eating his own share he pushed back his chair to go out.

Abbie followed him out of the back door and into the back jowler.

'Where you going to, then, in such a hurry?'

Sam tapped the side of his nose with his forefinger, 'That's for me to know and for you never to find out.'

'I will find out, I'll ask Sandra,' Abbie told him

determinedly. 'I know you tell her all your secrets,' she teased.

'You leave Sandra out of this,' Sam scowled.

'OK. I'll keep your secret if you keep mine!'

'That's a deal. Now I'm off, and you'd better start washing up those dishes or Mam will give you a belt round the ear like this,' he told her, playfully cuffing her ear.

As she washed up the pile of greasy plates and put them away, Abbie daydreamed about what life could be like if she lived in a house like the Ryans'. Everything there was so clean and shining, there never seemed to be any shouting or squabbling, and Peter always had shoes and socks to come to school in and usually looked cleaner and tidier than anyone else.

Abbie liked him a lot; he was always so nice to her. He wouldn't let anyone bully her. He even took her side whenever Billy came out into the street shouting at her for something she was supposed to have done wrong. She sometimes thought he was as nice, or even a tiny bit nicer, than Sam was, and yet she loved Sam more than anyone else in the world. She'd never been afraid of him like she was of Billy.

Sam and Billy were still out when she went to bed that night. Her mother had gone upstairs earlier, complaining that sitting in a chair only made her ribs ache worse. Abbie had made her a cuppa and taken it up to her in bed, but Ellen complained that it didn't taste right.

'Billy'll be bringing me back a bottle of stout so

I'll wait and have that,' she'd muttered, pushing the tea aside.

Abbie intended to stay awake until Sam came in, so that she could get him to tell her where he'd been. She wondered if he'd gone out with Sandra on their own and that was why he wouldn't say where he was going.

She didn't want him getting too friendly with Sandra because then he'd have less time for her. It was all right for Sandra; her mammy kissed and cuddled her and worried about her, and even took her out when she wasn't working. She wished her own mammy was like that, instead of always being tired and grumpy.

Despite her determination to stay awake, Abbie drifted into sleep, still thinking about the good times she and Sam had when they went out with Peter and Sandra as a foursome.

Chapter Six

Abbie was quite relieved when the summer holidays were over and it was time for school to restart, since anything would be better than the sheer drudgery of having to tackle mounds of housework every day and getting the family's meals ready. It wouldn't be so bad, she thought, if her mammy was pleased with what she did, but usually she did nothing but grumble.

When she'd cleaned the windows, even though she'd rolled up old newspapers and used them to shine the cracked, scratched glass, like Mrs Ryan had told her to do, her mammy had complained that they looked streaky.

It wasn't her fault that after she'd lugged all the dirty sheets, towels and vests all the way to Frederick Street wash house, and boiled them all for almost an hour, that she found there was a red handkerchief mixed in with them and everything was streaked red.

She still couldn't see what all the fuss was about, since it was the first time that any of their clothes had been boiled for months and months. Her mother usually put dirty clothes to soak in the same water as they'd used when they'd had their weekly bath. She would leave them there in the tin bath to soak overnight, but sometimes she forgot about them for days. When she eventually rinsed them out they were such a dismal grey that she was ashamed to hang them out on the clothesline stretched across the jigger. Instead, she'd drape them on the guard around the fire after they went to bed, and leave them there to dry. Often they were still there days later.

Abbie wished they had an airer in their kitchen, the same as the Ryans and the Lewises had. They lowered it down to put the wet clothes on and then pulled it back up to the ceiling when the clothes were on it, and left them there until they were dry.

Even when she'd made some briquettes from the coal dust and wet newspapers, her mam had grumbled that they were too small to be any good.

At playtime on the first day of the new term back at St Anthony's, Abbie and Sandra looked for Sam, but he kept well out of their way.

'He said not to expect him to talk to us any more,' Abbie told Sandra as they walked round the playground, hand in hand.

'Why not?'

'He said that the other boys would tease him if they saw him talking to us.'

'That's daft! He's your brother and we've always talked to him at playtime.'

'I know that, but it's different now he's older and in the top class.'

'I'm beginning to hate school,' Sandra sighed. 'I don't even like the teacher we've got this year. Sister Mary is so strict!'

'I bet we're going to find the work's a lot harder, too,' Abbie agreed.

'The minute I'm old enough I shall leave and get a job,' Sandra vowed.

'I bet your mam won't let you. She'll want you to go to a commercial college, and learn to type and do shorthand and things like that.'

Sandra pulled a face, but before she could express her opinion on the matter the bell went, and they had to go back to their classroom and Sister Mary, and no more talking was allowed.

The two girls settled in far quicker than they had anticipated. The lessons were more difficult, but they had both expected that, and the routine seemed to be as dull as ever.

It was better than being at home, though, and if she worked really hard, Abbie thought, then maybe she'd be able to get a good job, like Mrs Lewis was always talking about, when she left school.

One Tuesday, a few weeks later, there was an unexpected excitement. At the beginning of afternoon playtime, two policemen arrived. They looked so imposing, in their navy serge uniforms with bright silvery buttons and their big dome-shaped helmets, that everyone stopped what they were doing and watched as they walked across the school yard.

They were met by one of the Sisters and taken inside. Almost immediately the bell went, but instead of going back into their classrooms they were all told to line up outside.

'What's going on?' Sandra whispered, as she and Abbie were jostled into line by the rest of their class.

There was an immediate call for silence. Then Mr Tomlinson, the headmaster, appeared, alongside the two policemen. 'The police have come here to inform me that a bicycle was stolen yesterday evening from Monks's Cycle Shop in Great Homer Street, and that one of the pupils from this school is responsible. Now, I want that boy or girl to step forward and own up.'

He stopped speaking and waited expectantly. There were whisperings and nudges and the sounds of suppressed laughter, but no one moved or spoke up.

'Silence!' His voice brought immediate quiet.

'For the last time, I am giving the culprit the chance to come forward.'

Still no one spoke or moved, so he turned to the policemen. 'You have a name?'

They nodded, and one of them took his notebook from his top pocket and read out, 'Peter Ryan! Is there a Peter Ryan here?'

Abbie and Sandra squeezed hands and stared at each other in shock. There must be some mistake. It couldn't be Peter, he never got into any trouble.

They watched in disbelief as Peter stepped forward. In his grey shorts, navy blue V-necked ribbed jumper and white shirt, he looked to be one of the most respectable boys in the school. He even had on proper black shoes and knee-length grey socks.

'Is your name Peter Ryan?'

They watched as Peter nodded. He tried to speak, but his voice seemed to have dried up and though his lips moved, no sound came out.

'Did you steal a bicycle from a shop in Great Homer Street last night?' the policeman demanded.

Peter shook his head. 'No,' he croaked. 'Why would I want to do something like that, I've got a bike already.'

Some of the older children started laughing, but they were quickly silenced as Mr Tomlinson glared in their direction.

'Can you tell us where you were last night?'

'At home, of course!' Peter mumbled. 'Where else would I be?'

'Right. We don't need lip from you!' He looked Peter up and down carefully and then referred back to his notebook. 'You answer the description we were given of the boy who was in the bicycle shop around the time the bike went missing,' he said ominously. 'You'd better tell us exactly what you did when you left school yesterday afternoon.'

Peter bit his lip. 'The usual. Walked home with my friends and then went out on my bike with Sam Martin for a bit, and then I went home for tea.'

'So you admit you were riding a bicycle?'

'Yes, but it was my own bike.' He stopped and stared boldly at the policeman. 'It was my own bike, I've had it for almost a year. My dad bought it for me the last time he was home from sea.'

'And did you go out again after you'd had your tea?'

Peter looked uncomfortable. 'Only for a few minutes. I'd chipped some of the paint on the back mudguard so I nipped out to get some touch-up paint.'

'Did you get it from Monks's in Great Homer Street?'

Peter nodded.

'So who was your accomplice?'

Peter looked puzzled. 'I went there on my own.'

'And while Mr Monks went through to his storeroom at the back of the shop to fetch a tin of black enamel, you stole a bike from the front of the shop. Right?'

Peter shook his head. 'Of course not,' he said indignantly. 'I wouldn't do a thing like that. I've already told you I have a bike, so what would I want with another one?'

'Stop lying, son. You stole a bike, admit it. You wheeled outside one of the bikes that were on display in the front of the shop, propped it against the kerb, went back in, paid for your tin of enamel, and then came out of the shop and rode the bike away, as bold as brass.'

'No, I didn't. Someone else was in the shop at the same time, he'll tell you I didn't do anything like that.'

The policemen exchanged knowing looks. 'Are you going to tell us what you did with the bike?'

'How can I when I didn't take it?' Peter protested, his voice quavering.

One of the policemen placed a hand firmly on Peter's shoulder. 'Come on, we're taking you back to the police station with us for further questioning.'

He turned and thanked the headmaster for his cooperation. 'The rest of you remember, if you steal or do anything else wrong, then we will get to hear about it and come after you,' he warned.

With Peter walking between them, the two policemen started to move towards the school gate.

'Stop, stop, you can't do this, he's not done anything wrong, he never does anything wrong!'

Her dark hair flying, her blue eyes blazing, Abbie pushed her way through the lines of other pupils and chased after the trio. She clutched at Peter's jumper, trying to pull him away from the policemen.

'And who are you?' One of the policemen grabbed her firmly by the arm, halting her in her tracks.

'I'm his best friend.'

'I see!' The policeman regarded her sternly. 'And can you tell me where Peter Ryan went yesterday evening after he visited the cycle shop in Great Homer Street?'

Abbie hesitated, wondering if she should lie, but afraid they would only find out if she did and take her along to the police station as well. 'No!' she said miserably. 'He's already told you, though, that he was at home with his mam most of the evening, and that's where he usually is.'

The policeman frowned. 'I think you are wasting our time,' he said gruffly. 'We've had information from someone who was in Mr Monks's shop at the same time. Come on,' he took Peter firmly by the arm and began to walk off.

Abbie grabbed at the policeman's stiff blue jacket to try and stop him. 'He's not done anything wrong,' she insisted, pummelling with her fists on the policeman's back, 'he's already told you that!'

He tried to shake her away but she grabbed him more tightly, latching on to one of the silver buttons on his jacket. As he pulled back, the button tore away from the blue serge.

Angrily, he prised it from her fingers. 'Get back with the rest of your bunch before I run you in as well,' he barked.

Tears streaming down her face, Abbie turned away and followed the other children back into the school. She was shaking with anger that Peter should be taken away. It wasn't fair. She was sure that he wouldn't dream of pinching a bike. He didn't even nick other kids' balls or tops or anything. And, as he'd told the scuffers, he already had a bike, so why would he want another?

The incident was the talk of the school. Abbie found herself publicly reprimanded by the headmaster, and ridiculed and teased by all the other kids for sticking up for Peter. Even Sandra ignored her and pulled her hand away when Abbie went to take it as they crowded back into the classroom.

That night she didn't wait for Sandra, but ran home as fast as her legs would take her. She didn't go straight to her own house, but went to Mrs Ryan's, banging on the door as if the devil himself was on her heels.

She breathed a sigh of relief when Maggie Ryan answered the door because she had been afraid Mrs Ryan might have been called down to the police station and still be there.

'Is Peter here?' she asked anxiously.

Maggie Ryan shook her head. Her eyes were red-rimmed and puffy from crying and for once she wasn't smiling. 'They've kept him at the police station,' she said. 'Do you want to come in? Your mam won't be home from work for a while yet, will she?'

'No, and our Sam's out doing his deliveries.'

'Come on in, then, and I'll find you a biscuit or a piece of cake.'

'He didn't do it, Mrs Ryan. I know Peter wouldn't do something like that,' Abbie told her as she followed Maggie Ryan through to the living room.

'Peter told me how you stuck up for him,' Maggie said with a gentle smile.

'It didn't do any good, though, did it,' Abbie muttered stubbornly. 'They still took him away. Wouldn't they believe you, either?'

Maggie shook her head. 'They said they had proof, but they wouldn't say what it was. Peter has to stay there until they've finished their enquiries and then he will have to appear before a magistrate. His dad will be out of his mind with worry when I write and tell him.'

'Perhaps you shouldn't tell him,' Abbie said sagely.

Maggie smiled. 'We'll see, luv. The trouble is his boat docks in a couple of months' time.'

'That's ages away! By the time he comes home it will all be forgotten and someone else's name will be mud,' Abbie said hopefully.

Abbie was wrong. Since there was only his mother's word that he had been at home that night, the police insisted that he had been the one who stole the bike, and they thought he probably had an accomplice who had actually taken the bike while Mr Monks was serving Peter. Since they couldn't locate the bike, and Peter wouldn't admit to an accomplice, they adjudged he was guilty.

Later, when Peter appeared before the magistrate, even though the police still couldn't trace the bike, he was found guilty and sent to a reform school for three years.

Abbie and Sam were both convinced he was innocent. Sandra wasn't sure and said that if he did do it then he was a fool to get caught.

Remembering how close they had come to being wrongly accused of pinching things in Bunney's store, and probably would have been if Mrs Ryan hadn't spoken up for them, Abbie thought that Sandra was being very unfair and told her so.

She was so annoyed with Sandra that she refused to play with her that night and went home early. She liked Peter a lot, and next to Sam she thought he was the nicest person in the world.

Abbie was so upset that she couldn't get to

sleep that night for thinking about Peter and what might be happening to him. Sam felt the same, and without her having to ask him he came into her room and they curled up together for comfort, until they heard Billy and their mam coming down the road, roaring drunk.

'Where have they found the money this time, to go boozing this early in the week?' Sam murmured.

Abbie stared at him, wide-eyed. 'I wonder if it was Billy who stole that bike?' she whispered. 'He was having a good laugh when I was telling you about Peter being kept in custody and having to go before the magistrate, and he was in Monks's shop around the same time.'

Sam shook his head. 'He wouldn't let Peter take the blame, that would be low even for Billy,' he muttered.

'Well, they've had a skinful, and I don't know where else they'd get the money from,' Abbie persisted, as the noise from downstairs became louder and more raucous.

'You mean you think Billy pinched the bike then sold it to someone?'

She nodded. 'That could be why the police say that they can't find it.'

Sam looked doubtful.

Abbie struggled to her feet. 'I'm going downstairs to ask him.'

'Abbie! Don't be so stupid! He's drunk, he might hit you, you know what he's like.'

'I don't care! Peter is in a reform school being

64

punished and Billy's out enjoying himself, swilling beer,' she declared angrily.

Before Sam could stop her she was running down the stairs. Reluctantly, he followed her, fearful of what might happen.

'What the hell're you doing down here?' Ellen muttered as she turned and saw Abbie in the doorway.

'I want to ask Billy where you got the money from to go to the boozer tonight.'

'You cheeky little brat!' Ellen's massive hand swung out, but Abbie ducked and it went over her head.

'Well?' She faced Billy. 'Where did you get the money?'

'Abbie!' Sam shouted a warning but he was too late.

'You were the one that stole that bike, weren't you, Billy? And you've sold it, and that's where you got the money from for you and me mammy to go boozing.'

Billy's sallow face turned a dark red colour, his small dark eyes glittered menacingly and he let out a low growl as he lunged towards her.

Abbie stepped back out of reach and Sam grabbed her by the arm and pulled her towards the back door. Seconds later they were out in the back jigger, running barefoot down the alleyway towards Great Homer Street with Billy in hot pursuit.

Sam pushed Abbie behind some sheets of rusty corrugated iron that were propped against one of the walls and shushed her to silence.

They crouched there, shivering with fright as they heard Billy pounding to the end of the jigger and then back again. As soon as Sam felt they were in the clear, he took her hand and ran with her to the other end of the alleyway and then round the corner into Scotland Road and finally back into their own street.

'We can't go back indoors tonight, he'll murder us,' Sam told her.

'I'm sorry, it's all my fault,' Abbie whimpered. She felt cold and frightened and her bare feet were sore and hurting. 'What are we going to do?'

Sam's face was grim. 'There's only one thing we can do, he told her. 'We'll go to Mrs Ryan's, and see if she will take us in.'

Chapter Seven

Abbie missed Peter far more than she would admit to either Sandra or Sam. Because Sam had begun to spend a lot of time with Sandra, her friendship with Peter had grown closer. Now, with him gone, she was more lonely than ever.

All three of them talked about Peter a lot, wondering how he was getting on. They asked Mrs Ryan to take messages when she went once a month to visit him. They sent along comics and sometimes a Fry's chocolate bar as well, which Sam paid for out of his Saturday earnings.

Abbie spent more and more time with Mrs Ryan, because when they came out of school in the afternoon Sandra now went straight to the corner shop where her mother worked. 'I have to, because me mam says she wants to keep an eye on me so's I don't get into trouble like Peter Ryan,' Sandra confided to Abbie.

'Peter didn't do it, he didn't steal that bike,' Abbie told her emphatically.

'Well, if he didn't then who did? And if you think you know who did steal it, Abbie Martin, then you ought to go and tell the police.'

'No good doing that if I haven't got any proof, is it,' Abbie said miserably.

'Well, you seem to think you know who it might be?' Sandra persisted.

Abbie shook her head. 'I'm not saying.'

Sandra looked at her shrewdly, her grey eyes wary. 'It wasn't Sam, was it?'

'Of course not!' Abbie's face coloured up with indignation. 'You know quite well that Sam wouldn't do a thing like that!'

She had to bite her tongue not to confide in Sandra that she and Sam both thought it might be Billy. Sam had warned her not to breathe a word to anyone. They were both quite sure that he was involved, though.

That was a night neither Abbie nor Sam would forget in a hurry. They'd still been talking things over when Billy and their mother had arrived home so drunk that they could hardly stand up. They'd fallen through the door into the passageway and cursed each other for a good ten minutes as they'd tried to pick themselves up.

Then they'd started pushing and shoving each other so hard that in the end it had come to blows, and Sam had had to step in and stop them. He'd got a kicking from Billy, as well as a black eye, the result of his mother's elbow jabbing him in the face.

Ever since then Billy had been surly and aggressive, cuffing Sam round the ears whenever he got the chance. Abbie felt his small mean eyes following her whenever she was in the same room as him, and she knew she only had to do or say something that annoyed him and she'd feel the force of his hand around her own ears.

As it was, he vented his spleen on her by making her clean his shoes, and iron the white cotton shirt that he wore at the weekends when he went out drinking. No matter how well she did these jobs he was never satisfied. If his boots didn't gleam enough he made her polish them again, and if there was a crease down the sleeve of his white shirt he threw it back in her face and told her to iron it properly.

Abbie couldn't see that it mattered if there was a crease since he always had his jacket on anyway. Ironing was not something she was very good at. She found heating up the flat iron over the coal fire, and then making sure it was perfectly clean before she began using it, was tricky. More often than not she burned herself, either lifting it off the trivet or when she was cleaning the bottom of it and around the edges with a piece of old towel.

Sometimes she forgot to spit on it, to test it and make sure it wasn't too hot, and then there would be a brown singe mark on whatever she was ironing. Yet, if she didn't have the flat iron hot enough then it was a waste of time using it because it wouldn't remove the creases.

Although her mother usually left a pile of washing or ironing for her to do when she got in from school, and also expected the table to be laid and the kettle boiling, Abbie still managed to fit in a visit to Maggie Ryan's most evenings.

To do this she worked out a clever plan. She dashed home from school and filled the big iron kettle and put it on the trivet over the fire. If it wasn't quite boiling when she got back from Mrs

Ryan's then she poured the water from it into the tin kettle they used on the gas ring. She always made sure that she was back home in time to be in the middle of whatever other chore it was she was supposed to be doing when her mother and Billy came in from work.

'You'll have to buck your ideas up, young lady, when you come to leave school,' Ellen would grumble, when she found her doing the ironing on a corner of the table or leaning over the sink up to her elbows in dirty sudsy water. 'If you go to work in a factory where you're on piece work you'll starve to death, the time it takes you to get anything done.'

Abbie would concentrate on what she was doing and say nothing. Sometimes Ellen would let it pass, at other times she'd yell at her, 'Answer me when I speak to you, you insolent little brat!'

As winter approached and it was dark earlier and earlier in the evenings, Mrs Lewis insisted on Sandra staying indoors after tea.

'Is your mam trying to stop us seeing each other or something?' Abbie asked. 'Sam was saying he hasn't seen you for ages, either.'

Sandra went bright pink and avoided Abbie's eyes. 'I told you, she's worried about me getting into trouble.'

'We don't get into trouble, though, do we!'

'Only because we don't get caught! Look what happened when we went into town together. And then there was that time when we tied Mrs Kelly's door knocker on to Mr Parsons's door handle so that when he came out and shut his door her knocker banged.'

'That was ages ago,' Abbie said indignantly, 'when we were in infants' school, and it wasn't us, it was Peter and Sam who did that.'

'We were out playing with them! My mam says that Mrs Kelly is always going on about it whenever she comes into the shop.'

Abbie shrugged. 'It didn't work properly, anyway. If Mrs Kelly had any sense she would have known that it wasn't really anyone knocking on her door.'

'She told my mam she was frightened out of her life because she thought it was the scuffers coming after her Liam.'

Abbie laughed. 'Serve her right, he's always in trouble. He does cruel things like tying a tin can on to a cat's tail and picking up dog turds and putting them through people's letterboxes.'

Deprived of her playmate, and anxious to get out of her own house after she'd washed up the dishes and put them away after their evening meal, before she was landed with more chores or in trouble of some kind, Abbie would sneak down the back jigger to the Ryans' house.

Maggie was always pleased to see her and when Michael wasn't there she would sit and listen to her, show her photographs of Peter and Michael when they were small, and talk to her about everything under the sun.

One evening Abbie had even confided in her that she couldn't understand why her own mammy was always so cross with her and didn't seem to want to spend any time with her.

'I think that perhaps my sister Audrey dying so young upset her a great deal,' Abbie sighed.

Maggie Ryan looked startled, but said nothing.

'I don't know anything about what happened, because nobody ever wants to talk about it,' Abbie went on. 'It was around the same time as I was born, wasn't it?'

'More or less,' Maggie Ryan agreed evasively.

Skilfully, Maggie changed the subject. 'Now, didn't I say we'd make some of those fairy cakes you like so much? We'd better get started or they won't be cooked before you have to go home.'

Whenever she was baking, or preparing a meal for herself and Michael, Maggie would let Abbie help and would teach her how to cook and make cakes.

Usually, too, there was a sample to be enjoyed at the end of their task. If Abbie couldn't wait until the cakes or pies were cooked and ready to eat, then Maggie Ryan always saved her a taster until the next time she popped in.

The only thing that spoiled this wonderful friendship for Abbie was Michael Ryan. He was an older version of Peter. He was good-looking, tall and lean with black hair and eyebrows and deep blue eyes. He said very little, even to his mother, and seldom spoke to her except to mutter 'Hello' or 'Goodbye'. He made Abbie feel uncomfortable because he seemed to watch her closely all the time she was in their house.

When she first started going there every evening

she tried to get him to talk to her by asking him about his work.

'Do you like being a porter at Lime Street station?' she asked shyly.

He shrugged, and took a packet of Lucky Strike cigarettes out of his pocket and lit one.

'Do you want to be a guard or an engine driver and travel on the trains someday?' she asked.

He took a deep drag on his cigarette. 'Not really,' he said, and blew out a cloud of blue smoke.

'You could see lots of other places, if you did,' she gabbled on.

Michael shrugged. 'Only different stations.'

'Is it hard work being a porter?'

'It's just a job.'

'Do you meet lots of interesting people?'

He shrugged again. 'They're only on the platform for a few minutes so I wouldn't know if they're interesting or not.'

She waited hopefully for him to go on, but he didn't. He concentrated on lighting a fresh cigarette from the stub of the one he'd just finished.

After that she confined herself to saying 'Hello' or 'Goodbye', the same as he did.

She remarked on it once to Maggie Ryan, and Maggie had merely smiled.

'Perhaps he doesn't like me coming here,' Abbie said worriedly.

'No, of course he doesn't mind,' Maggie Ryan assured her.

'He's not friendly like Peter,' Abbie persisted. 'I miss Peter a lot!' she added wistfully.

73

'Take no notice of Michael. He's a man of few words and a bit on the shy side,' Maggie said reassuringly.

'Is that why he hasn't got a girlfriend?'

Maggie Ryan looked taken aback. 'I don't know whether he has or not,' she said slowly. 'He certainly hasn't brought one home yet.'

After that, Abbie decided not to visit when Michael was there, if she could help it. His presence definitely seemed to mar the atmosphere between her and Mrs Ryan, and that was so special she didn't want it spoiled in any way at all.

Instead, she counted the days left until Peter came home. Mrs Ryan helped her to make a chart and every time she visited they marked off the days.

'It's going to be a big chart,' Mrs Ryan sighed. 'Peter won't be home until 1929, just before his sixteenth birthday in September.'

'Shall we plan a very special birthday for him?' Abbie suggested.

'We can, but it's an awful long time away.'

'We could have a party. Some of the friends he had at school could come, and, of course, Sandra and Sam. I could help you to get everything ready and do some extra baking.'

'That's a great idea! You make a list of the people we should invite and a bit nearer the time I'll buy extra food for the store cupboard each week. We'll have a special baking session a few days before he's due home so that there's plenty of cakes and little pies . . .'

'And could we have jelly and custard?' Abbie

interrupted wistfully. 'Sandra's mam used to make it as a special treat on my birthday when I was little, but she doesn't do it any more. I can still remember what it tasted like, though.'

'We'll go even better,' Maggie Ryan promised. 'We'll make a trifle with sponge cake and tinned fruit in it, and decorate the top with real cream. How about that? And we'll make a big birthday cake and you can help me decorate it, and we'll put Peter's name on it in coloured icing.'

Chapter Eight

Maggie and Abbie planned the party for when Peter would be released in September 1929 over and over again. They constantly changed the menu and even the names of the people they would invite. It was a bit like playing a game, and one they both thoroughly enjoyed.

Since it was such a long time away, Maggie suggested they should keep it a secret until nearer the date of Peter's release, so whenever Michael was around they talked about something else.

When that happened, Abbie hugged the secret to herself and elaborated on their plans when she was at home and in bed. It was like living in another world; one of her own making where everything was exactly as she wanted it to be. In her dream world she was wearing a lovely blue dress that matched her eyes and she had on shiny new shoes, and Peter told her how pretty she looked.

Abbie was now on such friendly terms with Maggie Ryan that she no longer knocked on the door when she visited. Instead, she simply called out 'Hello' as she opened the back door and went in, so it was quite a shock when she walked in a few nights before Christmas to find Paddy Ryan in the kitchen.

He was away at sea for such long stretches that for a minute she didn't recognise him. She had forgotten that he didn't look a bit like Michael and Peter. He had thick copper-coloured hair and a dark red beard, and the most massive shoulders and muscled arms she had ever seen. His face, what she could see of it, was weather-beaten, and his dark grey eyes were sharp and penetrating.

'And hello to you, young lady,' he grinned, 'how can I help you?'

'I . . . I've come to see Mrs Ryan,' Abbie told him, her face going red.

'Visitor for you, Maggie,' he bellowed.

Maggie came rushing into the kitchen looking very flustered, a worried frown on her face. 'Hello, Abbie,' she hesitated, looking anxiously at her husband and then back at Abbie. 'I was just coming round to tell you . . .'

'Abbie? Abbie who? It's not Abbie Martin, is it?' Paddy Ryan challenged. His welcoming smile changed to a heavy scowl.

'It's all right, Paddy, Abbie's only popped in for a second with a message for me.'

'A message? What sort of a message? What the hell is she doing walking into my house without even knocking? Come to that, what is she doing under my roof at all?' The affable look had gone from his face; his eyes were no longer friendly, but steely grey as they darted from Abbie to Maggie and back again.

'It's all right, Paddy,' Maggie Ryan murmured soothingly, 'I can explain.'

'Bloody well get on with it then, and it had

77

better be good,' he growled, his hands clenching into fists as if he was having difficulty containing his temper.

Abbie reached behind her for the handle of the kitchen door. 'I'll come back some other time,' she said hastily as she backed away. Paddy Ryan looked so fierce and angry that she felt herself trembling all over. For a minute she'd been afraid he was going to attack her.

She was used to her mammy screaming at her, and Billy shouting and swearing at her, but there was something so intense about Paddy Ryan and the way he was looking at her that she felt sure he meant to do her some harm.

She couldn't think why. As far as Abbie knew she'd never spoken to him before, so she had no idea how she could have upset him.

'You'd better go, Abbie,' Maggie Ryan whispered. Her face was white, her lips trembling, and she avoided Abbie's eyes.

Abbie didn't stop to question why Mr Ryan was so angry. She felt so scared she couldn't get out of the Ryans' house fast enough.

Paddy Ryan was probably so upset about what had happened to Peter that he didn't want to see any of Peter's friends, so that was the reason he didn't want her there, she reasoned as she ran back home, her heart still pounding.

Christmas 1926 was on a Saturday, and it was the most miserable one Abbie had ever known. Paddy Ryan was still at home, which meant she couldn't go round to the Ryans' house and she had been looking forward to doing so. She knew there wouldn't be much celebration in her own home, apart from her mammy and Billy getting drunk, and she couldn't stop thinking about all the treats Maggie had promised her.

She had helped Maggie to make a Christmas pudding and a Christmas cake and she'd been looking forward to tasting them. They had been planning that on Christmas Eve they would make a batch of mince pies, and Maggie had said that Sam could come round, as well as on Christmas Day.

'It will have to be fairly late on in the day, because in the afternoon I'm going to visit Peter,' Maggie explained. 'I'll leave everything prepared ready, and when I get back I'll be able to tell you how Peter is getting on.'

Now, with Paddy Ryan at home, that was going to be impossible, Abbie thought sadly. He had seemed to be such a nice man when she'd walked into the kitchen. A beaming smile, a hearty greeting and then, the moment he had heard her name, he'd become a bad-tempered ogre. She kept asking herself why? She hadn't said or done anything to upset him. Maggie had looked so flustered that she hadn't dared ask. She couldn't put it out of her mind, though, and once Paddy Ryan went back to sea she would certainly ask Maggie what had gotten into him causing him to have acted the way that he did.

She knew that Sandra had invited Sam to her place on Christmas Day, but so far she didn't know if he had accepted or not. If he went, then it meant she was going to be on her own. Except, of course, for her mammy and Billy, and with Christmas Eve being on a Saturday they'd both have a hangover until the middle of the morning and then they'd probably be in a drunken stupor for the rest of Christmas.

Unless Sandra asked her to come round as well, and somehow she didn't think that would happen. Lately, Mrs Lewis seemed to think that it was better for the two of them to be kept apart in case they got into any trouble. Why Sandra would get into trouble going out and about with her, and yet it was all right for her to go out with Sam, Abbie couldn't work out.

As predicted, Abbie found herself staying at home with her mammy and Billy on Christmas Day. Both of them were bad-tempered, having had far too much to drink the previous night. Her mammy had bought a chicken, but made no attempt to cook it.

'If you want it then you'd better stick it in the oven before you go to Mass,' she told Abbie. 'And stick some spuds in alongside it as well.'

'And mind there's some stuffing and some good thick gravy,' Billy told her.

'I'm not sure how to make stuffing,' Abbie replied.

'Then bloody well find out. Go and ask Maggie Ryan, you're as thick as thieves with her most of the time.'

'I can't go down there, Paddy Ryan is home from sea.'

Billy gave a nasty laugh. 'Doesn't want you around the place, eh, kiddo! Hear that, Mam?' He turned to Ellen, a smirk on his face. 'Paddy Ryan doesn't like the look of Abbie's face.'

'Huh! That's not surprising. Told you to sling yer hook, did he?'

Abbie shook her head. 'Not really. He didn't seem very pleased to see me, though.'

Billy and his mother exchanged knowing glances.

'Then you'd best stay home where you belong and do a bit more for your own folks, hadn't you, instead of gallivanting out all the time,' Ellen told her. 'Now get on and see to that chicken or else there'll be nothing for any of us to eat.'

Abbie didn't see or hear anything from the Ryans all over Christmas and the New Year. The weather was cold and miserable and she felt desperately lonely.

She saw hardly anything of Sam because he spent more and more time with Sandra. They had plenty to be excited about because on Monday, January 2nd, he would be starting work full time at Nelson's Jam Factory.

The whole thing had come as a surprise. One of the travellers who called at the shop where Mo Lewis worked had said there would be a vacancy at the factory after Christmas. He'd said if she knew of a likely lad then he'd put in a good word for him.

It was a chance in a lifetime. A job being handed out on a plate, when half the boys who left school couldn't find work, and more and more men were being laid off because of the rising unemployment.

Sandra had been in the shop and overheard

their conversation, and said she knew someone who was working as a delivery boy and was looking for better employment. The upshot had been that Sam had got the job.

It meant that, in future, instead of Sam being at home in the early evening to take her part when her mother and Billy arrived home, she would have to face them on her own.

Sam would come in soon afterwards, but he would probably be tired out from his long day and in no mood to listen to her trivial problems. Like his mother and older brother he'd be ravenous and expect to find his meal on the table. Later in the evening, when normally they would have had time to talk to each other, Sam would be going round to see Sandra.

Now that he was about to start work, Sandra went round telling everyone that Sam was her boyfriend. Abbie thought she was being stupid since she was only eleven, and they wouldn't be old enough to marry for years and years. When she said this to Sam, Sandra accused her of being jealous.

'You'll see things differently when Peter comes home,' she retorted smugly.

At school, Sandra began to avoid Abbie and go around with a bunch of other girls, arms linked, all singing and sniggering together. Sometimes the song was 'I can't give you anything but love', or else, 'Let's do it, let's fall in love'.

Abbie tried to pretend she didn't care what they were doing or what they were saying. Deep down, though, she felt lonely and unhappy and longed for Peter to come home from reform school, but it seemed to be a lifetime away. She missed him so much, and she wanted to be reassured that he was still her best friend, the same as before he was sent there.

If the day ever came when he told her that he loved her then that would be the happiest day of her life. When that happened she would sing 'Let's fall in love' at the top of her voice, even though she knew she'd be out of tune and sound more like a frog croaking than a nightingale warbling.

Chapter Nine

Christmas had been dismal, but the start of 1927 was even worse for Abbie. Her mother and Billy had celebrated New Year's Eve, which had fallen on a Saturday, with a drinking binge that had started on the Friday night.

Sam had been late coming home because he and Sandra had gone into town to see the New Year in, so there had been no one she could turn to when Billy and her mammy had arrived home, roaring drunk, very early on Sunday morning.

Their New Year resolution seemed to be to see how much booze they could get down them in one night, Abbie thought miserably. She cowered under the bedclothes with her hands over her ears as they shouted and yelled at each other and sang rowdy songs that ended in bursts of raucous laughter.

When she finally heard them stumbling up the stairs she prayed that neither of them would come into her bedroom.

When she came downstairs on New Year's Day she had to pick her way over discarded coats and boots, pools of vomit, and a broken chair. The living room was in such a state of disorder that it looked as though they'd been robbed.

Except that they had nothing worth taking,

Abbie thought bitterly, as she set about clearing out the ashes and stirring the fire to life with bits of rolled-up newspaper and firewood. Resignedly, she set about clearing up the mess before she went off to Mass.

If her mammy used one quarter of what she spent on drink and cigarettes on making their home comfortable, it could be every bit as nice as the Ryans' or Lewis's, she thought wistfully. They could have a rug on the floor to take away the chill that went through your feet and legs first thing in the morning. They could have pretty matching cups and saucers, instead of a collection of chipped mugs and battered cups that didn't match up with any of the saucers. They could have proper sheets and woollen blankets on the beds instead of having to use old coats for extra warmth.

The list was endless. She could go on and on, but what was the point. Practically every penny Billy and her mam earned, and some of Sam's wages, went on beer and cigarettes, and she couldn't see that changing. She supposed she should be grateful that her mammy paid the rent regularly. At least she kept a roof over their heads, even if half the time their bellies were empty.

She wondered if things would be any better, now that Sam had a better job and would be bringing more money home each week. He'd be expected to hand it over, of course, and she wondered if it would be set aside for housekeeping or used as extra beer money.

She was pretty sure she knew the answer, but

Sam might have something to say on the matter and if he did then she'd certainly back him up.

In some ways she wished Sam hadn't got the job at the Nelson's Jam Factory. She knew he had been lucky getting taken on since there were dozens of boys in Liverpool who would have jumped at the chance. It meant, though, that he would have to travel to Aintree each day, so he would be going out of the house even earlier than her mammy and Billy. That meant she'd be expected to clear up and tidy the house all on her own before she went to school.

1927, Abbie decided, was going to be anything but a happy new year. She wished she was old enough to leave school but it would be another year and a half before that was possible.

Perhaps if she could make the house nicer, Abbie thought, as she continued to clean out the ashes, then Sam wouldn't want to go out with Sandra every night. Her mammy might even begin to take an interest in making the place more comfortable once Sam started bringing more money home.

It would be Sam's fourteenth birthday in ten days' time, so perhaps she'd try and put on a special tea for him and ask Sandra to come round. She'd keep it a secret and ask Sandra not to breathe a word about it to Sam.

She planned all the details in her head as she cleaned the place up. Then she made a cup of tea and took it upstairs to her mammy so that she could tell her all about her wonderful idea.

Ellen looked terrible. Her face was yellow, there

were bags under her eyes, and her hair was so tangled and matted that it looked as though it hadn't seen a comb in weeks.

'Happy New Year, Mammy, I've brought you up a cuppa,' Abbie told her. She felt so full of hope for the future that she leaned over and kissed her mother's cheek.

Ellen pushed her away. 'Gerroff with you! What you after, smooching around me like wet echo. If it's money then you can forget it, I'm bloody skint!'

Abbie pulled back as if stung. 'I don't want money!' she muttered, her happy mood shattered. 'I wanted to tell you what I thought we could do for Sam's birthday.'

Ellen heaved herself up in bed, took the cup of tea and slurped a mouthful. 'What do you mean, do for his birthday? He's got his present and a damn good one it is and all.'

'Oh!' Abbie looked taken aback. 'I didn't know you'd bought him anything.'

'Buy him anything?' Scowling, Ellen pushed her hair back out of her eyes. 'He don't need me buying him anything. He's got his birthday present, the lucky little bugger, he's got a decent job at long last and it's been handed to him on a plate.'

'That's not a present, well, not a present from us, is it!'

'It's all he's going to get so he'd better make the best of it!'

'I thought that perhaps we could put on a nice tea for him and ask Sandra to come round and . . .'

87

'Have Sandra Lewis in here scoffing my grub! You must be out of your mind, girl. If she wants to have her tea with Sam then she'd better be the one to invite him to her house. Her mam's got a sight more food in her pantry than I've got in mine. Gets it all cut price from that corner shop where she works!'

'I don't know anything about that . . .'

'No, you don't know anything about most things. Now bugger off and clean up downstairs and let me get some bleedin' shuteye. My head's thumping like a steam hammer without listening to your stupid twaddle.'

Nothing more was said by either of them about it, and Sam's birthday would have passed by unnoticed had it not been for Sandra inviting him to her house for a meal.

'She said you can come as well if you like,' Sam told Abbie.

Abbie hesitated, wondering if it meant that she and Sandra could once more be good friends.

'If she wants me to be there then why couldn't she ask me herself?'

Sam shrugged. 'I don't know. Ask her yourself!'

'Won't I be in the way if it's special for the two of you?' she asked tentatively.

'Sandra's mam will be there as well, so of course you won't be in the way.'

Abbie's face lit up with a wide smile. 'Then I'd love to come. Do you want me to tell Sandra or will you?'

'She's taking it for granted that you'll come.'

Abbie boiled up a kettle of water and washed

her hair in the sink, rinsing it three times to make sure there was no soap left in it. Then she rinsed out Sam's best shirt and a blouse for herself and dried and ironed them.

She felt really excited. She hadn't been out anywhere all over Christmas. The winds blowing in from the Mersey had been icy, making it too cold to walk around the streets, so she'd stayed indoors, and now she was fed up with her own company and was really looking forward to going to Sandra's place.

Abbie felt a sharp stab of jealousy when she found that Sandra had bought Sam a present. She would have loved to have been able to give him one but she had no money.

Sandra's present wasn't very big, but it was wrapped up in glittering gold paper and tied with an elaborate ribbon bow.

When Sam opened it Abbie heard him catch his breath in surprise as he pulled out the shiny new mouth organ.

'This is great!' he exclaimed, his brown eyes shining. Eagerly, he put it to his lips and began to play. The tone was beautiful, soft yet powerful.

Sam stopped and examined it carefully. 'This is a double reed *Echo*,' he said in awe. 'Gosh! Thanks, Sandra. It's the very best you can get!'

'Well, I didn't think you'd want one of those cheap *Bandmaster* mouth organs like the rest of the boys have,' she sniffed. 'Go on, play us something.'

'He can't play,' Abbie told her.

'Yes I can! Well, a bit. I ought to practise first, though!'

'Rubbish. I'd sooner hear you play that thing badly than listen to you whistling,' Sandra joked. 'When you were on your delivery bike I always knew it was you coming along the road by the way you whistled,' she told him archly.

'All delivery boys whistle. It's to make sure people get out of our way, especially when we're riding on the pavement,' he grinned.

'Yeah, but none of them whistle as badly as you used to! I'm glad you won't be doing that any more.'

The tea was terrific. Abbie's eyes widened when she saw the loaded table. Mo Lewis had brought home all sorts of tasty things to eat from the corner shop where she worked. Little chocolate cakes, a swiss roll that had jam and cream in it, chocolate biscuits, and some little tiny biscuits with coloured icing stars on the top.

To start off their meal, Mo Lewis cooked a pan of sizzling pork sausages and served a mountain of chips to go with them.

As they sat happily round the table, laughing and joking and tucking into the plentiful spread, Abbie felt she had never enjoyed herself so much and wished things could be like this in her own home, even if it was only on special occasions.

Her bubble of happiness burst when Sandra began pointing out how different she was from Sam. Abbie felt as if a black cloud had suddenly descended, and all she wanted to do was get out of the house.

It was so silly really, she told herself, Sandra didn't mean to make her feel like that. It had been a light-hearted remark but it ruined the occasion for Abbie.

'You and Sam don't look a bit alike,' Sandra said in a puzzled voice. 'Sam's hair is brown and so are his eyes. Yours aren't! You've got black hair and blue eyes.'

'Sam takes after Mammy,' Abbie told her. 'She's got brown hair and brown eyes.'

'And so has our Billy,' Sam pointed out.

'You're as tall as Sam, even though he's two years older than you,' Sandra persisted.

'Mammy's short. And so is Billy,' Abbie reminded her.

'Was your dad tall, then? And did he have black hair and blue eyes?'

'I don't know!' Abbie grinned. 'I never met him, did I!'

'Why? Did he die when you were very little?'

'That will do, Sandra,' Mo Lewis interrupted. She shook her blonde head slightly and there was a warning in her grey eyes as they locked with Sandra's.

'Sorry! I just wondered. No one ever talks about him, and I've never seen him, and now Abbie says she hasn't either,' Sandra said with an innocent smile.

'That's because he cleared off when Abbie was a couple of weeks old and we've not heard from him since,' Sam said sharply.

'Oh!' Sandra clapped her hand over her mouth. 'I didn't know that or I wouldn't have brought it up. I suppose you must take after him in looks, Abbie, that's why you have such black hair. Was he a gypsy?'

Abbie felt too choked to answer. Sam reached out and squeezed her hand, and his brown eyes were full of concern when he saw how upset she was.

'Stop teasing her, Sandra,' he warned. 'Dad went into the Army and he was listed as "missing" when the war ended.'

'That certainly wasn't a very nice thing to say,' Mo Lewis agreed. 'Now, if we've all had our fill, what about you helping me to clear the table and wash the dishes, Sandra?'

'I'm going home, Sam,' Abbie told him the moment they were left on their own. 'I wish I hadn't come. Fancy Sandra asking if Dad was a gyppo!'

'Don't be daft. She was only pulling your leg.'

'Well, I didn't like it. It was a horrible thing to say. You stay here if you want to, but I don't want to be here a minute longer.'

'Sandra's got all sorts of games for us to play and she has a new record for her wind-up gramophone of "Bye Bye Blackbird" for us to listen to. And she'll put on the other one you like singing along to, "When the Red Red Robin comes Bob Bob Bobbin' Along".'

Abbie shook her head. 'I don't want to listen to any of them.'

'Not even if I play an accompaniment on my new mouth organ?' he grinned.

'No, not even if you do that,' she said tearfully. 'I'm going home and I'm going right now.'

Chapter Ten

No, not even if you do that,' she said tactfully.
'I'm going home and I'm going right now.

Abbie had never seen Sam so happy. He seemed to find his new job perfect in every respect.

The Nelson preserving company had only been established for about eight years at its site in Long Lane, Aintree, but already it had become a household name for quality, and was famous worldwide for its jams.

Sam was so intrigued by what they produced that he didn't seem to be able to stop talking about it. Each night when he came home he had something new to impart to Abbie as he washed his face and hands at the kitchen sink and waited for her to put his meal on the table.

'They use countless different types of fruit and it comes from all over England, and they also ship in strawberries and raspberries from eastern European countries. You should see all the other fancy fruits, like apricots, that they import, too. They bring in huge crates of bitter oranges to make marmalade,' he went on, his round face glowing with excitement. 'The colours and the smells when they open up the crates of different fruits makes your head swim!'

'So what do they do with them all?'

'The fruit goes into enormous copper pans and they are boiled up in those, along with the finest crystal sugar, to a special recipe for each type of fruit . . .'

Abbie clapped her hands over her ears. 'You sound as though you are reading it from one of their labels,' she exclaimed.

'I've read them so many times I know it off by heart,' he grinned.

'So what happens to the fruit when it's taken out of the pans?' she asked.

'The pans have special spouts, so that when the fruit is properly cooked and about ready to set then it's poured out of the pans and into seven-pound tins or one- or two-pound jars.'

'Isn't that dangerous?'

'Of course it is! The jam is boiling hot, so the pans have to be tilted very carefully to make sure there's no splashing and that the jam doesn't spill over from the tins or jars. The people doing that are properly trained and very skilled.'

'What happens next?'

'When it's been poured into the big tins or small glass jars, you mean?'

Abbie nodded.

'The tins and jars are stacked in wire cages until they've cooled off. After that, all the containers are sealed and then they pass along an assembly line where girls label each one according to what sort of jam is inside it. Then they pass them along to the packers who crate them up. Then they stick on a label showing the shop or destination they're going to on the outside of the package.'

'So what's your part in all this?'

Sam grinned. 'I shovel the fruit out of the casks,

where it's been stored from the moment it arrives at the factory, into the copper pans. Girls and women do all the packing and labelling stuff. The men do all the heavy work like lifting the crates and loading the lorries when the crates are ready for delivery.'

'So how many women and girls work there?' Abbie asked.

Sam puffed out his cheeks and looked thoughtful. 'Hundreds! They all wear white overalls and white turban things over their hair. They stand in long lines, putting the lids on and making sure the seals are tight before they pass them along to the girls who put the labels on.'

Abbie listened with interest, but inwardly she resolved that when she left school she'd make sure she didn't go to work in a factory.

The only good thing she could see about Sam's job was that, unlike Billy, he was always in the dry and working in a nice clean place. That, and the regular pay packet he received every Friday. Ten shillings a week, every week, less the money for his insurance stamp, seemed to be an awful lot of money to Abbie.

At the end of the first week Ellen demanded that he should hand his pay packet over unopened, but Sam refused to do so.

'No, Mam! You tell me how much you want me to pay for my keep and I'll give you that and keep the rest,' he told her.

'I want the lot!' she told him brusquely. 'You hand it over to me and I'll give you some pocket money back.'

Sam shook his head. 'That's no good. I have to pay out for tram fares every day and I need something to eat and drink at midday.'

'Take some bleedin' sarnies and a bottle of cold tea, like other lads do.'

Sam pulled a face.

'That's what the rest will be doing!' Ellen insisted.

'Maybe, but they probably have a mam who makes up their sarnies and has them all ready by the time they leave home in the morning.'

'If you're too bloody idle to make your own then get your sister to make them for you, she doesn't do much else,' Ellen told him.

Sam still wouldn't agree to hand over his pay packet.

'If you don't I'll chuck you out, and then you can see if Mo Lewis will take you in as a lodger,' Ellen threatened.

Sam remained tight-lipped. 'You tell me how much you want from me and I'll hand it over,' he told her stubbornly.

'Right, if that's the way you want it then let's have eight shillings.'

Sam shook his head and his mouth tightened. 'That doesn't leave me enough for my tram fares, let alone spending money.'

'Money to waste on that Sandra Lewis, you mean,' Billy sneered. He had been listening to their argument with a cynical smile on his face.

'No! Money for ciggies and beer.'

Billy's lips curled. 'You're too young to drink!'

'You used to go out drinking with mam when you were fourteen,' Sam reminded him.

The row went on for almost a week. When she realised Sam was refusing to give in to her browbeating, Ellen finally agreed he should turn over seven shillings a week.

'You pay for your own grub at midday, though,' she told him.

'I only need a cob of bread, I can have all the jam I want to put on it,' he grinned. 'Tell you what, you give me the bread and I'll bring you home some jam every week. There's always dented tins or cracked jars going for free.'

Sam was as good as his word. From then on they never went short of jam or marmalade. Abbie knew that he also brought some home for Mo Lewis. In fact, he spent so much time round at Sandra's house, and had so many meals there, that Abbie thought it should be Mo Lewis who received his seven shillings a week.

It was the second week in February 1927 before Paddy Ryan went back to sea, and until then Abbie felt she dare not go and knock on Mrs Ryan's door.

She'd not even bumped into Mrs Ryan all over Christmas and the New Year, and she was desperate to know how Peter was. She'd asked Sandra a few times if either her or her mother had heard, but they hadn't seen anything of Mrs Ryan either.

'My mam said that the whole lot of them had gone over to Ireland to see Paddy Ryan's old folk,' Sandra said.

'If that's true,' Abbie said worriedly, 'then it means that Peter hasn't had any visitors since Christmas. I wish I'd known and then I would have gone along to see if they would let me visit him.'

'Of course they wouldn't. You're not a relation!' Sandra told her. 'They're awfully strict about such things.'

'It might have been worth a try.'

'I think you're mad to go on holding a torch for him. He won't be home for another couple of years, and by then he'll probably have forgotten you.'

'Of course he won't. I send messages with his mam every time she goes to visit him, and he sends me messages back.'

'He'll have changed, though! Locked up in there all that time with ruffians of every description, he won't be the same Peter Ryan that we used to know.'

Abbie's blue eyes misted. She didn't want to believe Sandra. She carried a picture of Peter engraved on her brain. Even at this minute she could see his face, his very dark hair that he wore brushed back but which always fell forward over his forehead, his straight dark brows framing his intensely blue eyes, his wide smile and firm chin. He was much better looking than Sam, as well as being head and shoulders taller than him.

She wondered if he had grown any more, if so he would be nearly six foot by now. She was glad about that because she was tall, much taller than Sandra and taller, even, than Sam was.

She was pretty sure he would never let himself be influenced by the type of boys he had to associate with, even if they were rough and uncouth.

'He'll be nearly sixteen by the time they let him out,' Sandra commented. 'He'll have a job finding work. His reputation will be against him for one thing.'

'He doesn't have to tell them he's been in reform school!'

'Don't be daft! It will be on his records. Anyway, they'll want to know what he's been doing with himself since he left school.'

'Out of work and looking for a job like most of the other school-leavers.'

Sandra looked smug. 'Yes, Sam's been dead lucky, thanks to me and me mam getting him the job at Nelson's.'

'Well, he must be good at it or they wouldn't be keeping him on there, would they,' Abbie retorted sharply.

'I've been thinking I might go there to work when I leave school,' Sandra went on. 'I'd be able to keep an eye on Sam and see he behaves himself with all those girls he has to work alongside.'

'Good luck to you! I wouldn't work in a factory if you paid me!'

'Oh my, Miss Hoity-Toity, and where do you think you'll go to work, then?'

'Frisby Dyke's, or somewhere like that.'

'Bit behind the times, aren't you, luv,' Sandra said loftily. 'They're in real trouble and about to go bankrupt!'

'Well, there's other big stores, Lewis's or Bon Marché, I'm not too fussy.'

'You mightn't be, but I bet they are and they may not want someone whose boyfriend has been in reform school.'

Abbie's cheeks went scarlet. 'You do talk rubbish, Sandra Lewis,' she said hotly.

'It's been a long time since you were last here – I've missed you,' Maggie Ryan commented when, eventually, Abbie went round to see her.

'I wanted to come before, to find out how Peter was the last time you saw him.'

Maggie shook her head despondently. 'I'm worried about him,' she admitted.

'Why? He's not ill, is he?'

'No, but he's changed such a lot, Abbie. You'd hardly know him!'

Abbie's heart thumped anxiously. 'In what way?' she asked tentatively, and gritted her teeth as she waited to hear the answer.

'All the fun has gone out of him,' Maggie said sadly. 'He's so serious, as though he has the cares of the world on his shoulders.'

'He probably hates being in there, that's why!'

Maggie pushed her dark hair back from her face, and her eyes were puzzled. 'No, I don't think it's simply that, luv. He seems to be so sombre. Keeps telling me about all the studying he's doing. In fact, he never even mentions how long it will be before he's released. He's working away all the time at some exam or other. I can't make head nor

101

tail of it, but he seems to think it is very important.'

'I didn't know they studied and did exams while they were in reform school.'

'Oh yes. Education is considered to be very important. If you work hard you get points or something, and that all goes to help when your case comes up for review.'

'So, if he's working so hard, does that mean he will be released earlier?'

Maggie looked taken aback. 'I never thought about that, Abbie. I'm glad you've mentioned it. I'll ask him, next time I go in to see him.'

'Apart from that, Mrs Ryan, how has Peter changed? Does he look different?' Abbie asked anxiously.

Maggie Ryan sighed. 'Well, he's grown quite a bit; he's a lot taller than his dad now. And he's broadened out as well. He's quite a handsome-looking lad, in fact,' she added proudly.

Abbie's heart beat faster. 'He always was, but it sounds as though he's improved even more,' she smiled.

Chapter Eleven

The next few years flew by, and all Abbie could think about was how much she was missing Peter. She still counted the days to his release, but at the very start of 1929, she also began to mark off the days until she left school. Because her birthday was not until July she was expected to stay until the summer holidays. Sandra's birthday was in May, but her mam thought it would be a good idea if she stayed on until the end of July as well.

'The sooner you leave school and start earning some money, the better off we'll all be,' Ellen told Abbie. 'It's a pity you can't find yourself a Saturday job, like our Sam did. Lazy lump, lying around the house all the time.'

'Will you be better off?' Abbie questioned. 'When I start work I won't have time to do all the cleaning and washing and ironing,' she pointed out.

'Less of your bleedin' cheek,' Ellen flared. 'Who the hell do you think you're talking to? I put the food on the table and buy all your clothes so the least you can do is pull your weight around the place.'

'I do more than pull my weight, as you put it, I practically run this house,' Abbie reminded her.

'Most of my clothes and shoes come from Paddy's Market and are someone else's cast-offs!'

Over the last couple of years, Abbie had come to realise that no matter how hard she tried she would never be able to win her mother's love and approval, and now she no longer tried to do so. She was taller than her mother and her two brothers, and she no longer felt intimidated when her mother and Billy began shouting and swearing, whether it was at her or each other. Generally, she simply ignored their outbursts and filled her head with other thoughts.

Most of the time she thought about Peter, who was due for release in September, and about the difference between her home and the Ryans'. She had long since stopped comparing her mam with Peter's mam because there was such a vast difference between the two women.

Ellen was a tough sort of person; cold, aggressive, untidy and raucous. She wasn't interested in cooking, or making their home comfortable. Maggie was the exact opposite. She was warm-hearted, her shoulder-length curly black hair was always clean and shining, her blue eyes continually sparkling, and she had a warm, ready smile. She was a good homemaker, and an excellent cook.

Maggie Ryan had shown her more love and affection since Abbie had been visiting her regularly, while Peter had been in reform school, than her own mother had shown her all her life, Abbie thought sadly.

She still couldn't understand why Paddy Ryan had taken such a dislike to her. Maggie didn't seem to want to discuss it, but she was sensible enough not to take offence. Without being asked, she steered clear of the Ryan house whenever Paddy was at home.

As summer heightened, Abbie started thinking more and more about where she was going to go to work. She turned a deaf ear when her mother kept hinting to Sam that he should ask if they were taking on school-leavers at Nelson's. Although Sam still seemed to like his job there, and he had been promoted to helping on the vans, she still didn't intend to go and work in a factory if she could help it.

Maggie Ryan said that with her lovely dark looks and tall figure she would easily get a job in one of the Lyon's Corner Houses, but she didn't really fancy being a Nippy, either.

Sandra said she wouldn't be going to work in a factory after all. Her mam was going to ask Mrs Pringle, the woman who owned the hairdressing salon in Great Homer Street, if she could start there as an apprentice. Mo Lewis went every fortnight for a marcel wave, and sometimes to have her fair hair bleached with peroxide.

Abbie looked at Sandra enviously. A hairdresser! She had never thought of trying to do something like that, but it certainly sounded better than working in a factory.

'If she wants more than one girl to start there, perhaps she'd take you on as well,' Sandra suggested. 'Shall I get my mam to ask her?'

'That would be wonderful,' Abbie agreed, her eyes shining enthusiastically.

Suddenly, life seemed to be full of promise. Since Sam had been working, and had had some money in his pocket, she'd seen hardly anything of Sandra because Sandra had been out with Sam all the time. If she and Sandra were working together, though, it might put things back on the old footing. She hoped so, they'd been such close friends when they'd been younger that she missed seeing her every evening and sharing secrets.

When Sandra said that her mam was going to ask Mrs Pringle the next time she went to have her hair done, Abbie could hardly wait to find out what the answer was.

She could tell by the look on Sandra's smiling round face that the news was good, the moment she saw her.

'So, when do we start, do we have to go and see her for an interview first?'

'No! Normally we would have to, but my mam is such a special customer, and Mrs Pringle has known her for such a long time, that she took my mam's word that you would be suitable. She didn't need any sort of reference for me, of course. She's cut my hair ever since I was about six years old, so she's known me for as long as she's known my mam.'

Abbie looked enviously at Sandra's shining fair hair, which was cut in a sleek bob. 'That's probably why it always looks so nice,' she told her.

Sandra studied Abbie's 'pudding basin' cut critically. 'Perhaps you ought to try and do something to your hair before you start work. It badly needs cutting. Would you like me to do it for you?'

'Could you!' Abbie's face lit up. This was like old times, doing things for each other, sharing things and taking an interest in each other.

'Come round this evening after tea. Tell your Sam I won't be going out tonight.'

'Shall I tell him why?'

Sandra shrugged her plump shoulders. 'No, keep him guessing, do him good.'

'He might be worried?'

'So? You shouldn't let boys know everything, or take you for granted, Abbie. You've got to have a life of your own, you know.'

Abbie bit her lip and said nothing. If Peter was interested enough to ask, she would certainly tell him where she would be and what she would be doing.

'Haven't seen you here for quite a while,' Mo Lewis greeted Abbie when she turned up about half past seven.

'Sandra is going to cut my hair,' Abbie told her. 'Thank you very much, Mrs Lewis, for speaking to Mrs Pringle. I'm really looking forward to starting work there.'

'That's all right, Abbie.' Mo Lewis gave her a fleeting smile. 'I hope you will behave yourself and work hard, and not let me down,' she added.

'Of course I won't. I'm very grateful.'

'Come on, we don't want to take all night doing your hair,' Sandra said impatiently. 'Come into the kitchen.'

Sitting on a hard kitchen chair with a towel tied

round her neck, Abbie felt apprehensive as she heard the scissors snipping away. Sandra tilted her head first one way and then the other. She wished there was a mirror so that she could see exactly what Sandra was doing.

When Sandra finally finished and handed her a small hand-mirror, Abbie gasped. She looked so different. Her face-framing bob and central parting were gone. Most of her hair was swept back behind her ears in a ragged, uneven style, and there was a badly chopped-off fringe covering her forehead.

'Well? Do you like it? It makes you look more grown-up.'

Abbie turned her head this way and that. 'It's so different I don't know what to say,' she murmured.

Mo Lewis was taken aback. 'You don't sound very grateful! I think our Sandra has done a good job. It shows she's cut out to be a hairdresser.'

Abbie wasn't so sure. Her hair didn't feel right, and she couldn't wait to get home and take a good long look at herself in the mirror.

When she did she was aghast. She couldn't possibly go to work in a hairdresser's looking like that! She didn't even fancy going to school in the morning with her hair in such a state.

Biting back her tears she slipped out of the house again. It was late, but she was sure Mrs Ryan wouldn't mind the intrusion, and there was no one else she could think of who would be able to help her.

Maggie Ryan gasped and then started laughing when she saw Abbie.

'Oh my goodness, what have you been doing?'

She listened sympathetically as Abbie explained about the forthcoming job and Sandra's attempt to cut her hair so that she would look better.

'If I was Mrs Pringle I would send you packing before you started work,' Maggie told her. 'With hair like that you'd frighten off all her customers!'

'Can you do anything to put it right?' Abbie begged.

'I'll try! Come on into the kitchen.'

Once again, sitting on a hard chair with a towel round her neck, Abbie listened to the snip of scissors and wondered what on earth she was going to look like this time.

'There you are!' Maggie held out a hand-mirror for her. 'Does that look any better?'

Abbie studied the results with relief. The style remained the same, but this time her hair was cut smoothly into the nape of her neck. It was all the same length and hung neatly behind her ears. The heavy ragged fringe had been transformed into a neat wispy one that curved over her right eye.

'It's wonderful, thank you so much! I could never have gone out looking like I did.'

'Well, it's not all that much different,' Maggie said modestly. 'I've tidied it up, that's all.'

They looked at each other and grinned conspiratorially. 'Our secret?' Maggie said.

'You mean let Sandra think that this is how she actually cut it!'

'I don't think she will say anything, do you?'

'I don't know what I would do without you,' Abbie told her. Impulsively she flung her arms round Maggie Ryan's neck and hugged her.

If Sandra noticed the improvement she said nothing. Even though she knew she looked better than she had ever done in her life, Abbie still felt nervous when, a week later, she and Sandra started work.

Maggie had bought her an Amami shampoo, and shown her how to comb her hair after washing it so that it hung sleek and smooth. She had also helped her to make a new dress from a length of lovely blue material Abbie had bought in the market with money Sam had given her for her birthday.

In the window of the salon there were two models' heads. One had a smooth blonde wig that showed the perfection of a marcel wave that cost one and sixpence, while on the other one there was a dark brown curly wig advertising the advantage of a steam perm at nine shillings and sixpence. On shelves down one side there was a display of hairnets; coloured ones to sleep in at night, and very fine ones to protect the hair during the day. On shelves on the other side of the window, combs and brushes were displayed, and Amami shampoos at fourpence each, in different coloured sachets for blondes, brunettes or redheads.

The salon itself was a long narrow room that was spotlessly clean. There was a reception desk immediately inside the door. At the far end of the room there were two wide white bowls side by side, where the apprentices washed the customers' hair. The rest of the room was divided up into eight curtained-off individual cubicles, ensuring that whatever treatment the customers had done was carried out in complete privacy.

Alice Pringle was a forbidding-looking lady in her late forties. She was immaculately dressed in a smart white blouse and a plain black skirt. Her brown hair had a rigid marcel wave, and her frosty smile was turned on and off like a light, depending on who it was she was dealing with. Her manner with her staff was stern and cold; with customers, smooth and ingratiating.

'Well, Sandra,' Mrs Pringle looked down at the gold watch on her wrist, 'I'm pleased to see you have arrived on time. Bad timekeeping is something I will not tolerate.' She looked Abbie up and down. 'And this is your friend. Hmm! You are rather tall to be a hairdresser, young lady. I hope you won't be complaining of backache every whipstitch.'

Without waiting for an answer she signalled to a red-headed girl in her late twenties. 'Beryl, come and take charge of these two new girls. Find them some overalls and show them what to do.'

'Yes, Mrs Pringle.' Beryl hurried across the salon.

'They can start by washing the dirty towels from yesterday.' She turned to Sandra and Abbie. 'I'm sure you both know how to use a dolly-tub so get on with it.'

It was mid-morning by the time they had finished and hung the towels out to dry on a line stretched between two posts in the yard at the back of the shop.

'While those are drying you can sweep up the floor, and wash out the basins after each customer,' Beryl told them. 'At lunchtime, you make tea for the rest of the staff and then you can stop for fifteen minutes to eat your own snack.'

It didn't sound too bad, but they found there were countless other tasks which Beryl didn't bother to mention. They were constantly being asked to run errands for other members of the staff, or even for some of the customers. They were expected to keep the floors in each cubicle clean by continually brushing up hair. Half the time they didn't know which cubicle they were needed in, and if they went into the wrong one the assistant working there told them off.

In the afternoon they had to bring in all the towels they had washed in the morning and hung out to dry, fold them up neatly and stack them away on a shelf. At the same time they had to collect up all the towels that had been used during the day, wash them, and hang them to dry in readiness for the next day.

By the time the salon closed at seven o'clock that night, both Sandra and Abbie felt dog-tired as they made their way home.

'It's a lot harder than I thought it would be,' Sandra grumbled.

'Perhaps working in a factory might be easier after all,' Abbie giggled.

Sandra sniffed. 'You go and do that sort of work if you want to, but my mam says I am worth something better than that, and after her getting us the jobs I'm sticking it out. It's bound to get better.'

Chapter Twelve

Although there was another young apprentice and four qualified hairdressers working at Mrs Pringle's salon, Abbie and Sandra seemed to be the ones who were sent to wash out the towels and make the tea. After the first few days, however, most of the others who worked there became a little more friendly towards the two newcomers.

Mrs Pringle spoke to them only very occasionally, and then it was usually because there was an errand she wanted one of them to run, but they sensed she was watching them closely.

On the Thursday morning she instructed the senior stylist, Marcia, to let Beryl, the other junior, attend to the towels.

'I want you to instruct Abbie and Sandra on how to shampoo,' she told her.

'Do you want them to practise on each other?'

'No, Mrs Harding will be arriving in five minutes' time and she has agreed that they can try out their skills on her. Let one of them apply the shampoo and let the other one rinse, and report back to me on how they get on,' she ordered.

Although it looked fairly simple, Marcia turned it into a complicated art-form.

'Before you start to shampoo you must make sure that the client is well protected,' she instructed. 'Use two towels. A small thin one, which you tuck inside their collar, and a large thicker one over that. You must make sure that the thick towel completely covers their shoulders and protects the front of their clothes. Do you understand that?'

Both girls told her they did.

'There is a right and wrong way to apply shampoo,' she continued. 'First you must carefully measure it out into the palm of your hand, and then it must be massaged into the scalp using firm yet gentle movements. Every strand of hair must be perfectly covered to make sure it is clean. Rinsing off is equally important. Every particle of shampoo must be removed. Remember that the hair must be squeaky clean. You then wrap a clean towel around the client's head and move them into one of the cubicles ready for the stylist.'

Again, both girls murmured that they understood what she was telling them and assured her that they had no questions.

'Right. Well, we will see how you get on with Mrs Harding. I'll stand behind you so that I can be sure you are doing it properly, and if anything goes wrong I can deal with it.'

Sandra placed the towels round Mrs Harding's neck as they'd been told to do and then reached out for the shampoo.

'Wait,' Marcia held her arm. She studied Sandra's plump little hand and then turned to Abbie. 'Hold your hands out,' she ordered.

Marcia nodded her head as if reaching an

important decision. 'You have much longer fingers,' she told Abbie, 'so I think you will be much better at massaging the shampoo into the scalp. Anyway, you do it this time and we'll see how you get on.'

Abbie felt nervous as she tipped shampoo into her hand. She knew Sandra was scowling, annoyed because she had wanted to be the first one to do it.

As she gently but firmly worked up a lather, and made sure it covered every part of Mrs Harding's scalp, the woman murmured her appreciation.

'There, I thought you would be best for that job,' Marcia exclaimed, pleased by her decision. 'Now, Sandra, let's see how well you can rinse it all off. Squeaky clean, mind!'

Sandra picked up the rubber attachment that was fixed to the tap, digging Abbie hard in the ribs to make her move out of the way. As she did so, a jet of hot water shot out of the spray nozzle at the end, missing Mrs Harding but soaking Marcia, who screamed as the hot water hit her full in the face.

Abbie grabbed at the hose to try and deflect the spray away from Marcia, but Sandra pushed her out of the way causing the water to shoot straight at Mrs Harding, soaking the front of her clothing.

Mrs Pringle, hearing all the screams and commotion, came hurrying out of her office to see what was going on. She arrived on the scene at the precise moment that Abbie grabbed the spray.

After that it was bedlam. All the staff seemed to

be milling around Marcia and Mrs Harding, everyone trying to help. Countless dry towels were passed from one to the other. Marcia was calmed within a few minutes, but Mrs Harding remained very irate.

'Look at the state I'm in,' she ranted. 'My blouse and skirt are completely ruined, and I'm soaking wet right through to my knickers!'

Even though it was a blazing hot August day, she claimed she would probably catch her death of cold from being soaked to the skin like that.

Mrs Pringle did her best to calm her down. Brenda was dispatched to make Mrs Harding a cup of tea to counteract the shock she had suffered. More towels were handed to Mrs Harding to wrap round her shoulders to keep her warm. Mrs Pringle assured her that a taxicab had been called to take her home and that she would pay for it.

Then Mrs Pringle turned on Abbie, blaming her for the whole incident.

'I didn't do anything wrong,' Abbie protested, her voice trembling and tears streaking down her cheeks. 'I grabbed hold of the spray to try and prevent Mrs Harding from getting wet. If you ask Marcia I am sure she will tell you the same thing.'

Mrs Pringle refused to listen.

'Ask Sandra, then,' Abbie told her. 'I'm sure she will tell you it was all a dreadful accident.'

'I'm not interested in what Marcia may have to say, or what she may think. I have already spoken to Sandra. The poor child is distraught and from what she has told me it is obvious that you were to blame. She says you deliberately pushed her.'

Abbie felt angry about the injustice of the accusation. After so many years of being brow-beaten by her mother and Billy, Mrs Pringle's raised voice and angry stance had less effect on her than it would have had on most young girls.

Automatically, she straightened her shoulders, standing so tall that her eyes were on a level with those of Mrs Pringle. 'That is not true,' she said firmly, her dark head held proudly. 'All I did was to try and turn the spray away so that the water went into the washbasin and not over anyone.'

'So why did Mrs Harding and Marcia get soaked to the skin, then?' demanded Mrs Pringle.

Abbie met her accusing gaze with a contemptu-ous look. 'It happened because Sandra tried to twist the hose out of my hand,' she explained angrily.

'That's quite right, that is what happened,' Marcia piped up.

Mrs Pringle looked flummoxed. She waved a hand imperiously to quieten Marcia. Realising that she was probably in the wrong, but having no intention of admitting this, Mrs Pringle glared at Abbie and said frostily, 'Report to my office, Abbie Martin, we'll finish this discussion in pri-vate where there will be no further interruptions!'

Once they were in her office, and Mrs Pringle was seated behind her desk, she wasted no time in venting her spleen by dismissing Abbie and telling her to leave the premises immediately.

'And don't expect any wages or a reference,'

Mrs Pringle told her. 'In fact, I ought to make you pay for a new blouse and skirt for Mrs Harding, as she is one of our most valued customers and I doubt if she will ever put a foot over our door again.'

'She probably won't when she hears how unfairly you've treated me,' Abbie told her quietly as she turned on her heel and walked out.

Once she was standing on the pavement outside the hairdresser's, Abbie's bravado evaporated. She'd been working there less than a week and already she'd been sacked!

She wished there was someone she could talk to. Someone who would understand her predicament and advise her on what she ought to do. Mrs Pringle was in the wrong. It had been Sandra's fault. Yet Sandra had blamed her and played the innocent.

As she walked down Great Homer Street, turning her back on Pringle's Hairdressing Salon for good, Abbie had to admit that it would probably have been even worse for Sandra than for her if Sandra had been the one who'd got the sack. Sandra really would have been in deep trouble, because her mother knew Mrs Pringle well and had asked her to give them the job.

She would be in hot water herself when her own mother got to hear about what had happened. She'd never wanted her to go there in the first place, but Abbie had always vowed that she would never work in a factory. Now, she thought miserably, it looked as if she'd have to go back on her promise to herself.

Too upset to go home, she decided to walk into the centre of Liverpool and look at the shops.

She gazed into the windows of the big department stores, wondering if the day would ever come when she would be able to afford to buy some of the wonderful clothes on display. As she stopped to look in the windows of Frisby Dyke's, she remembered telling Sam and Sandra that one day she intended to work there.

And why not, she asked herself. She'd never wanted to be a hairdresser. Why didn't she go in and ask if there were any jobs going. She had nothing to lose.

She stared at her reflection in the glass window, then, smoothing down her dark hair and straightening her dress, she marched boldly into the store.

Once inside she had no idea what to do next. Taking a deep breath she marched up to one of the shop-walkers. 'Do you have any jobs going?' she asked quickly, before her nerve deserted her.

He looked at her, startled. 'You'd have to ask in the office. Top floor. Take that lift over there and it will take you all the way up there.'

Once she was inside the lift she felt so scared that if it had stopped at any of the intermediate floors she would have got out of it and run. As it was, when it bumped to a stop and the doors opened she found herself right outside the General Office.

Knees knocking, she pushed open the heavy wood and glass door, and found herself in front of a polished mahogany counter. The girl perched on a high stool behind it gave her an encouraging smile.

'I . . . I wondered if there were any jobs going?' Abbie stuttered.

'You mean here, in the office?'

'No. Down in the shop, serving behind the counter,' Abbie said quickly.

'All those jobs have already been filled by this year's school-leavers,' the girl told her.

'Thanks!' Shoulders dropping, Abbie turned away. She should have stuck to her guns and come after a job here the day she left school, and not bothered with the hairdresser's, which was not what she had wanted anyway, she thought despondently.

'Wait a moment,' the girl called out as Abbie reached the door. 'I've just remembered, one of the new girls didn't turn up. She met with some kind of accident. I don't think anyone else has been taken on in her place. Hang on a minute and I'll ask.'

She was back in seconds. 'Miss Breck says she'll see you. Will you follow me,' she said, and opened a door that led into a corridor. When they stopped outside another door, the girl tapped lightly and then opened it and indicated to Abbie that she should go in.

The woman sitting behind the desk was in her thirties. Abbie had never seen anyone who looked so neat. Her brown hair was drawn back into a bun from her oval face, which was as smooth as ivory. She was wearing a dark grey costume the same colour as her eyes, and a white blouse which was buttoned right up to the neck.

'You are looking for work?'

Abbie nodded.

Miss Breck drew a notepad towards her and picked up a pen. 'And what is your name?'

'Abbie Martin.'

'Where have you been working until now?'

'I . . . I've only just left school.'

'I see! When were you fourteen?'

'On the eighteenth of July.'

'And you want to be a counter hand?'

Abbie relaxed. 'Yes, I've always wanted to work here, ever since I was quite small,' she replied, smiling.

Miss Breck studied her more closely and Abbie pulled back her shoulders, glad she was wearing the new dress Maggie had made for her, and that she had washed her hair only the night before when she'd gone to the public baths so she knew it was clean and shiny.

Miss Breck smiled kindly and indicated to Abbie that she should sit down. 'Well, we finished taking on new junior staff in July but we do still have one vacancy. It's in one of the fashion departments so we need someone who looks attractive and has a nice manner.' She studied Abbie carefully. 'Where do you live?'

'Bostock Street.'

'I'm not sure where that is?' Miss Breck remarked.

'It's one of the roads between Great Homer Street and Scotland Road.'

The smile vanished, and a frown marred the smoothness of Miss Breck's ivory face.

'I see!' She twiddled the pen between her thumb and forefinger thoughtfully. Then she looked up and scrutinised Abbie once more. 'Well, you certainly look quite respectable, and you appear to have a nice personality, so I think we can give you a trial. You will be on probation, you do understand that? If, after the first month, we decide you are not satisfactory, then you will have to go.'

Abbie nodded vigorously. 'I understand.'

'You will be paid five shillings a week during your first month. After that, if your work is satisfactory, we will increase your wages to seven shillings. Deductions will be made each week for your Insurance Stamp. Your hours are from eight o' clock in the morning until seven at night, Monday to Friday, and until nine o'clock on Saturdays. You will have a half-hour break in the middle of the day; this will be on a rota system with the other members of your department. There is a rest room where you can eat your sandwiches or you can use the staff canteen. Is there anything else you wish to know?'

'It all sounds perfect,' Abbie said enthusiastically. Her relief at getting a job overshadowed everything else.

'Right. You can start next Monday morning, then. Report to Miss Webster in the Coats department. Do you know where it is?'

'No, but I am sure I can find it. I'll go and have a look now, while I'm here, to make sure I know where to go on Monday.'

'Yes, well I think it might be even better if I took you there myself and told Miss Webster who you are. It might save a lot of time and misunderstanding on Monday morning.'

Chapter Thirteen

Abbie walked home on air. Her head was spinning, her heart was singing, and she couldn't wait to relate all her day's adventures to Maggie Ryan.

Her only worry was how she was going to explain to her mam at the end of the week when she had no money to hand over. Perhaps, though, when she heard that she would be earning five shillings a week, and not three and sixpence, she wouldn't take it too badly.

Since she never goes to a hairdresser's herself, it probably won't worry her too much when she hears that I've been sacked from Pringle's, even before I've been there a week, she told herself.

Frisby Dyke's! The name repeated itself over and over in Abbie's head. It was where she'd always dreamed of working, though she'd never even thought about which department. To be starting in Coats was even better than she could have hoped for.

Maggie Ryan was as pleased as Abbie when she heard the news.

'That's wonderful, luv. Far better than working at a hairdresser's. You've more chance of getting on and being promoted. Better money as well! I'd say it was a lucky break for you, and I wouldn't let what happened at Pringle's bother you any more.'

'When I was a small kid I always said I wanted to go and work at Frisby Dyke's,' Abbie smiled.

'Well, there you are, then, it was meant to be.'

'Will you tell Peter when you go in to see him next time?'

'Of course I will, luv. He'll be as pleased as punch for you. Now that you've left school they may let you visit him. Would you like me to ask, next time I go there?'

'Would you!' Abbie's eyes shone with excitement. 'I'd like that more than anything. It would have to be on a Sunday, of course, because I'll be working every day for the rest of the week.'

'We'll try and fix something up,' Maggie promised. 'Anyway, he'll be home soon. All you have to do now is tell your mam about what has happened.'

Abbie's eyes clouded. 'That's not going to be easy.'

'Rubbish! She'll be delighted when you tell her about your new job.'

'I'm not so sure. Mrs Pringle hasn't paid me, so mam'll have plenty to say about that!'

Maggie looked thoughtful. 'Need you tell her that bit?'

'I shall have to, because she's already told me I've got to hand over two shillings and sixpence a week.'

'Oh, I see!' Her face brightened. 'I know what we can do; I can lend you the money you should have earned. How about that?'

Abbie stared at her, open-mouthed. 'You'd do that for me?'

'Of course!'

'I promise I'll pay you back,' Abbie assured her.

'I know you will. Shall we say at a shilling a week, then if you give your mam the two and sixpence she's expecting you'll still have some spending money left over.'

'Thank you, Mrs Ryan, thank you so much!' Abbie hugged her. 'You really are my guardian angel,' she said gratefully.

'I'll get you the money right now,' Maggie smiled as Abbie released her. 'You can hang on to it until "handover" day, but at least you know you'll have it ready,' she smiled.

Ellen and Billy were already there when Abbie reached home. As soon as she walked through the door Ellen launched into a diatribe about the fire being out and Billy was cursing loudly because there was nothing ready to eat.

'Well, I'll be here tomorrow when you get in and your meal will be ready and waiting for you, and on Saturday as well,' Abbie told them.

Ellen stopped what she was doing and stood there with her hands on her hips, glaring at Abbie. 'Why's that?' she demanded.

Abbie told them. She recounted her story in detail. The only thing she omitted was the fact that Mrs Pringle had refused to pay her.

Instead of her mother being riled, as she had expected, Ellen rocked with laughter. And so did Billy. It wasn't the raucous laughter that she was used to hearing from them when they came home late at night in a drunken stupor. It was real laughter, as though they were both amused and pleased about what had happened.

'Oh my God!' Ellen wiped the tears from her eyes. 'You're a right caution! I wish I'd been there to see it all happening.'

'So what are you going to do now?' Billy asked. 'You going to stay home and look after this place and cook our food?'

'She certainly bloody well isn't,' Ellen rasped. 'Our Sam can ask around and see if he can get her taken on at Nelson's, or at one of the other factories out at Long Lane.'

'There's no need for him to do that,' Abbie told her quickly. 'I've already got another job. I'm starting on Monday at Frisby Dyke's.'

'You're doing what?' Ellen's mouth gaped in surprise. 'How the hell did you manage that?'

Abbie shrugged. 'I went in there and asked for a job.'

'And you got it just like that?'

'I was lucky. One of the new apprentices hadn't turned up because she'd had an accident, and I've got the job instead of her.'

'They're dead posh in there,' Billy muttered. 'I've never fancied the place, not with that dolled-up fella in the doorway, bowing and scraping, the silly old sod.'

'Yeah, it's posh all right!' Abbie said. 'Ever so. I suppose you mean the doorman, the man who is all dressed up in a frock coat.'

'Isn't that the place where, when you leaves the shop, they gives you a special handle with their name on it to hook your parcels on to carry them home?' Ellen asked.

'Yeah!' Abbie smiled and nodded.

'Wonder they bloody well let you in!' Ellen exclaimed. 'Probably only because you was dressed up, like.'

'The lady who interviewed me was ever so nice,' Abbie told them.

'Did you have to tell her where you live?'

'Of course. I don't think she really knew where it was, though!'

'I bet she didn't. Uppity they are, those who work in there. And most of the customers are toffs, or come from Wallasey and think they are! You'll be expected to do a lot of bowing and scraping, you know! I bet you won't like that.'

'Have to put up with it, I suppose,' Abbie grinned. 'I start on Monday in the Coats department.'

'Wait till I tell the other shawlies down at the cotton shed that you're going to work at Frisby Dyke's!' Ellen guffawed. 'That'll give them something to think about. Going up in the world, that, and no mistake!'

'Something to go out and celebrate,' Billy grinned. 'You going to treat us, kiddo?'

'No I am not!'

'Hoity-toity already, are we,' he leered. 'I suppose you'll make out you don't recognise me if I walk into the store!'

Abbie felt hot waves of embarrassment sweeping over her as she regarded the scruffy, unshaven figure in front of her. With his greasy trousers tied under the knee with old shoelaces, his grubby shirt frayed at the collar, and a button hanging by a thread from the cuff of his filthy jacket, he looked more like a down-and-out than a working man. Her mother, in her long coarse black skirt, stained blouse and black shawl, didn't look much better.

Not for the first time, Abbie longed to be able to get right away from her slummy home and surroundings. Their place was probably the most run-down house in the whole of Bostock Street, she thought, as she looked round the shabby living room.

Mo Lewis and Maggie Ryan both kept nice tidy homes. It wasn't simply that their front steps were cleaned with pumice stone twice a week, or that their washing was sparkling white, and not a dull, dirty grey collection of rags, when they hung it out on the lines stretched across the back jowler between their street and Kew Street.

There was more to it than that. When you went in the door of the Ryans' or the Lewis's you were met with a smell of furniture polish and good cooking, not a damp rancid smell like there always was in the Martins' house.

The entire atmosphere was different, too. There was a feeling of friendliness and warmth that made you feel cosy and welcome, even if you were only staying for a few minutes.

Even the rent man wrinkled up his nose, signed their book to show they'd paid, and didn't hang around in their place any longer than he had to do.

Sam never brought Sandra home with him, and

Abbie wondered whether it was because he was ashamed of the dump they lived in, or whether it was because Sandra wouldn't come there. Their home being so shabby could be one of the reasons why Billy never brought a girl home, either. Most chaps of his age, except Michael Ryan, were married or going steady.

To do that, of course, you had to be in love, but love was something that Billy and her mam didn't seem to know the meaning of, as far as she could tell. She couldn't remember the last time her mam had hugged her or kissed her. Even when she was quite small, her mam had never tucked her up in bed and kissed her goodnight.

Maggie Ryan had shown Abbie more affection than any of her own family had ever done, apart from Sam. Sam would still hug her now and again, when he could see that she was particularly down in the dumps, but even with Sam there was less of that these days, now that he was going out with Sandra.

She longed for Peter to come home. He'd be almost sixteen when he was released, and, even though she hadn't seen him for three years, and his messages had become few and far between, she hoped he hadn't changed all that much.

In the past he'd always been telling her how much he cared about her, but Maggie had said several times how much he'd altered, so Abbie couldn't help wondering if he would still feel the same way about her. It wasn't something that she felt she could ask Peter's mother to find out.

After her last visit Maggie had said, 'Do you

know, Abbie, Peter's become so serious that I sometimes wonder if I still know him!'

It seemed to worry her. Yet, she also seemed to be very proud of the fact that he was doing a lot of studying.

'I'm sure he's working far harder at his books in there than he would have done if he'd been at home. I suppose it's because there's not much else for him to do.'

'Better for him to be studying and reading than getting in with a bad lot and learning all their tricks,' Abbie had reminded her.

'Yes, there's that to be thankful for,' Maggie Ryan agreed. 'The only trouble is, I wonder what it means for the future. Several times he's talked of going to sea like his father does when he gets out, and that's something I don't want him to do. With two of my menfolk away at sea my life would be pretty bleak.'

Her own life would be bleak as well, if Peter went to sea, Abbie thought. Like Maggie, she hoped it wouldn't happen, especially now, when she had landed herself such a good job and there was such a bright future for them to look forward to.

Chapter Fourteen

Peter Ryan lay with his eyes wide open, staring into the darkness and listening to the ragged breathing of the other twenty boys in his dormitory. It was almost midnight on his very last night of incarceration.

At eight o'clock tomorrow morning, Friday 13th September 1929, he would be free, released into the outside world once again. In three days' time it would be his sixteenth birthday.

Never again would he have to wear the prickly khaki-green shorts and harsh yellow top that had become his uniform ever since he had entered the reform school two years earlier.

His first pair of long trousers, grey worsted ones that his mother had brought in for him, were in a brown paper parcel underneath his bed, together with a white shirt and a blue pullover.

As the door to the dormitory opened and a glimmer of light appeared, followed by the slow, measured tread of approaching footsteps, he closed his eyes quickly. All his other senses were alert, waiting and listening.

Slowly, Tobias Prescott's feet came closer. There was an accompanying sound of the thin cane he always carried being thwacked lightly but rhythmically against his trouser leg.

He would pause every now and then by one of the beds, and there would be a rustle as the coarse bedcovers were thrown aside. Then came the padding of a pair of bare feet as their owner scurried along the scrubbed wooden floor in the direction of the door.

Peter sensed Tobias Prescott's presence as he reached the foot of his own bed and paused. The man was grossly overweight and his breathing was heavy and laboured.

Ignore him; take no notice. Keep your eyes shut. Breathe slowly and steadily; pretend he's not there, Peter warned himself silently as he heard the cane whipping against the man's leg like a beating heart.

It seemed to be an interminable time before Tobias Prescott moved on. When he eventually did so, Peter felt his tense muscles relax. Opening his eyes a mere fraction, he looked on as Prescott stopped twice more. He watched with rising anger as he saw bedclothes being thrown back and frightened young boys, clad only in striped flannel nightshirts, scramble out of bed and run for the door, trying to escape the thwack of the cane on their bare legs.

Peter shuddered. That was mild compared to what they would endure before they crept back to their beds again, weeping, distressed and ashamed.

He remembered the first time it had happened to him. The selected boys were told to line up in the masters' common room, to lift their nightshirts up over their shoulders and to bend forward, hands on their knees, their bare backsides exposed.

They'd been left standing like that for about half an hour, heads hanging so that the blood rushed to their faces making their eyes bulge.

Then Tobias Prescott had walked down the line, wielding his cane. Each boy received five stinging strokes. He'd had so much practice that he was an expert in making every stroke felt. The cane was so thin that it was like a whip. It seared the flesh, stinging like a wasp and drawing blood.

Anyone who cried out, or moved, received an extra lash. As the air reached the cuts, the pain became excruciating, but there would be another slash of the cane for any boy who dared to jerk away or straighten up.

Five minutes, ten minutes, or even longer, they were left standing there, bending forward, their hands on their knees. The ungainly stance ensured that every scrap of self-esteem and dignity was eroded. And then came the final punishment, and that was even more degrading.

Peter had been so utterly shocked that he had almost fainted.

He had told his mother about a great many of the indignities he had suffered, but never about that. He knew she would find it so terribly repulsive that he couldn't find the words to do so.

Instead, each time it took place he refused to acknowledge what was happening. He tried to pretend it wasn't him or his body that was being treated so vilely, and he refused to dwell on it afterwards. He confined each incident to the darkest corner of his mind and kept them there, locked away even from his own thoughts.

His attitude separated him from the others. They talked about what had been done to them. For some it cleansed the incident from their mind. Others revelled in what had happened and covertly indulged in a replay with each other, of what had taken place.

Peter wanted no truck with what they were doing. He regarded their behaviour as an endorsement of the abomination that they were being subjected to by Prescott, the master in charge of their dormitory.

Isolated and scorned, he spent long, lonely hours on his own. He used much of the time to mentally rebel against the injustice of what had happened that had brought him into such a place.

Someone had lied and told the police that they had seen him taking the bicycle he'd been accused of stealing. His mother had said that both Sam and Abbie were convinced that it had been Billy. They were sure that he'd been the one who had stolen the bike, but they had no proof.

Peter thought a lot about Abbie and wished she was allowed to visit him. His mother brought messages from her every time she came in, and continually told him that she had grown into a lovely girl.

Peter listened avidly to news about her. She was the only girl he'd ever really known well, certainly the only one he'd ever cared about. He wondered how she felt about him. If she was as pretty as his mother claimed, then she must have plenty of boyfriends, he reasoned. He'd not seen or spoken to a girl since the day in the Magistrate's Court when he'd been found guilty.

Knowing what he did now, he worried that Abbie might be suffering unspeakable abuse from her brother Billy and be afraid to tell anyone. If she did, he wasn't sure if Sam would be a match for Billy. Sam wasn't very tall or very muscular, and Billy was such a mean, nasty character. When he was under the influence of drink he seemed to lose all self-control, and was aggressive even towards his mother.

Peter's memory of Abbie was so different from his mother's description of what she was like now. He remembered her as a skinny kid who always looked so frightened and wistful, because she was always being shouted at by her mother and bullied by her older brother. He remembered how he used to put his arm around her shoulders and promise to protect her from the world for the rest of their lives.

He smiled to himself at the memory. He'd been pretty puny himself in those days. Now, he was over six-foot tall, broad-shouldered and muscular. It was his physique as much as anything that had kept him safe from bullying and abuse. He was bigger and taller than most of the other boys, and many of the masters. His fearless attitude of looking them straight in the eye, even though he might be quaking inwardly, had stood him in good stead, except where Prescott was concerned. And even Prescott had not singled him out for special attention for the last six months.

He wondered how Abbie would see him when he was released. His mother never mentioned that she had any other boyfriends. She always said how much Abbie was looking forward to him coming home. He wasn't sure, though, if that was true, or whether she told him that to keep his spirits up.

He had given quite a lot of thought to his own future. Not all the masters were depraved like Tobias Prescott. The master who was in charge of their education, Mr Walters, was elderly, grey-haired, and concerned for their mental welfare rather more than their physical well-being.

'You've got a good brain, young Ryan, why don't you make use of it,' he said quietly after the first lesson Peter had attended.

So Peter had. He'd worked at his studies, not only in class but in his spare time as well. Mr Walters had encouraged him. Yesterday, at his final lesson, aware that it was the eve of his discharge, Mr Walters had wished him well in the future and given him a folded piece of paper. On it was a name: Frank Lewis.

'That's the name of a man at the Royal Liver Friendly Society. Go and see him as soon as you get out of here and he will give you a job as a clerk.'

Peter had been grateful, but doubtful of his chances. Three years in a reform school was hardly a good recommendation.

'Thank you, but won't I need a reference?'

Mr Walters shook his head. 'Don't worry about

that, my boy. I've already spoken to Frank Lewis about you. Good luck.'

Peter still couldn't believe it would be possible to walk straight into a job, not these days when there were hundreds of men and boys unemployed in Liverpool, the same as in the rest of the country.

To work at one of the most prestigious new buildings in Liverpool, to be able to live at home with his mam and to see Abbie regularly, all seemed too good to be true.

On the one occasion when his father had been on shore leave and visited him, he had expressed such disgust that one of his sons should be in such a place that Peter wondered if he would ever manage to rid himself of such a stigma.

'You'll have to go to sea when you get out of here. No one in Liverpool will take you on,' Paddy Ryan had warned. 'Go to sea, sign on for a long trip so that everyone here forgets all about you. When you come home again in a couple of years' time, then, with any luck, they'll have forgotten all about your past.'

Peter knew that going to sea was the very last thing he wanted to do. Months spent aboard ship in a confined space with only men for company would be like another sentence. The only thing that had kept him sane while he'd been in the reform school was the thought of being back at home again once his punishment was complete.

Each day, as he downed the thin watery porridge at breakfast-time; the grey-looking stew made mostly of vegetables with a few lumps of meat that was little more than gristle and fat at midday; or the slice of dry bread and margarine served as an evening meal, he yearned for his mother's home cooking.

The memory of the bowls of rich tasty scouse, the steamed puddings, the fruit cakes and scones that he'd taken for granted when he'd been at home, not only made his mouth water, but gave him something to look forward to in the future.

He'd made a calendar, a list of all the days he had to endure before he would be free again, before he would enjoy the blissful comfort of his home and be able to talk and laugh with Abbie. Each night he marked off one more day. Tonight he'd marked off the very last one.

With a contented sigh he turned on to his side, ready to sleep, knowing that when he woke it would be to a new life and freedom.

Chapter Fifteen

Working at the Frisby Dyke emporium was like entering another world for Abbie. The people she found she would be working with were all so prim and proper. They spoke in quiet, refined voices and wore such smart clothes that Abbie realised from the outset that she was going to have to tread warily. Even though she was wearing the blue dress that Maggie had made for her, she knew she didn't quite measure up to the others.

Her very brief experience at Pringle's Hairdressing Salon had taught her how important it was to be careful not to do anything to upset those in authority.

She had no idea at all what her duties would be when she reported to Miss Webster, but she was quite unprepared for the look of horror on Miss Webster's face as she hurried her off the shop floor and into the stockroom.

'My goodness! Thank heaven there are no customers to see you dressed like that,' she exclaimed. 'Now, remember to stay in here out of sight until you are fitted with a uniform. There's plenty for you to do. You can start by unpacking those boxes,' she went on, indicating a stack of very large cardboard boxes. 'It's the new stock of winter coats. Put each one on to a hanger and then on to one of the mobile rails, ready to be taken out into the showroom once any creases have dropped out of them.'

The woman handed Abbie a box of shaped wooden hangers, each one printed with the company's name, and bustled away leaving her to tackle the mountain of boxes.

The pile reached almost to the ceiling and Abbie was trying to reach the top one to start unpacking when another consignment was wheeled in.

'You're new!' the young man pushing the forked trolley commented, as he deposited his load on to the floor at the far end of the stockroom. 'Need some help?'

He was wearing a uniform of brown trousers and a brown jacket with 'F.D.' embroidered in gold thread on the top pocket. He had red hair and freckles and he didn't look to be very much older than Abbie was, but he was so tall that he had no difficulty in picking the top four boxes off the pile and putting them on the ground by her feet.

'Is that enough or shall I get another pile down?' he asked.

'I think I can manage to reach the others, thank you very much.'

'They're quite heavy, perhaps I'd better lift a few more down for you,' he insisted. 'I'm Jamie Greenslade, by the way,' he told her with a friendly smile. 'I work in the warehouse so we'll probably be seeing quite a bit of each other as I'm always bringing new stock up here.'

Abbie smiled shyly. 'Thank you for your help, Jamie.'

'I was hoping you were going to tell me your name?' he grinned.

'It's Abbie. Abbie Martin.'

'And this is your first day! It must be,' he smiled, 'because you're wearing your own dress, and it suits you. That blue is the same colour as your eyes!'

Abbie felt her cheeks burning. 'I think I had better get on with the work I've been told to do,' she said quickly, and began to fiddle with the thin string around the top package.

'Here, let me show you the easy way to do that,' he told her. Expertly, he slid the string to one corner of the box and slipped it off the edge so that it fell in a tangled heap on the floor and the lid could be lifted off without any difficulty. 'Break your nails trying to undo the string on each parcel,' he warned. 'You straighten the string out afterwards and then it is saved and sent down to the packing room so that it can be reused.'

'Thank you, I'll try and remember.' Abbie smiled nervously. 'I really should get on now and do the work I've been told to do.'

'I'll see you again, then.'

Without waiting for her to say anything he wheeled his trolley away. Left on her own, Abbie began unpacking a coat from each of the boxes as she had been instructed to do.

They were all so beautiful that they took her breath away. Jewel colours, wonderfully soft,

143

warm fabric and, in some instances, trimmed with fur collars and cuffs.

They must cost the earth, she thought, smoothing them on to the hangers and then arranging them on the rail.

She stacked the boxes one on top of the other against one of the walls, smoothed out the tissue paper into neat sheets, and laid out the lengths of string beside them.

She was on the last box in the pile she'd been told to unpack when Miss Webster returned.

'My goodness! You are a tidy worker,' Miss Webster smiled. 'Are you as good at wrapping up parcels as you are at unwrapping them?'

'I . . . I don't know. I've never tried.'

'Well, never mind about that at the moment. Run along to Gowns. Miss Miller is waiting there to fit you with a uniform. Do you know where it is?'

Abbie shook her head. 'No, but I am sure I'll be able to find it.'

'It's on the floor below this one. Don't take all morning about it as there's lots here to be done.'

Miss Miller was a thin, angular woman in her late fifties. Her grey hair was drawn back in a severe bun and her dark eyes were sharp and cold. She was wearing the regulation high-necked black dress and looked extremely forbidding.

'Abbie Martin? This way.' She turned on her heel before Abbie could reply and stalked off into the staff room at the rear of the department. Abbie hurried after her.

The minute the door closed behind Abbie, Miss

Miller produced a tape measure and expertly measured Abbie's bust, waist and hips. With equal speed she selected a black blouse and skirt from a rail. 'Try that on, it should fit!'

'You mean now?'

'Of course I mean now! We can't have you wandering around the store without a uniform. That dress barely covers your knees!' she added in shocked tones.

Shaking with nerves, Abbie pulled her own dress over her head and took the garments that Miss Miller held out to her. As she stood there in her cami-knickers and lisle stockings, which were held up by pieces of elastic as garters, she was conscious of the look of disapproval on Miss Miller's face.

'You are quite well developed, so you really should be wearing a liberty bodice or one of these new-fangled brassieres,' Miss Miller stated in an extremely critical voice.

Abbie kept her head lowered, biting her lower lip to avoid her embarrassment. No one had ever seen her undressed before, except Maggie Ryan when she had been trying on the blue dress Maggie had made her for her birthday. Then she had been wearing a liberty bodice and navy cotton knickers. Maggie had given her the cami-knickers, saying that she had bought them for herself, but that they were too small. Abbie knew they were a little on the large side for her, but she hadn't minded that. The feel of the soft silky material against her skin, after the stiff prickly knickers she had been wearing, was wonderful.

145

'You'll need to wear a slip under your uniform,' Miss Miller went on, 'otherwise you'll find it clings to your legs in a most unpleasant way. Have you got one?'

Abbie shook her head.

Miss Miller tut-tutted in disapproval. 'What do you young girls spend your money on,' she admonished. 'What you are wearing underneath is as important as what you are wearing on top. Now remember that in future.'

Abbie nodded.

'Right, well into those clothes and let's see how they look on you.'

She drummed impatiently on the back of a chair as Abbie put on the straight black skirt, which hung several inches below her knees, and then the black top, which buttoned up to a high banded neck and had long sleeves that fastened with buttoned cuffs.

'Tuck the top inside the skirt,' Miss Miller ordered. 'There, that looks better!' she commented, once Abbie had done so. 'Now you look like one of our girls.'

Abbie smoothed the waistband and then undid the top button of the blouse because she felt as if it was choking her.

'No! That stays done up,' Miss Miller told her sharply. 'Turn round so that I can check if the skirt is hanging right at the back.' She gave it one or two small sharp tugs, then stood back, a satisfied look on her angular face.

'Now, look in the mirror and take note. I expect to always see you looking as trim as you do now.'

146

Abbie stared at her reflection in disbelief. She could hardly recognise the tall, slim figure, dressed almost to the ankles in black, that was staring back at her. She had never worn black before, and it made her skin look so white and her eyes such a bright blue that it seemed to transform her features. She looked solemn, but she also looked elegant, and it rather took her breath away.

'When you've quite finished admiring yourself you'd better get back to your work,' Miss Miller told her caustically.

'Here,' she handed Abbie a package. 'That's another top. You needn't unwrap it as it's exactly the same as the one you have on. You are only issued with one skirt, but you get two tops. They must be changed regularly, at least once a week, and they should be washed very carefully and properly ironed. Is that understood?' She gave her a crumpled piece of brown paper. 'You'd better wrap your own dress up in that, and don't forget to take it home with you tonight, otherwise it will go out with the rubbish.'

As she made her way back to the Coats department, Abbie felt that every eye was on her, even though she knew that, now she was dressed exactly the same as all the other counter assistants, she simply blended into the general background.

'Ah! That looks better,' Miss Webster greeted her. 'We won't have to hide you away in the stockroom any more.'

The rest of the day passed in a whirl of activity. Abbie made tea, swept the floor, dusted counters and fitments. In between, she held pins for the alteration hand, who was called in to make an adjustment to a coat that didn't quite fit one of the customers, and then she had to clear up the pins and lengths of cotton that were still on the floor afterwards.

She also discovered that after the store closed there was still work to be done. All the coats that were out on display had to be covered over with dustsheets, and every counter cleared. Whatever was on display had to be put away safely in drawers or glass cabinets.

Everyone had a part to play and, even though it was only her first day there, she found she had to help tidy up the stockroom so that everything was put away and the room was as neat and tidy as if it had never been used.

Then and only then could she leave.

'Is that your dress and second top in those parcels?' Miss Webster asked her, as she was about to walk out.

'Yes!' Abbie said in some surprise.

'You had better open them up so that I can check the contents.'

Abbie's face flamed. 'Why? Do you think I am pinching something?' she asked indignantly.

Miss Webster sighed. 'No, of course not, Abbie, but it is one of the rules. Before you take anything out of the department I have to check and issue you with a receipt, which you must then show to the doorman as you leave the building.'

When she finally made her exit from the Frisby Dyke building, Abbie had another surprise. Jamie, the boy from the warehouse, was waiting for her.

'Hello,' he grinned. 'I didn't like the idea of a pretty girl like you having to walk home on her own after her very first day at work. Shall I carry your parcels for you?'

'No thank you!' Abbie clutched the two parcels tightly to her chest. 'I can manage quite well.'

'You said that this morning, but in the end you let me lift down some more boxes for you.'

'Well, they were heavy and these aren't,' she told him primly.

'You look different in your uniform, you know,' he told her. 'Very prim and proper,' he added with a cheeky sideways look of appraisal. 'Are you in a hurry to go home?' he asked when she made no reply. 'If not, we could go and have a coffee at the Kardomah.'

Abbie stopped, and turned and faced him. 'Look, Jamie, I was grateful for your help this morning but I've already got a boyfriend.'

For a moment he looked taken aback. Then he laughed. 'I was asking you to go for a coffee, not to marry me,' he called back over his shoulder, as he stalked off in the opposite direction.

Chapter Sixteen

Did she have a boyfriend? Were things still going to be the same between her and Peter when he came home? It was something that bothered Abbie all the way back to Bostock Street.

She quite liked Jamie and she wondered if she had acted rather rashly in turning down his offer of friendship. As a new girl, who knew no one else of her own age working at Frisby Dyke's, perhaps she had been rather too hasty in spurning his attentions.

Still, Peter would be home in a few weeks and then she would know exactly where she stood. Three years was a long time, he had probably changed a great deal. For that matter, so had she. She'd been a skinny unattractive schoolgirl when he'd gone away and now she was almost grown-up.

She caught a glimpse of her reflection in the shop windows as she walked along Lord Street. In her long black skirt she certainly looked different, and she wasn't at all sure she liked what she saw. She hoped she wouldn't meet Sandra on her way home. She'd been quite envious about the dress Maggie had made for Abbie and she'd be bound to have something disparaging to say about her new black look, Abbie thought self-consciously.

Thinking of Sandra reminded her of the fracas there had been at Mrs Pringle's. She wondered if she ought to go and see Mo Lewis and tell her she was sorry about what had happened, since she'd been the one who'd helped her to get the job there.

What had happened had been Sandra's fault, she reminded herself, so perhaps it would be best to say nothing. She still didn't know what Sandra had told her mother and she didn't want to say something that might get her into any trouble. As things were, she felt she probably had the better job now, and that was probably why Sandra was avoiding her.

Even though Sandra was no longer very friendly towards her, Abbie knew she was still as thick as ever with Sam. The two of them seemed to be so full of each other that they had no time for anyone else. Abbie couldn't help feeling a little bit miffed about this because she and Sam had always been so close when they were younger.

At one time they had shared all their secrets and comforted one another when things were bad at home. Now, she hardly ever saw him, and when she did he was usually getting ready to go out with Sandra and wasn't very interested in what was happening in Abbie's life.

Even when she had told him about her new job he had merely raised his eyebrows in surprise. 'Frisby Dyke's, eh! Going up in the world, aren't you. You'll have to learn to talk posh if you want to get anywhere there.'

She wondered if he was jealous. Sam wasn't a rough, tough type of character. She was surprised that he had settled down to working in a factory as well as he had done. Perhaps it had something to do with the fact that most of the other workers were women. The wages were better, too, than what he would get working in a shop, and, if Sandra was to be believed, Sam was saving up so that as soon as she was seventeen they could get married.

A half smile played on Abbie's lips as she recalled the plans she and Sam had harboured for so many years. When Billy and their mam had been so drunk they couldn't stand up and were shouting and bawling at each other, the two of them had clung together and said that as soon as they were old enough to go out to work they would set up home together and move right away from Bostock Street. And Peter had always said he would come with them. In his case it hadn't been because he was unhappy at home, but because he had wanted to be with her.

Abbie wondered if he still wanted to be with her, and whether he had thought about her while he was in the reform school, as much as she had about him.

He hadn't written to her. Maggie said it was because all their letters had to be read by the teachers and headmaster before they were posted, and Peter didn't want them to know about his feelings or private life.

'He doesn't write to me much, either, luv,' she'd said when Abbie's eyes had filled with tears.

'He could give you a note to give me,' Abbie

had pointed out. 'You get to see him every month.'

'No, luv, it would be difficult. There's a master on duty all the time I'm there. He walks up and down between the tables and we're not allowed to pass anything at all between us.'

'You take cake and sweets and stuff for him.'

'I have to hand them over when I go into the building and they are given to him later after they've been inspected,' Maggie told her.

'You never said!'

Maggie sighed. 'No, luv, there's a lot that's gone on in there that I've never said anything about, to you or anyone else. No point in making you more unhappy than you already are.'

There was so much to learn, so many new faces to remember, that the next few weeks at Frisby Dyke's flew by. Any day now Peter would be home and he'd be able to tell her what it had been like in reform school. Even more important, she would be able to find out if he still felt the same way about her. Maggie kept saying he'd changed. That he was so much more serious than he had been. From the little she had gleaned from Maggie about what it was like in there, then it was no wonder all the laughter had gone out of him.

She hoped, though, that he wasn't too serious. She and Maggie were still planning a welcome home party for him, because it would be his sixteenth birthday on the Sunday after he came home.

'He'll be released on the Friday so it won't give him very much time to come to terms with being back at home,' Abbie said thoughtfully. It would also give her a few evenings to get to know him again, she thought. One more week of waiting, that was all.

Like Maggie, she was on tenterhooks. During the day, her mind was fully occupied in learning about her new job and memorising the names of all the new people she was meeting.

She'd been relieved to find that Jamie hadn't taken offence by her refusal to have a coffee with him. The next day he greeted her with a wide smile and was as chatty and helpful as he had been on her first day.

In the days that followed, Jamie introduced her to several other members of staff who were about the same age as them, and this had helped a great deal in putting her at ease.

Miss Webster and most of the other senior staff frowned upon too much fraternising. There were occasions, though, when she was sent to another department with a message or goods, and it was reassuring to see a face she knew when she got there. It also helped when she passed people in the corridor or on the stairs, because she often recognised them and knew which department they worked in.

When a crowd of them met up in the staff restroom, Abbie tended to listen and say as little as possible. Some of those with posh accents, she discovered, came over on the ferryboat from Wallasey each day. Others lived in the better parts of Liverpool, like Aintree, Edge Hill, or Aigburth.

She envied them as they talked about their

semis and big detached houses, but she was careful never to mention where she lived. She was afraid someone might know that Bostock Street was a row of terraced houses off Scotty Road, and everyone knew that was the most notorious part of Liverpool.

Jamie had told her he lived in Wallasey, in Palmerston Road. From what he said about his home life she was sure that, like most of the others she had met at Frisby Dyke's, he would have been slightly shocked if he heard she came from Bostock Street, one of the slummiest areas of Liverpool.

Peter was released the following Friday. She would have liked to have been there when he arrived home, or better still to be at the gates when he was released, to be the one to greet him first. Knowing that was impossible, she went off to work with a heavy heart and found it difficult to keep her mind on what she was doing.

When she eventually left work that night she didn't stop to join one of the long queues of people waiting for a tram, but ran most of the way home. It was a warm September evening, but a fine mist was falling, and by the time she reached Bostock Street her uniform was clinging to her and her hair was hanging in rats' tails.

She knew she ought to go home first and change, before knocking on Maggie's door. In her dreams about her reunion with Peter she had envisaged that she would be wearing the lovely blue dress Maggie had made for her, and that her hair would be sleek and shining as it framed her face.

That would take precious minutes and her need to see Peter mattered more than anything else did in the world. Yet she felt nervous and shy, and although she usually walked in the back door she couldn't bring herself to do so.

Her heart was beating so hard that it sounded as loud as the knocker did as she rapped on the Ryans' door. She had her fingers crossed, praying it would be Peter not Maggie who opened it.

In her dreams, his face lit up with happiness the moment he saw her and he pulled her into his arms as if he couldn't wait a moment longer to hold her close. Then his lips covered hers as she melted into his embrace and he whispered how much he loved her. With his arm around her shoulders he led her into the living room and they could hardly answer each other's questions for the need to kiss and kiss again.

Peter did answer the door. For a moment he stood there, a tall, lean figure with broad shoulders, looking down at her enquiringly, waiting to know what she wanted. His pale face was sombre, his mouth a thin line. If it hadn't been for his thick dark hair and vivid blue eyes she would have thought it was a stranger.

'Welcome home, Peter!'

'Abbie? I didn't recognise you! You look so . . . so different.'

'So do you!'

They stared at each other in bewildered silence.

'You'd better come in, you look half drowned. Mam's in the kitchen,' he added awkwardly.

Maggie, hearing Abbie's voice, came out into the passageway. 'Heavens above, girl, you're soaked to the skin. You'd better run home and change, hadn't you. Why don't you come back after tea and then you can have a good long talk with Peter.'

Too choked to answer her, Abbie nodded.

'See you later, then, Abbie. You and Peter can have a good chat and catch up,' Maggie said again as she left.

She didn't answer. Her mouth was so dry that she couldn't even swallow. The ground seemed to be spinning before her tear-smeared eyes. This wasn't how it was supposed to be!

All her dreams evaporated into the mist. To think she'd turned down the chance to go for a coffee with Jamie Greenslade because she had wanted to stay true to Peter. She'd told Jamie she had a boyfriend. Now she wasn't sure if Peter was even a friend! He'd been so cool towards her, cold almost. He hadn't even recognised her, well, not at first. He didn't even seem pleased to see her. They might as well have been complete strangers.

When she reached home she ran straight upstairs to her bedroom. She leaned her arms on the rickety chest of drawers that served as a dressing table and stared into the flyblown mirror hanging above it.

Her reflection sent a shudder of hopelessness through her. What on earth had she expected? She sat there, staring deep into her own despairing blue eyes, wondering who she was and what she could ever hope to have from life. Her hair hung in rats' tails around her face, her uniform clung to her body like a black shroud, and she had a haunted look that was almost frightening.

No wonder Peter hadn't recognised her, or, if he had, that he had hidden his feelings from her. Seeing her standing there on the doorstep so bedraggled must have been a terrible shock for him. It had probably shattered all his dreams, that is if he had ever harboured any, she thought bitterly.

Feelings of self-hatred flooded over her. Perhaps this was why her mam had no time for her, why Billy treated her as if she was something revolting he had trodden in.

The only person in the world that she could think of who really cared about her was Maggie ... and she had more or less told her to go home and come back when she had tidied herself up.

Chapter Seventeen

Peter had changed so much she'd hardly recognised him, Abbie thought ruefully, as she changed out of her wet clothes into the pretty blue dress and went back round to his house.

This time, however, he certainly seemed more pleased to see her, and gradually, as they talked and exchanged memories, and Abbie related her experiences at the hairdresser's and told him about her new job at Frisby Dyke's, some of their former rapport returned.

She still wanted him to tell her what his feelings for her were, but she realised that he wasn't likely to do that with Maggie sitting there. Instead, she listened to what he was prepared to tell them about his stay in the reform school, and plied him with questions about what he was planning to do now that he was home.

'First thing Monday morning, I'm going for a job,' he told them.

'You should have a word with Sam and see if there are any jobs going at Nelson's Jam Factory,' Abbie suggested. 'There's an awful lot of chaps on the dole, you know. Things have got worse since you've been inside, haven't they, Maggie?'

'Yes, unemployment figures are up,' Maggie

agreed. 'It mightn't be as easy as you think to get fixed up, Peter.'

'Oh, we'll see,' he said quietly.

'I hope you don't find that you have to go to sea like your dad suggested,' his mother said worriedly.

'I don't think I'll be doing that!'

'Well, don't be too sure,' she warned. 'I don't want to sound depressing, but as Abbie has said there's an awful lot of men and boys out of work. Lads coming up to twenty who've never managed to find work since they left school.'

Peter adroitly changed the subject. He asked Abbie how Sam and Sandra were, and about some of the people he had known while at school. His mother told him about the proposed party she was planning for the coming Sunday but he shook his head. 'No, Mam, I don't want to do anything like that. I simply want to slip back into my place here as if nothing has happened.'

'But Peter, we've planned it all. We were only waiting for you to come home so that we could invite everyone.'

He frowned anxiously. 'You haven't done so yet, though, have you?'

'No! We left that until the last minute in case you didn't get out on the day you were supposed to. Abbie is going to contact everyone; Sam and Sandra will help her . . .'

'No! There isn't going to be a party, or a fuss of any kind. Is that clear?'

He rose, and walked up and down the small

room agitatedly. 'I'm sorry if it's spoiling your plans, but that's the way I want things to be.'

Maggie looked very taken aback. 'Well, if that's what you want, luv, then of course I won't organise anything. I thought you would enjoy having all your old friends round, having a nice meal and catching up with all that's been happening.'

'No!' This time his voice was so hard and authoritative that Abbie and Maggie exchanged surprised looks.

'Would you like me to ask Sam and Sandra and Abbie round for tea on Sunday, then, seeing that it's your birthday?' Maggie persisted.

Peter crossed the room and took her by the shoulders. 'Can't I make you understand, Mam, I don't want any special tea or party. I don't want to celebrate my birthday, I want to slide into the background without anyone noticing. I want it to be as though I've been on a holiday, or away on a trip like Dad, and come home again. I don't want a barrage of questions about what it was like in there. I don't want people staring at me and questioning me as if I've come from another world. Answering all the questions you two have fired at me has been bad enough. I want to be left alone to get on with my life. Is that understood?'

Abbie stood up. 'I think I'll be going,' she said, her voice unsteady. This was the second time tonight that all her hopes and plans had been trampled in the mud, and she didn't think she could take any more.

She felt sorry for Maggie because, like her, she

had been looking forward to putting on a party for Peter, to spoiling him and making a fuss of him, and now he had made it quite clear that he didn't want any of it. He resented their interference in his life and in the plans he had obviously already made.

As she walked the few yards back to her own house, Abbie wondered where she came in his scheme of things. He certainly wasn't aching to take her in his arms, or to tell her he loved her as she had been dreaming he would do. She was burning up with her need for him to do so, but there was such a coldness about his manner that she was too intimidated to even kiss him on the cheek in case he rejected her.

On Saturday, Abbie had to work until nine o'clock, and she felt so tired when she left the store that she went home and straight to bed. She'd have plenty of time to see Peter the next day, Sunday, she told herself.

When she did call at his home in the middle of the morning, hoping he would walk to church with her, Maggie said he'd been to early Mass and now he'd gone for a walk.

Abbie hoped he'd call and see her later, but although she waited in all day he didn't show up. Pride wouldn't let her go to the Ryans' house again that day.

For all Peter's aloofness, however, Abbie couldn't keep away from the Ryans' house. She called round on Monday evening when she had finished work, but Maggie said he wasn't in. He'd gone out early in the afternoon and hadn't come back yet. Even as they were speaking, Peter came in. He looked confident and pleased with himself as he told them his news, that he was starting work on the following Monday.

'You've got a job already? How have you managed that? Where is it?'

He held up his hand, warding off the questions fired at him by his mother and Abbie as if they were blows.

'I've got a job with the Royal Liver Friendly Society,' he told them.

'You mean the insurance company in that big building down at the Pier Head? The one with the Liver birds on the top of it?' Abbie exclaimed in astonishment. 'What're you going to be doing there, then?'

'Working as a clerk.'

'They're ever so posh! I thought you had to pass your School Certificate before they'd even look at you,' she said in surprise.

'I *have* passed it.'

Abbie stared at him in disbelief. 'When did you do that? You weren't even in the top class at school . . .'

'I passed while I was in the reform school' he told her. 'I did a lot of studying and reading while I was in there, far more than I would have done otherwise. The master who taught us was very supportive and he recommended me for this job.'

'And yet you never said a word when we were saying about all the unemployment and how difficult it was for lads to get work!' Maggie said.

Peter shrugged. 'I've told you often enough that I've been doing a lot of studying.'

'You never mentioned anything about a job!'

'I've learned never to take anything for granted. If I'd told you that I was going after this job then you would have been all keyed up. As it is, I hope it has come as a nice surprise for you.'

'For me an' all,' Abbie breathed, as Maggie went off into the kitchen to put the kettle on. 'I never dreamed you'd be able to get a job like that, Peter. I thought you'd end up in a factory like our Sam, or working as a docker like our Billy.'

His mouth tightened and his blue eyes were icy as he stared back at her. 'You mean because I was sent to a reform school?'

She bit her lip, remembering how sensitive the old Peter had been. She didn't want to hurt his feelings, but he was quite right, that was what she had been thinking.

'No!' she defended. 'It's just that, what with the General Strike and the Depression and everything, and so many people out of work, I thought you'd be lucky to get a job at all.'

'Look, Abbie, I never took that bike. I was innocent, as you well know. I have been punished for something I didn't do, but I don't intend to let it make me bitter for the rest of my life,' he stated. 'Getting this job isn't pure luck, I've worked hard for it. Now I intend to make a new life for myself.'

'Does that new life include me, Peter?'

He shrugged. 'That remains to be seen. You're not the scrawny little schoolgirl I left behind. You have changed so much. You've grown up, you're beautiful and you've got your own life.'

'Not completely,' she said softly. 'I've dreamed of you coming home, Peter, of us picking up the threads. I've always loved you and I thought you cared for me in the same way.'

'You're talking about when we were kids.'

'We used to be so close, we shared all our secrets. Remember the times whenever my mam and Billy were legless after one of their drinking binges, and we came running to your mam for protection? Sam and me used to say that once we were old enough to work and earn money we'd run away from here and find a home of our own, and you always said you wanted to come with us.'

He smiled cynically. 'Kids' talk!'

'There was more to it than that!'

'Perhaps! Now you've got your own life, Abbie, your own friends.'

'Friends, yes. That's all they are, though. I've never gone out on a date because I've always thought of you as my boyfriend and I've stayed true.'

Peter laughed, a dry humourless sound. 'Love is a feeling I dispensed with a long time ago. Being shut up, a prisoner for all that time, not allowed visitors apart from a visit from my mother once a month, and from my father when he was home from sea, killed off any feelings I had for other people, Abbie,' he said bitterly.

'Oh, I thought about you from time to time,' he added, as if trying to quell the hurt he saw in her eyes, 'but that was all. Memories of how we played together, sometimes on our own, sometimes with Sam and Sandra, but it was as though it was someone else's life. Not mine! I knew that things between the four of us could never be the same again, so what was the point of hankering after them?'

'Now that you're home, do you feel the same? About us, I mean?' Abbie persisted.

Peter sighed expressively. 'It's nice to see you again, but quite frankly, Abbie, I'm a little scared of you. You are so worldly, so grown up and so very pretty, that I can't imagine why you would be interested in someone like me. You must meet plenty of young men who are keen to take you out and have a good time. I don't know how to enjoy myself any more.'

'Perhaps I can teach you!'

He shrugged. 'For the moment it's going to take all my concentration to cope with my new working life.'

'Well, perhaps I can help you over that.' She blushed furiously. 'If we saw each other in the evenings then we could talk about it, discuss any problems you're having. That might help you to settle in better, don't you think?'

His mouth tightened. 'You are trying to be kind, Abbie, but I've learned to fight my own battles and deal with my own problems. I prefer to do things that way.'

'Does that mean you don't want to see me any more?' she asked desperately.

'I'm sure I'll see quite a lot of you. You seem to

166

be good friends with my mother and I'm sure you'll be popping in to see her.'

His remarks made Abbie's hackles rise. 'Look, Peter Ryan, I've been carrying a torch for you throughout the time you've been away. I've never dated anyone else, because I thought it wasn't fair to do so with you shut away. I've had plenty of offers. Boys at work have asked me out, but I've always turned them down. I may not have visited you, but that was because the authorities refused to let me do so while I was at school. I've sent you messages and things whenever your mam has been visiting you, and I always came round to ask her how you were the minute she got home again.'

'Abbie! I'm sorry. I didn't mean to hurt you, I just don't want you building your hopes up about us, or our future together,' he told her.

'Oh, don't worry, you've made it quite clear that we have no future!'

He passed a hand over his thick dark hair. 'I don't know what to say. I'm so mixed up inside, Abbie. So much happened to me while I was in that place. You had to be hard in order to survive. There are things that happened to me that neither you nor my mam know about, and which I don't ever want to talk about.'

'You're not in that place now, though, are you,' she said quickly.

He stared at her, his handsome face haggard with indecision.

'Please, Peter,' she begged. 'You are the person I love most in the world! I've looked forward so much to you coming home. I really thought you would still love me, but even if you don't I'd like us to be able to go out together and have some fun. Won't you give it a try? It might help you to forget some of the bad things that happened to you.'

Chapter Eighteen

Abbie found that it took Peter several months to settle back into normal life, and even then their relationship was still on a formal basis. She wondered if they would ever regain the fun and the feelings of closeness they had known in the past, but she refused to give up hoping.

She still loved him with all her heart, and she was never happier than when they were together, whether it was at his home or when they went out with Sam and Sandra.

She hoped that seeing Sam and Sandra kissing and cuddling when the four of them went to the pictures, or on the rare occasion to a dance, would stir some passion in Peter. Apart from a cool kiss when they met or said goodnight, though, he seemed determined to keep his feelings tightly reined.

Abbie felt frustrated. She yearned for a display of deeper feelings of love from Peter. She wondered if there was something wrong with her, that no one seemed to show her affection the way she wanted them to do. Her mam had never loved her, never had any interest in what she did or what she thought about things. Billy either teased her or sneered at her. Sam, who had at one time been so close and protective, was now utterly besotted by Sandra, who was so possessive and jealous that she couldn't bear to see them exchanging confidences or laughing and joking together.

Abbie had hoped that she would be able to forget or ignore how unhappy she felt about losing Sam when Peter came home. She had envisaged that there would be the same kind of relationship between herself and Peter as there was between Sam and Sandra. She had planned and dreamed of their life together, once Peter was home again. She'd thought they would be inseparable, that he would never tire of telling her how much he loved her and how deep his feelings were for her.

Instead, even though she had been patient all these many months, he was so wrapped up in his job at the Royal Liver Friendly Society that he didn't seem to notice if she was around or not. Persuading him to go out with her was such hard work that she sometimes wondered why she bothered, especially when she often had other offers that she turned down.

As Christmas approached, she received so many invitations to parties from her friends at Frisby Dyke's that she decided to accept some of them, despite the fact that Peter said he didn't want to go with her.

Perhaps if she went on her own to some of the parties it would make Peter realise that she wasn't content to wait forever for him to pay her the sort of attention she desired. Instead of feeling so frustrated by Peter's behaviour, she'd make this new attitude her New Year resolution, she resolved.

Abbie kept to her New Year resolution, and from the very start of 1930 she concentrated on enjoying every moment, both when she was working and when she wasn't.

She concentrated heart and soul on partying and having a good time. She teased, cajoled, begged, or threw a tantrum when Peter wouldn't go with her, and then went on her own. Her mother became tired of her mood changes and threatened to kick her out if she didn't change her ways.

'I'll not stand for it any longer, you little slut,' she bellowed at her. 'You'll be fifteen on your next birthday, my girl, and unless you mend your ways then out of this door you go, bag and baggage. I'm not putting up with you coming home all hours of the night and morning, like you're doing these days, it gives the place a bad name.'

'It might do if you hadn't already done that,' Abbie told her derisively. 'At least I come home sober, not staggering all over the place and shouting the odds at the top of my voice for all the neighbours to hear, like you and Billy.'

Although Billy frequently raised his fist to her, and would quite happily have given her a hiding, his mother restrained him. 'Wait until her next birthday. Do it now and the scuffers'll claim she's only a kid and have you in the nick for hitting her. After July she won't be a kid any longer and then you can belt all hell out of her, for all I care.'

Abbie laughed off her mother's threats, but deep inside she felt hurt and resentful. She retaliated by doing less and less around the house. She kept her own room tidy, but that was all. She ate most of her meals out, either snacks in one of the milk bars near where she worked, or fish and chips that she bought on the way home. Towards the end of the week, when she had very little money left, she made do with a twopenny Mars bar. She looked forward to Sundays, when she was usually invited to a meal with Maggie and Peter.

At work, when she was finally allowed behind the counter to serve customers, she felt as if her life was changing for the better at long last.

She would never forget the thrill she felt the first time she actually made a sale. Bursting with importance, she loaded the customer's bill and money into the little round wooden container, screwing the lid back on and then putting it into the little metal cage above her head. Then she pulled the wooden handle that sent it winging its way along the wires suspended under the ceiling to the office. A few moments later it came winging back with a sharp pinging sound, and as she unscrewed the wooden ball, took out the receipt and change and handed them over to the customer, she felt as proud as any mountaineer who had scaled the highest peak.

When she had been given her promised pay rise after her trial period, her mother had made her hand it over for her keep. Since then, she had said nothing to her mother about the other rises she'd received. Instead, she used the extra money to buy herself pretty clothes and make-up.

She had become very friendly with two girls of her own age; Molly, who worked in the dress department, and Pearl, who was on the cosmetics counter. They kept her informed about all the wonderful bargains that were available when prices were reduced on shop-soiled items or end of season lines.

For her fifteenth birthday on Friday the 18th July 1930, she bought herself a brilliant red, Spanish-style, tiered skirt, and a low-necked black top trimmed with lace to wear with it. She combed her sleek black hair back behind her ears and pinned it in place with two red combs. Jamie gave her a single red rose and she pinned this high on one shoulder of her top.

'You look like a real Spanish dancer,' one of the girls told her as they all met up with Peter, Sam and Sandra after work at the Kardomah café.

'That's what she is,' Jamie laughed. 'Why do you think I brought my guitar along?'

'You can't play it in here,' Peter warned him, looking round the packed café.

'I know that!' Jamie laughed. 'I'm going to play it afterwards, though, and Abbie is going to dance for us, isn't that right?' He gave Abbie a wink that made her giggle.

'For goodness' sake you two, behave yourselves,' Peter told them in a disapproving voice. 'People are looking, you're showing us all up!'

'OK. Drink up and we'll move on,' one of the other boys told them. 'It's Abbie's fifteenth so we

173

ought to celebrate with a proper drink.' He looked at Peter, 'Are you coming?'

'Of course he is,' Abbie giggled, clutching hold of Peter's arm. 'He's my guardian angel,' she tittered. 'Peter makes sure I don't get into any trouble.'

'Oh, is that all,' laughed Pearl, 'I thought he was your father he's so staid!'

Still laughing and joking they made their way out of the Kardomah and into the nearest pub.

Knowing the devastating effect that having too much to drink could cause, Abbie had always sworn she would never get drunk. She found the very smell of beer and stout obnoxious, but it was her birthday and all her friends wanted to enjoy themselves.

When Jamie gave her a small glass containing a deep red liquid she took a tentative sip and found she liked it. This wasn't beer, it was smooth and as sweet-tasting as nectar. This was delightfully different! It wasn't drinking, not in the sense she recognised. She took another sip; it slid down effortlessly. She felt so happy and relaxed that she blithely accepted another and then another.

'You do know that's port you're drinking,' Sandra hissed. 'It can make you very tipsy indeed,' she warned. 'You'd better watch yourself, or you'll end up smashed out of your mind and rolling down the street like your mam and your Billy do most weekends.'

Peter took hold of Abbie's arm. 'Come on, I'll walk you home before you make a spectacle of yourself,' he told her firmly. 'You shouldn't be drinking at all, you're not old enough! You're only fifteen, remember.'

'Oh no you don't!' Her dark hair flying and her eyes sparkling dangerously, she pulled away from him. 'You go home if you want to, misery guts! This is my birthday and I'm going to enjoy it. Jamie's going to play his guitar and I'm going to dance. Isn't that right, Jamie?'

'Whatever you say, my Spanish beauty,' he chuckled, giving a low sweeping bow as he lifted the strap of his guitar over one shoulder and began strumming.

'Not in here you don't, mate,' the barman told him. Putting down the glass he was holding under one of the pumps, he dashed round to their side of the counter and began hustling them out through the door. 'Bloody load of rabble, that's all you are,' he stormed as he pushed them outside. 'Any more trouble and I'll call the scuffers, so don't try and come back in.' He looked at Peter, 'I'm surprised that you're associated with this lot, you look like a decent bloke,' he exclaimed, as he slammed the door behind them.

They crowded together on the pavement, laughing and giggling as they emerged into the warm July evening. It was not even properly dark and they all agreed it was much too early to go home. Arms linked, they surged like a tidal wave along the streets. Peter tried to pull Abbie to one side and reason with her, but it was pointless. She was in high spirits and determined to dance as she had said she would.

On the steps of St George's Hall they gathered

round in a group as Jamie once more began to strum on his guitar. He played 'Dancing on the Ceiling' followed by 'Puttin' on the Ritz' and then 'You Made Me Love You'. They screamed for more, they yelled for Abbie to dance for them, so she pirouetted and stamped her heels as Jamie strummed wild chords of music. With her full red skirt billowing in the evening breeze she twirled madly to the frenzied beat of his music.

Crowds streaming home from the pictures and pubs stopped to take in the spectacle, whistling and cheering her on.

Oblivious to them and to everything else that was going on around her, Abbie was taken by surprise when a hand grabbed at her arm, pulling her to a standstill.

'Gertoff,' she screamed, and tried to go on dancing. Then, suddenly aware that Jamie had stopped playing, she looked around in surprise and tried to steady herself. Her head was spinning and she found it difficult to stand upright and still at the same time.

'I think you've been celebrating rather too well, haven't you, miss,' the policeman holding her arm stated. 'Come on, let your friends take you on home before you do anything daft.'

Abbie grinned up at the tall, broad-shouldered figure in a blue uniform and high-domed hat. 'Thank you, officer, but it's my fifteenth birthday and I don't want to go home, not yet. I haven't finished celebrating. Look,' she waved her arm, 'all these people are my friends ...' She stopped and looked round her, puzzled. Everyone except

Peter had disappeared. It was as if the night had swallowed them up. A short distance away, Sam and Sandra were watching her antics uneasily. Only Peter remained, standing at her side.

'Abbie, come on,' Peter muttered worriedly as he took her arm.

'Yes, miss, do as your boyfriend asks,' the policeman insisted.

'Don't you want to know my name so that you can write it down in your notebook?' Abbie grinned. 'It's Abbie. Abbie Martin.'

'Right then, Abbie Martin, let's see you on your way home.'

'Aren't you going to arrest me?' she stuttered, looking up into his handsome, clean-shaven face provocatively.

His brown eyes twinkled. 'Not this time, but if I ever catch you dancing on the steps of St George's Hall again, or causing any more disturbances, then I will have to,' he told her severely.

He turned to Peter. 'I'll walk along with you to make sure there isn't any further bother. Do you have far to go?'

Peter looked embarrassed. 'Bostock Street, off Scotland Road,' he told him.

The policeman nodded. As they turned into Whitechapel he said, 'You should be able to manage to get her home safely from here.'

'Hold on!' Abbie grabbed at the policeman's arm as he was about to walk away. 'I told you my name but you haven't told me yours!' She squinted at the number on the shoulder of his blue uniform, 'I can't even read that in this light,' she announced.

'The name's Fisher. PC Fisher,' he told her politely.

'Aren't you going to wish me a happy birthday, then, PC Fisher?' Abbie challenged.

'Most certainly not!' he said firmly. 'You are not legally old enough to be out drinking, and if you cause any more disturbance then I will have to take you into custody,' he added gravely.

Abbie pouted. 'It is my birthday,' she persisted.

'I know!' He smiled. 'I'll wish you a happy birthday the next time we meet, providing you're sober! Now, let your friends take you home before you get into any more trouble.'

Chapter Nineteen

Sandra was furious. She could hardly wait until the policeman was out of earshot before she caught up with Abbie and began lambasting her.

'You idiot, Abbie Martin,' she railed. 'You could have got us all locked up with your daft carry-on. Behaving like that on the steps outside St George's Hall is enough to get us all in trouble.'

'Nothing daft about it at all,' Abbie defended. 'I'm only having a bit of fun and celebrating my birthday. I'm wearing a Spanish skirt so what's wrong with dancing a fandango.'

'Fandango! You're drunk!'

'Sandra's right. It's lucky for you that that policeman was in a good mood and not much older than us. If it had been one of the older bobbies we'd have found ourselves chucked into a cell for the night and up before the beak in the morning,' Sam agreed.

'Don't talk so stupid,' Abbie flared. 'We weren't doing any harm, only having a lark around and a good time. We hadn't robbed a bank or broken any windows or anything.'

'No, but Jamie was strumming his guitar like some demented banshee and you were cavorting as if you had lost your senses.'

'Sandra is quite right,' Peter said grimly. 'We

were causing a disturbance and that officer had every right to charge us. It's pure good fortune for all of us that he didn't.'

'Pure good fortune,' Abbie mimicked Peter's voice. 'Rubbish, and you know it. He was a good sport and he would probably have liked to have joined in. He would have done an' all, if he hadn't been in uniform,' she added with a grin.

'If, instead of being so lenient, he'd arrested us, think of what the results might have been,' Sandra went on, ignoring Abbie's light-hearted comments.

'Oh stop being such a misery guts,' Abbie scowled. 'You're ruining my night out.'

'If we'd been arrested then I would probably have lost my job and Sam might have, too,' Sandra pointed out. 'Peter most certainly would have been in serious trouble because of his previous record. You wouldn't be laughing, either, Abbie Martin, when we all ended up in court.'

'I would have told the magistrate that I didn't know any of you and that you were trying to restrain me, and then he would have had to let you all off,' Abbie giggled.

'You are impossible!' Sandra snapped. 'We should have cleared off like the rest of your so-called friends and left you to get on with it on your own.'

'Sandra's right,' Sam agreed. 'I thought you had more sense than to behave like that. I thought you'd seen enough of our mam and Billy getting drunk to never let yourself end up legless like them.'

'I wasn't legless! I was dancing a fandango! How could I have been doing that if I was legless?' Abbie argued petulantly, her lip quivering at the injustice of Sam's accusation.

'Oh leave her alone, Sam, she's still pissed out of her mind,' Sandra exclaimed witheringly. 'Are you going to see me home or do I have to go on my own?'

'Of course I'm going to walk you home, luv,' Sam told her quickly. 'I can't help being concerned about my sister, though, can I?'

'Leave her to Peter,' Sandra said scornfully, 'I don't want to have anything more to do with her.' Her voice broke and she began to sniffle. 'I don't know what my mam would say if she knew I'd been stopped by the police!'

'There's no need to say anything to her about it. It wasn't you that was doing anything wrong, it was our Abbie,' Sam protested. 'Don't get upset about it, luv.' He pulled out his handkerchief and dabbed away her tears. 'It's all over now, they don't even know our names.'

'Yes they do! Your Abbie was stupid enough to tell that copper her name.'

'Well, he didn't write it down so you can bet your boots he'll have forgotten it by now. Come on,' he took her arm, 'I'll take you home. You'll see Abbie back safely, won't you, Peter?'

'That's right, Sandra, turn on the waterworks, make sure you get every bit of sympathy you can squeeze out of our Sam,' Abbie said sarcastically. 'I suppose you think you're really clever because you've won him over to your side, and it's you

181

he's worrying about and not me. I've watched the way you make up to him. You think you've got him exactly where you want him, you weepy little wimp!'

'At least I have a boyfriend who wants to marry me and I can keep a job, which is more than you can do, Abbie Martin.'

'Keep a job!' Abbie's tone was scathing. 'Washing old women's hair all day! You call that a job? I call it skivvying. What I do is a job. Counter Assistant in the poshest store in Liverpool.'

'If it's the poshest store then why is it always in trouble. Everyone knows that Frisby Dyke's is going bankrupt and that they will be closed down soon. Then you'll be out of work again,' Sandra added spitefully, 'and being toffee-nosed won't be of much help to you then, especially if you have a prison record!'

'Prison record? I haven't got a prison record,' Abbie retaliated.

'You nearly had one tonight. I would never have forgiven you if you'd landed us all in court. If you think you can drag Sam down into the gutter with you and the rest of your drunken family then you've got another think coming.'

'Oh yes!' Abbie laughed derisively. 'You've got our Sam under your thumb, haven't you!'

'We're not having anything more to do with you. We're not going out with you ever again,' Sandra told her. 'Peter can do what he likes, but if he has any sense he'll drop you as well.'

'That's what you'd like to happen, isn't it, Sandra Lewis?' Abbie said contemptuously.

'You'll never get my brother to stop talking to me or going out with me, will she, Sam?' She looked imploringly at him, but he wasn't listening, he had already turned away from her and was trying to persuade Sandra to stop quarrelling.

'Come on, Sandra, let's go,' he muttered, taking her arm. 'We don't want that scuffer coming back and finding you two scrapping like alley cats or he might change his mind about letting us all off.'

'Letting us ALL off,' she screeched. 'You needn't drag me into this. It's your stupid sister that's caused all the trouble tonight. I'm never going to speak to her ever again, so you can like it or lump it.'

Flinging his arm away from her she started to stalk off. Sam ran after her, pulling on her arm, then slipping his arm round her waist and holding her tightly against his body as he matched his stride to hers so that they were walking in unison.

Tears flooded Abbie's eyes as she watched them. Sandra was right. Sam does care more for her than he does for me these days, she thought bitterly.

Sam had always been there for her; ready to protect her from the time she could crawl. In the past he would never have dreamed of walking off and leaving her like this.

Sandra, with her pale round face and big soft grey eyes, had stolen his affection. Her sweet, pretty, toadying manner had got under his skin. She'd seduced him!

Abbie felt she couldn't bear it. What had meant to be a night of celebration was turning out to be a parting of the ways. She would never feel quite the same about Sam. How could she, when he had let her down like this? As for Sandra, she would never speak to her again for as long as she lived.

'Do you want me to walk you home?'

Peter's subdued voice brought Abbie back to the present. Of course she expected him to see her home, but she wanted far more than that. She didn't want him to do it because he felt it was his duty, she wanted him to do it because of his feelings for her. There was a time when she had been so certain of his unwavering affection and had been sure he loved her deeply. She had considered herself to be his girlfriend and was confident that he would do anything in the world to please her.

Now she was no longer sure about that. Ever since he had come home from the reform school he had seemed cold and distant. Not really interested in her or her life. He was so serious, so unresponsive to her chatter. His mind seemed to be occupied by other things; his work, the night school he was attending, and his hopes of promotion.

He didn't talk to her about these things himself, she learned them from his mother. He didn't share his hopes and dreams for the future with her any more. She had no idea whether she featured in them or not.

She had always been sure of his love, and of Sam's, but now she seemed to have neither.

Maggie had changed, too. While Peter had been away she had been so welcoming, eager to share her thoughts and for them to do things together. Now, Maggie was so wrapped up in Peter, and everything she did was for his benefit.

At that moment, Abbie felt that if she disappeared off the face of the earth it wouldn't affect Maggie's or Peter's life one iota. Or Sam's, either!

She shrugged. 'Please yourself! Scarper like all the others if you want to,' she muttered belligerently.

'You know I wouldn't do that, Abbie. It's not safe for you to walk down Scotland Road on your own. Come on,' he took her arm. 'It's starting to rain, let's hurry or you'll get soaked and your new dress will be ruined.'

Peter's sombre mood sobered her. Without a word she fell into step alongside him. She was anxious to make amends for all that had happened that evening, for all that had gone wrong, but she couldn't find the right words.

She knew she had gone too far, but it had only been for fun, that and high spirits. Sandra's accusation that she'd been legless like her mam and Billy had rankled. She would never let herself be like them; she despised their behaviour and lack of self-control.

Sam taking Sandra's side had hurt. She had always depended on his support, but now, or so it seemed, she had turned him against her.

The fine drizzle became heavier, covering the wet pavement and reflecting the streetlights in a shiny black film. The rain clung to her face, to her painted eyelashes, so that she had to blink to see where she was going. She felt cold and miserable.

What had started out as a warm July night full of promise was now dank and depressing. She wished she had stayed at home.

When they reached Bostock Street, Peter made no attempt to walk all the way to her door with her. He paused by his own doorstep but didn't kiss her goodnight or ask her in.

'Night then, Abbie. See you later in the week, perhaps,' he said non-committally, shrugging his collar higher around his ears. 'I'll wait here until you reach your own door.'

'Oh don't bother,' she said dismissively. 'You might ruin your suit if you do.'

Hot tears were blinding her eyes as she stumbled the few extra yards to her own door. She went inside without even a backward glance.

Chapter Twenty

The display of affection between Sam and Sandra was in such stark contrast to the cool reserve that Peter showed towards her, that Abbie felt bitterly jealous.

Peter was so polite and formal that sometimes she wanted to scream. She tried to make him jealous by talking about Jamie and some of the other boys who had been celebrating with them on her birthday, but it had no effect whatsoever.

'Don't you lark around and have a bit of fun with any of the girls in your office?' she asked.

He shook his head. 'Certainly not! Mr Norris, the Senior Clerk, wouldn't approve of any nonsense of that sort,' he said coldly. 'Anyway, there are no girls in our department, only men.'

'There must be secretaries and telephonists working at the Royal Liver,' Abbie persisted.

'Of course there are, but I don't know any of them and have no occasions to speak to them.'

'So I'm still your only girlfriend, then?'

He frowned. 'Of course you are. Whatever makes you ask?'

Abbie shrugged. 'Nothing!'

'I'm not very good company these days, am I,' he said ruefully. 'I'm sorry, Abbie. I find it hard to let go and lark about like Jamie and the rest of the crowd you work with, because I think there's so much more to life than just having a good time. I want to get on in my job, to be promoted, to earn a good wage so that I have a secure future.'

Her blue eyes widened. It was the first time he had opened up and said that this was how he felt, or told her what was on his mind. He looked so serious in his dark suit, crisp white shirt, and sober blue-and-grey tie, that she often found it hard to believe that he was the same age as Sam. Now, listening to him making such solemn statements, he sounded like a man of thirty.

She couldn't wait to get away from Bostock Street and have a home of her own, but she wanted some fun first. She didn't want to be tied down to being a wife and mother for years and years.

'Perhaps you need to get out and have fun. We used to have some great times when we made up a foursome with Sam and Sandra.'

'I don't think that's possible, Abbie. I think they want to be on their own,' he told her, his handsome face serious. 'I think Sandra made it quite plain on your birthday that she doesn't like you coming between them.'

'Sam's my brother, and whether Sandra likes it or not she's not going to stop me seeing him,' Abbie said huffily. 'Anyway,' she went on, 'that spat between us was nothing. Sandra's like that. We're always falling out, but it soon blows over. She flares up over nothing and Sam feels he has to agree with her to keep the peace.'

Peter pushed back the lock of dark hair that had

fallen over his forehead. 'I don't understand such behaviour, Abbie,' he said wearily. 'I think we should all try and get along together.'

'That's what I'm trying to say. Let's go out as a foursome more often, and have fun.'

Peter shook his head. 'I have a lot of studying to do,' he prevaricated.

'So you don't want to go out and have a good time?' she persisted doggedly. 'Is that what you're trying to say? You'd sooner stay at home poring over dry as dust books than come out with me.'

'Of course I'm not saying that, Abbie. I do want to go out with you, but not every night of the week.'

'I see! So you want to come out with me when you are bored with your books. Great! And what am I supposed to do on the nights you want to stay in?'

He frowned. 'What did you do in the evenings while I was away?'

'Came round to your place to see your mam.'

'Well, there you are, then!' His face brightened. 'You can come round and see her while I'm studying. What could be better?'

'What could be better!' she mimicked, a scowl distorting her pretty face, her eyes glacial. 'I've already told you, Peter Ryan, what could be better. It would be better if you took me out more often, if we went to the flicks, or dancing, or even a walk and then dropped into the Kardomah or a milk bar.'

His face hardened. 'I've already explained to you, Abbie, that I have to study. I want to study,' he added, emphasising the word 'want'. 'It's for the future ... our future.'

Abbie bit her lip. It had been well over a year now since Peter had begun working at the Royal Liver and he was still spending most of his evenings studying. She had no idea how to deal with such dedication. She had thought that once he was settled she would be able to tempt him to reconsider his plans or at least modify them in some way so that they could see more of each other.

She shook her head, letting her dark hair fall over one eye provocatively. 'Please, Peter. After working all day I want some fun in the evenings. Can't we compromise? Can't you give up a couple of evenings a week to take me out?'

He shook his head firmly. 'No, Abbie. I'll take you out at the weekends, but during the week I want to study. Now that I'm going to night school two evenings a week I need the other evenings to do the homework they set. Surely you can understand that?'

She pouted prettily. 'I'm so lonely and fed up when I can't see you. I like your mam but I don't want to spend every evening with her!'

Visiting Maggie every evening while Peter had been away had been fine, because it was a way of keeping close to him. Now he was at home, although she still enjoyed Maggie's company, she wanted to be with him. She was jealous of Sandra and her hold over Sam. She wanted Peter to behave like a boyfriend should, and to give her the same sort of attention as Sam showed Sandra.

'Then go to night school, the same as I'm doing. I'm sure there's a course of some sort you could do that would help you to get promotion.'

Her winsome look changed to one of scorn. 'You must think I'm mad if you think I'm going to spend my evenings studying!'

'Then find something else to do that will make you happy,' he snapped.

'OK, I will.' She turned away from him, slamming the door as she left, not even calling out goodbye to Maggie.

She'd find something else to do with her evenings, she vowed, as she walked back down Bostock Street to her own house. And it wouldn't be cleaning up the hovel she lived in, either, she thought disdainfully as she looked round the squalid living room with its piles of dirty cups and plates scattered everywhere.

She'd show Peter Ryan that he wasn't the only pebble on the beach. She thought of all the invitations she'd had from Jamie and several of the other lads working at Frisby Dyke's. She'd always turned them down. In the beginning it was because she didn't think it was fair to Peter for her to go out with them when he was shut away in reform school.

He wasn't shut away now, but he might just as well be, she thought rebelliously. Well, she'd show him. She wasn't going to mope around every evening any more. She was going to do what she should have done a long, long time ago. Put herself first and have a good time.

You're only young once, she reminded herself.

From now on she'd accept every invite that came her way. She'd have a rip-roaring time.

Abbie tried to be patient. For the next twelve months she left Peter to study while she pursued her own social life. By the time Christmas 1931 came, Abbie was known to the entire younger element at Frisby Dyke's as a good-time girl. She'd go to anyone's party and she'd accept a date from anybody, except at the weekends. What she did from Friday to Monday morning, no one knew, but she was never free, no matter how alluring the invitation might be.

Because Christmas Day fell on a Friday it meant a really long weekend. They would close on Thursday night and not open up again until the following Monday morning.

There were so many parties planned for the Thursday and Saturday nights that Abbie was swamped with invitations. Everyone seemed to be staying at home on Friday, though, and celebrating with their families.

Her own Christmas Day was a complete blank, apart from going to Mass.

Sam had said he was going to Sandra's for his Christmas dinner, so Abbie waited hopefully for an invitation from Peter or Maggie to go to their house, and was bitterly disappointed when she didn't get one.

It meant spending Christmas Day with her mam and Billy. Her mam had bought a chicken for their dinner, and as usual was expecting her to cook it along with all the trimmings, but she felt it would be a complete waste of time. They would both be out cold from drinking themselves into a stupor the night before, and they'd push it around their plate because they had no appetite.

They'd be ready for a glass of port afterwards, though. Probably finish the bottle and she'd be left to clear away all the mess.

Life wasn't fair, she decided. She didn't blame Sam for wanting to get out, even if it did mean marrying Sandra and moving in with Mo Lewis. He'd be better fed and looked after there than he had ever been at home, she thought cynically.

Perhaps that was what she ought to do; get married!

The idea grew in her mind. She began dropping hints to her mother and Billy that she and Peter were thinking about getting married.

'I thought you'd have seen sense by now and stopped going around with that po-faced straight-jacket,' Ellen commented. 'I know you and him played together when you were kids, but I thought that now you were old enough to take your pick you'd take up with someone else.'

'Then you thought wrong,' Abbie told her defiantly. 'There's never been anyone else for me except Peter.'

'Oh no! Then what's the gossip I've heard down the cotton sheds about you being seen out with a different bloke every night?'

'A load of rubbish,' Abbie said defiantly, her face reddening. 'Whoever told you that?'

'Oh, word gets round, especially when you're making a spectacle of yourself. Make sure you behave yourself on New Year's Eve. We don't want to start off 1932 with your name splattered all over the *Echo*!'

'I've never had my name in the paper,' Abbie protested.

'Not yet, you haven't, but you got pretty near it with that bit of showing-off when you were celebrating your birthday outside St George's Hall a year or so back,' Ellen told her.

'How do you know about that? You've never mentioned it before.'

'Keeps me mouth shut when it's none of my business,' Ellen smirked. 'Anyway, I'm glad you've found yourself some new boyfriends and are playing the field before you settle down. It means you're not seeing so much of that Peter Ryan.'

'So why're you bringing it up now, then?'

'Just warning you to behave yourself on New Year's Eve,' Ellen told her. 'The scuffers have got their eyes peeled for anyone causing a disturbance.'

'It's you and Billy that need a warning,' Abbie retorted. 'I'm sick to death of being woken up in the middle of the night when you two arrive home legless and singing your lungs out. You're just as bad as our Billy. No wonder he can't find anyone to marry him.'

'What the hell would he want to get married for, when he has all the home comforts here and none of the responsibilities,' Ellen cackled. 'Billy's all right, so you leave him alone. He helps to keep a roof over our bleedin' head. We all know he likes his pint, so what? So do I!'

'We all know that as well,' Abbie agreed contemptuously. 'Everyone who lives in Bostock Street knows it. You make quite sure they do when you're pissed out of your head.'

'That'll do. You seem happy enough to stay here and yet you do damn all to help keep the place going. It's like a pigsty most of the time. All you use it for is a dosshouse these days,' she added angrily.

'Well, there you are. I don't like it here and you don't like me being here, so if I make a New Year resolution that I'm going to marry Peter Ryan and move out then we'll all be happy, won't we!'

'Anyone but him!' Ellen told her firmly. 'I told you before, forget that po-faced prig, you can do better than that for yourself!'

'You wouldn't be satisfied if I told you I was going to marry the Prince of Wales! I bet you think Sandra Lewis isn't good enough for our Sam, either.'

'Humph!' Ellen snorted. 'She's not given our Sam much choice, has she, the lying little bitch!'

Abbie's curiosity was roused. 'What do you mean by that?'

Ellen cackled and tapped the side of her nose with her forefinger. 'That's got you worried, hasn't it!'

'Not really, because I don't know what you're on about.'

'Why do you think Sam's in such a hurry to get

married? It's because he doesn't like the way Peter Ryan's always around at the Lewis's place.'

'Peter? Around at Sandra's?'

'He says he's looking for you. They know you're out with other fellas, but they don't split on you because Sam says Sandra feels sorry for him. Sam's in a hurry to get wed because he thinks Peter will take Sandra off him.'

'That's ridiculous!'

Ellen Martin grinned. 'Is it? Mo Lewis encourages her and Peter. She thinks he's much more respectable than our Sam and that he could provide Sandra with a better future. Our Sam's only a factory worker. Peter Ryan goes to work in his best suit and wears a smart trilby not a greasy old cap!'

Chapter Twenty-One

Abbie didn't want to believe her mother's insinuations. On New Year's Eve when she went to a dance at the Tower Ballroom in New Brighton with Peter, Sandra and Sam, she was aware of how well Peter and Sandra were getting on, and she wondered if, after all, there was some foundation for her mother's remarks.

She watched Peter and Sandra dancing together. Sandra barely reached up to his shoulder and Abbie noticed that he seemed to be looking down at Sandra in a way he had never looked at her.

That's because I'm on eye-level with him, she told herself, but she knew there was more to it than that. As she and Sam danced close to them she saw the warm smile on Peter's face and the concentration in his gaze, as if there was no one else in the world but the two of them.

She also noticed the flirtatious glances Sandra was darting up at Peter. There was a half smile on her lips and the hand that should have been resting on his shoulder was around his neck, as if she was going to pull his head down towards her at any moment and kiss him.

Sam seemed edgy and uncommunicative, which was unlike him, and Abbie suspected that he had noticed the closeness between Peter and Sandra, the same as she had, and was just as worried about it.

At the time, it didn't seem tactful to mention it; not on New Year's Eve. At midnight it would be 1932, the start of what she hoped was going to be a wonderful year. Peter would be taking some important exams after Easter, and if the amount of time he had spent studying had anything to do with it then he would pass with flying colours.

After that he was bound to get promotion. Once that happened, and he was earning a man's wage, then the possibilities for changes in her future as well as his were bright.

She'd enjoyed having a good time with the friends she'd made at work, but the endless hops at third-rate dance halls, visits to the flicks, or hanging out in a milk bar, were beginning to get a bit boring.

She'd be seventeen in July, time to start thinking of getting engaged and planning a home of her own.

Either that or looking for promotion at work. There were not all that many openings. She was too young to be considered for a Head of Department job, she hated sewing so she didn't want to become an alteration hand, and she didn't stand a chance of getting the one job she really coveted, being a mannequin.

There were only two of them in the whole store. Zara, who was the model for dresses, was in her twenties. She had a very good figure and was very pretty with long blonde hair and big grey eyes. Abbie knew that the chances of ever getting her job were nil. She was walking out with one of the Accountants and it was rumoured that he was about to be made a Director, and that was how she had got the job in the first place.

Minette, who modelled the coats and outerwear for their department, was almost forty, and all Abbie's friends said she would be far better. She was tall enough, slim enough and she had the looks. The only trouble was that she was too young to even be considered for the job.

Weighing everything up, Abbie decided, the best thing she could do was settle down with Peter. It wouldn't be a very exciting future, but it would be a secure one. He'd be a hard worker, and he'd always be reasonably well paid at the Royal Liver Friendly Society, so they should be able to afford to move away from the slummy Scotland Road area, perhaps over to Wallasey.

She could never understand why Maggie hadn't moved out of Bostock Street years ago. Abbie was sure she could have afforded to do so.

After all, Michael was still living at home and he had a good steady job as a railway porter at Lime Street station. Maggie herself had now started working part-time as a cook, and Paddy Ryan must be pretty well paid because he was a Chief Petty Officer. Maggie didn't smoke and only took a drink on special occasions.

On Christmas Day, when she and Peter had taken Maggie with them to Sandra's place in the evening for a drink, Maggie had had one small glass of port and then said she felt tipsy after it!

She'd seen her own mam down half a bottle of the stuff and it hadn't had any effect on her at all!

Maggie had said that she felt so strange that Abbie had offered to take her home and see her into bed. Peter had stayed at the Lewis's, she remembered, which was unusual because Peter was usually very protective towards his mother.

She'd stayed with Maggie for almost an hour because Maggie kept feeling sick. When she left, Peter still wasn't back, so she was surprised when she went home and found Sam already there.

'Is the party over?' she asked. 'I just popped in to pick up my cardigan because I was feeling cold, and then I was going to come back to the Lewis's.'

Sam shrugged. 'I'd had enough!' he muttered.

'Peter's still there, though, isn't he? He hadn't arrived home when I left Maggie.'

'Yeah! He's still there, but I'm off to bed. I shouldn't bother going back if I were you. Sandra and her mam will think you're still with Maggie Ryan,' he added.

She hadn't known what to make of this, or what to do, so she'd gone to bed herself. Christmas Day had always been something of a let down, ever since she could remember, and as she still wasn't getting on too well with Sandra she wasn't keen to go back to her house.

Now, as she sat there on her own watching the way Peter was holding Sandra, and the look on her face as she gazed up into his eyes as they circled the ballroom to the strains of 'Dancing in the Dark', Abbie wondered whether her decision on Christmas night had been wise. Her mother had been right. It would seem that Sandra had obviously got to know Peter extremely well while she'd been entertaining him on her own.

Not a good start for 1932, Abbie thought angrily. She may not find Peter terribly exciting but she regarded him as hers. She always had, and she certainly wasn't going to let Sandra steal him away.

She had no intention, either, of letting Sam be hurt. He adored Sandra; he'd never been out with any other girl. He'd saved hard ever since he first started work and he'd confided in Abbie that he was about to buy Sandra an engagement ring.

She wondered if he'd already done so. If so, was he planning to propose to her tonight, on New Year's Eve.

She felt uneasy; she didn't want him to see Peter and Sandra dancing together so intimately, and she felt it was up to her to do something about it.

The band was still playing 'Dancing in the Dark'. Pushing her way across the crowded dance floor she tapped Peter on the shoulder. 'This is our favourite tune, shouldn't you be dancing with me?'

Sandra glared at her and clung more tightly to Peter. Abbie was afraid she was going to cause a scene, or refuse to let him go, but when Peter smiled down at her she seemed to melt. With a little giggle she released her hold on him and walked away. Peter looked so uncomfortable that, against her will, Abbie found herself saying, 'Do you think we should make sure she is all right?'

They found Sandra and Sam sitting together, so

instead of dancing they stayed with them, having a drink until it was time to herald in the New Year. As the four of them linked hands for 'Auld Lang Syne' the atmosphere was uneasy. It was as if they were all slightly on edge and not happy about being in each other's company, Abbie thought uncomfortably.

Two months later, on St Valentine's Day, when once again the four of them were at the Tower Ballroom, Abbie discovered the reason for Sam's moodiness.

She thought at first that he was irritated because Peter was dancing with Sandra, but as she sat having a drink with him she was shocked when he revealed the real reason for his concern.

'Sandra's preggers.'

Abbie spluttered into her shandy. 'Am I hearing right?' she asked, her blue eyes wide with amazement.

Sam ran his hands through his short brown hair. 'Yeah! Bloody lovely, innit!'

'What're you going to do about it? Get hitched?'

'Have to in the end, I suppose,' he said gloomily. 'Trouble is she wants a roof over her head, first.'

'Nothing wrong with that! You could live at Mo Lewis's place for the time being if you have to, though. I'm sure she wouldn't mind,' she added quickly as she saw a heavy frown darken Sam's features.

'Sandra wants a place of her own, a corpy house and all the trimmings; you know what she's like.

202

What's more, she says she doesn't want kids, not for a while, anyway.'

Abbie laughed. 'She hasn't got much choice if she's already in The Club, has she!'

'She wants rid of it, so can you help?' he asked abruptly.

Abbie stared at him, open-mouthed. 'What makes you think I know how to go about doing something like that?'

He shrugged. 'You've been knocking around with Peter for years and you've never fallen for a kid so you must know something.'

'Yeah! Like keeping me legs crossed for one thing,' she told him tartly. 'I haven't slept with Peter Ryan or with any other bloke.'

Sam looked at her through hooded eyes. 'So who do I ask, then?'

Abbie played with a strand of her hair. 'You could ask Mam, she's bound to know someone.'

'I don't think Sandra would go for a backstreet job! Anyway,' he rubbed a hand over his face, 'I don't fancy some old shawlie messing her about. Too bloody dangerous!'

'Get something from the chemist, then.'

'Like what?'

'I don't know!'

'I can hardly go in and say "me Judy's in the Puddin' Club, so what can you dish out to get rid of it, whacker?" now, can I.'

'Then she'll have to go to the doctor and ask him to help her.'

'They're not allowed to do abortions, so it

would have to be a backstreet quack, though, wouldn't it?'

Abbie shrugged helplessly. 'Unless you have some sort of grounds why she can't have kids.'

'Like what?'

'I don't know! Heart trouble, liver trouble, insanity? You tell me. Mind,' she nodded in the direction of where Sandra and Peter were dancing, 'she looks too fit and healthy to be able to convince them about any of those things . . . except perhaps of sanity!'

'Bitch!' Sam scowled at his sister and took a long drag on his cigarette. 'Come on, our Abbie, you must know someone or something. How about all those smartarses you mix with at work? Surely one of them must have some answers.'

'I'll ask around,' Abbie promised, 'but I can't promise anything. The best thing you can do is get hitched. At least you're covered, then, if she can't find a way to get rid of it. Has she told her mam yet?'

'Christ, no! Mo Lewis will do her nut. You know what she's like, and she's got Sandra's dad under her thumb so he'd raise the roof as well. He's such a wet echo he'll side with her. I don't want to be around when they find out!'

'When is it due?'

'Sandra says around the end of August or the beginning of September. She's not too sure.'

'She'll have to do something pretty quick, then, or it'll be too late,' Abbie warned. 'I'll ask the girls at work but don't get your hopes up.'

'What about Maggie Ryan. Do you think she might know someone?'

'She's the last person you want to ask, she's too strict a Catholic for anything like that!'

'Yeah! You're probably right,' Sam said sheepishly. 'The trouble is, Abbie, I can't think straight, not since Sandra told me the news. I don't know what to do for the best.'

'Nip off and get spliced on the quiet, that's the best advice I can give you,' Abbie stated firmly. 'If you and Sandra are married then she might feel differently about having the baby.'

'I don't think so,' Sam said gloomily. 'She wants to have a big white wedding and everything.'

'Even if it means her kid's a little bastard?' Abbie asked cynically.

'I don't think she sees it like that. She just doesn't want to have kids until she can have everything nice for them. You know, the big pram to push 'em out in, the cradle and shawls and all the rest of the fancy gear.'

'Then she should have kept her legs crossed and you should have had more sense. It's her own fault! She's a tease. Look at the way she's flirting right this moment!' Abbie said angrily, looking across the dance floor to where Sandra and Peter were dancing cheek to cheek.

Chapter Twenty-Two

Sandra's outspoken fury, when she returned to where Sam and Abbie were sitting and discovered that Sam had taken Abbie into his confidence about her being pregnant, made Abbie cringe.

Sam was taken aback and Peter was shocked, but Abbie felt a sudden hatred towards the girl who had been her friend since childhood. To blame Sam for what had happened was so unfair.

It was as much Sandra's fault as his, and while she could understand Sandra might be a bit put out by the news being made known, Abbie still didn't think it warranted tearing Sam apart in public. After all, she reasoned, Sam had only told her in the hope that she might be able to help. Now, she decided, she wouldn't lift a finger to help Sandra. If she did and it went wrong, then Sandra might publicly berate her like she had done Sam, and Abbie wasn't standing for that.

She had to admit to herself that she felt secretly rather pleased that Peter was seeing for himself how churlish Sandra could be, without any need for her to say a word.

He had gone as white as a sheet when he heard Sandra admit that she was pregnant, and he'd looked absolutely thunderstruck when she had let fly at Sam because he had mentioned it.

Even so, Abbie felt sorry for her. She knew how worried she would be if she ever found herself in that sort of predicament. She told herself she was being mean not to try and help Sandra in some way, since they had, after all, been friends since schooldays.

'I've been telling Sam that the best thing you two can do is get married,' Abbie said quietly when Sandra finally stopped ranting at Sam.

'Oh, you did, did you! So we have your permission, do we!' Sandra sneered. 'And what business is it of yours? Your Sam getting me in the family way can hardly bring disgrace on the Martin name, can it, not with a drunken mother and layabout brother like you two have.'

Tears streamed down Sandra's face and she sobbed noisily like a small child. When Sam tried to take her into his arms to comfort her she fought him off like a wild cat and turned to Peter, clinging to his arm and burying her tear-stained face in his shoulder.

Abbie felt her anger rising. There was a limit to her sympathy. As she saw Peter patting Sandra's shoulder and mopping at her face with his handkerchief, while Sam slumped dejectedly, elbows on his knees and his head in his hands, she felt she had had enough.

'I'm off home,' she stated. 'Are you coming, Peter?'

He looked unsure. She knew he was embarrassed by what had happened, but she was also aware that it was Sam, not him, who should be comforting Sandra.

She put a hand on Sam's shoulder. 'See you at home later,' she said quietly.

He looked up, grabbing hold of her arm to stop her going. 'You will ask around, see what you can find out? You promised,' he added as he saw the look of hesitation on her face.

'You needn't bother!' Sandra flung at her. 'I don't need your help. And don't go opening your big gob and spreading rumours about me, neither.'

Abbie shrugged. 'All right, if that's the way you want it!'

Sandra's small round face twisted grotesquely. 'Don't come the holier-than-thou act with me, either, because I know different. I've heard of the way you carry on with the lads at Frisby Dyke's!'

Abbie felt outraged. Sandra, not content with messing up her own life, was doing her best to spoil things between Peter and me, she thought bitterly.

She'd never tried to hide the fact that she'd gone out with Jamie and his friends. They'd gone to the flicks, dancing, and to milk bars, but it had always been in a group and she'd never let any of them lay a finger on her.

None of them had ever seen her home or even kissed her goodnight because she had always made it plain that Peter was her steady boyfriend. Judging by the look on his face she was going to have quite a job convincing him of that, she thought angrily.

'I'm going.' She stood up and walked towards the door, her eyes sparkling with tears. She didn't wait to see if Peter was following her. She didn't care. Not about Peter, or Sandra, or even Sam at that moment.

She'd never speak to Sandra again as long as she lived, she resolved, as she left the Tower Ballroom and ran along the promenade and on to the pier to catch the boat back to Liverpool.

The strong wind coming off the Mersey was icy, and Abbie couldn't stop shivering. She found herself a corner seat inside one of the covered saloons and hunched there worrying about Sam and Sandra until she felt the boat grate against the Liverpool landing stage.

In the days that followed, Sam badgered her persistently to find out what Sandra could do to get rid of the baby, but Abbie remained resolute.

'If she wants my help then she can come and ask for it herself,' she snapped. 'And she can apologise to me in front of Peter, and take back all she said about me.'

'She didn't say anything about you except that you went out and had fun with the boys at work.'

'Boys and girls! Remember that. We went out as a group. There was no pawing. No pairing off, no sneaking off into dark corners, no pinching each other's partners.'

'If you're still sore about Sandra making up to your Peter then forget it,' Sam scowled. 'I've already told her that she wasn't playing fair and she's said she's sorry and promised not to do it again.'

'Only because she knows she hasn't much

chance with him now that she's got a bellyful. Another couple of months and she'll be the size of a house, and no chap will give her a second look!' Abbie said spitefully.

'Another couple of months and it will be too late for you or me to do anything to help her,' Sam muttered. 'Come on, Abbie, we've always looked out for each other, don't let me down over this one.'

By the time Abbie agreed to help it was far too late. She did find out the name of a woman living in one of the nearby streets, but when Sandra went along the woman took one look at her and shook her head. 'You're too far gone for me to touch you, luv,' she said firmly. 'What are you, five months?'

'No, not even four,' Sandra lied glibly. 'Can't you even give me something to take?' Sandra begged. 'Some medicine or pills, like. You wouldn't be involved, then, if anything went wrong,' she added hopefully.

'Need bloody elephant pills to shift what you've got in there!' the woman told her coarsely. 'You'd better find some poor bugger daft enough to marry you and give it a name before it's too late! That's the best advice I can give you.'

A month later, Sam and Sandra were married in a registry office. There was no fuss and no invitations.

Sam wore his one and only suit. It was navy blue and too short in the sleeves and in the legs because although he hadn't put on any weight he had grown taller since Billy had handed it down to him.

Sandra wore a loose-fitting, button-through, green cotton dress that concealed her bump, and a beige swagger coat over it. She didn't have a bouquet; there were no flowers of any sort, and no confetti afterwards.

Neither Mo nor her husband Dan were exactly pleased about Sandra marrying Sam Martin. Although she'd been going around with him ever since she was at school, Mo had always looked on her friendship with him, Abbie, and Peter Ryan as kids growing up together.

She knew she'd been naïve. Dan had warned her often enough in the past that she was building up trouble, but she had always laughed and reminded him that there was safety in numbers. She had never seriously thought that Sandra would ever marry Sam, and she knew Dan had never thought Sam was good enough for their Sandra.

In fact, as she had seen the interest Sandra had been showing in Peter Ryan lately, she'd thought that Sandra was growing up at last and had seen for herself that she could do better than Sam Martin. Peter had been in trouble, of course, but he was well over that.

Every time she saw him she thought how smartly dressed and well-spoken he was. He appeared to be such a serious young man, and seemed to have very good prospects for his future.

She and Dan weren't thrilled at the idea of having a grandchild, either. They'd had heated words over Sandra and Sam moving in to live with them. Dan didn't approve, but as Mo said, where else could they go. She certainly didn't want Sandra living at the Martins' place.

'It's better for them to move in with us than into that dump,' Mo told him. 'I've never understood how Abbie has turned out as nice a girl as she has, with a mother like Ellen Martin.'

'Never mind about that, is Sandra going to stay home and look after this baby?' Dan asked worriedly.

'That goes without saying!' she told him emphatically.

'It's only temporary, mind,' Mo warned Sandra and Sam when she agreed they could move in. 'I want a promise from you both that you'll try and get a place of your own as soon as possible.'

'Of course we will! The minute we're married and can go on the list, we'll put our name down for a nice little corpy house as far away from Scotty Road as we can get,' Sandra told her.

'Well, mind you do,' Mo insisted. 'Me and your dad are too old to start having screaming kids around the place. I never have liked small babies. They're nice enough when they get a bit older, but not when they keep you awake half the night, squalling their heads off and needing to be fed and have their nappies changed every five minutes.'

Sam wanted Peter to be one of the witnesses but Abbie was dead set against it. 'Let's keep out of it,' she told him. 'Sandra has tried to come between us as it is, and I don't want to have anything more to do with her.'

'You still talk to Sam!'

'He's my brother, I'll always be there for him,' Abbie told Peter.

'Even when he's married to Sandra?'

Abbie shrugged. 'He's got to do his duty for the baby's sake. Doesn't mean I have to be her friend, though, does it.'

Peter had kept his own counsel about the newlyweds after that, and Abbie never ventured any further information. Neither of them went to the wedding.

Ellen Martin was furious when she found out that Sam was not only getting married but that they were moving in with Sandra's mam and dad.

'That's his pay packet gone! That only leaves our Abbie and she barely tips up enough to cover her food,' she fumed as she told Billy the news.

'Then make her pay up a bit more. She must have had increases in her wages during the time she's been working at Frisby Dyke's,' Billy muttered.

'Yeah! You're right! Look at all the clobber she's bought herself and the way she's always out gadding about. You don't do that on peanuts.'

'Probably gets the boys to pay for her, if I know our Abbie, like all the rest of the young bints these days. That's all most of them want a bloke for is to pay for them when they go out,' Billy remarked sourly.

'She's smart, she knows what she's doing. Got her head screwed on, I'll say that for her. You don't see her getting caught out. Still looking for Mr Right is our Abbie.'

'Well, she won't find him while she's knocking

around with that bloody Peter Ryan. I thought you would have put a stop to that before now. Great pansy! Have you seen the way he goes to work these days, all dolled up in his pinstripe suit, stiff white collar and a bowler hat?'

'I see him down by the Liver Buildings now and again.'

'A proper day's work on the dockside would kill him,' Billy said scornfully.

'He's clever from what our Sam says.'

'Yeah? All this studying at night school, though, what's he think he's going to do, end up as General Manager of the Royal Liver Friendly Society?'

'According to what Maggie Ryan tells everyone, when he passes his next exam he'll be promoted to Manager of a department,' Ellen said, as she helped herself to a cigarette from Billy's packet that was lying on the table.

'Forget about him, he's nothing to us,' Billy said with a surly laugh. 'What's important is that our Sam's gone, so that means Abbie'll have to dib up more ackers. Get what you can off her now, before she moves out.'

'She can't get spliced until she's eighteen, not without my say-so,' Ellen said smugly.

'That won't be so very long, though, will it!'

'At least another year. Abbie won't be seventeen until July.'

'So that leaves plenty of bloody time for her to get knocked up like that Sandra Lewis,' Billy prophesised.

'She'd better not! I hope she's got more sense than to let that happen!'

Chapter Twenty-Three

As a treat for her seventeenth birthday in July, Peter took Abbie to the new Grafton Ballroom.

They both dressed up for the occasion. She wore a floor-length dress, a stunning creation in shimmering pale turquoise with a fitted top and very full skirt, which she'd bought at a special staff-discount price.

It was cut daringly low at the back, almost to her waist, so, although it was sweltering hot, Peter persuaded her to keep on the lacy white stole that Maggie had tactfully offered her in case later on in the evening it turned cool.

Peter wore a black suit, and a white shirt that was frilled down the front, and he had smart silver cuff-links and a silver pin in his grey silk tie.

He looked so handsome that Abbie's heart beat faster. Tonight was going to be a very special occasion, she was sure of that, and she could barely wait for him to find the right moment to propose.

She was seventeen at last, so now Peter could ask her to marry him with a clear conscience.

She smiled to herself; he was such a stickler about such things. As soon as they were officially engaged she was sure he would show her more affection. Once she'd promised to marry him he would feel free to be more demonstrative. They'd be able to behave more like Sandra and Sam towards each other.

Thinking of them brought her up with a start. She wouldn't let things go quite as far as Sandra had! At the moment, eight months pregnant, she looked like a hippo, with her bulging stomach and rolling walk. Her round face was so bloated that all her pretty looks had gone.

For a second, Abbie felt guilty that she hadn't done more to help Sandra earlier in the year. It wasn't her conscience that had stopped her from helping Sandra to get rid of the baby, it had been jealousy. She hadn't liked the way Sandra had flirted with Peter whenever they'd gone out together over Christmas and the New Year.

For a horrible moment she'd actually thought that perhaps Peter was going to drop her and take up with Sandra, and she knew that would have had a devastating effect on Sam as well as her. He'd adored Sandra, ever since they were small kids, in fact, the same length of time as she and Peter had been close.

That was all in the past now, she thought, as she looked across the table at Peter. She was the lucky one, not Sandra. Peter was tall, good-looking, smartly dressed, and now that he had been promoted to Head of a department he was earning good money. She was pretty sure he wouldn't want them to get married until she was eighteen, so that meant they had a whole year to save up and plan their future together.

A whole year to wait, but at least at long last

he'd be free to show his feelings. There would be no more chaste kisses on the cheek, or a gentle hug, but real snogging sessions. She'd be able to tell him how much she loved him and, best of all, he'd do the same in return.

She really longed to hear him express his feelings for her, to feel wanted and loved. To know that her thoughts and her every action mattered to him. Sam had been the only one who ever came anywhere near to doing that. She could never remember her mam ever hugging or cuddling her, not even when she had been very small and had fallen over and hurt herself, or when she wasn't feeling well.

Maggie had been more affectionate towards her, and more interested in her than her own mam had ever been. That was until Peter came home. Now he was the centre of Maggie's life and she couldn't do enough for him.

Sitting at one of the little round tables at the side of the dance floor, sipping the glass of sweet white wine that Peter had ordered, Abbie waited expectantly for him to lean across the table, take her hand in his, and pop the question. She had seen him slip a small box into his pocket before they left the house so she knew he had the ring. She wondered if he was nervous, but from the confident way he had studied the wine list before ordering she was pretty sure that Peter could handle any occasion quite calmly.

That was the difference between them, Abbie thought reflectively. Peter was so cool and concise, he always thought things through, never rushed into any situation until he was quite sure he was doing it right. Sometimes she wished he would throw caution to the wind and be a little more reckless.

She took another sip of her wine and, as she put her glass down, a thought came unwillingly into her mind. Perhaps it was as well that Peter was so cautious. If he had been the reckless type then he might have dropped her and dashed off with Sandra, and she wouldn't be sitting here now, on the verge of becoming engaged to the handsomest man in the room.

Her nerves were on edge as she waited for Peter to say the words she was longing to hear.

She tried to catch his eye, but he was staring at the whirling couples on the dance floor and she wondered if he was waiting for a more intimate moment. Was he waiting until he was holding her in his arms so that he could whisper the magic words seductively into her ear?

'Shall we dance?' she suggested.

His sweeping dark brows drew together in a frown. 'Wouldn't you prefer to finish your drink first?'

Abbie shrugged, letting the lacy shawl slip so that her bare shoulders gleamed in the artificial light.

'I thought you might like to,' she murmured. She lifted her wineglass and held it out towards him. 'To us!' she grinned, then raised it to her lips and drained it.

The wine waiter appeared at her side by magic and began refilling her glass, but Peter reached out and held his hand over the top of it. 'I think you should go easy on the wine, you're already looking a little flushed, Abbie,' he cautioned.

Deftly she moved the glass from under his hand and held it out towards the waiter. 'To the brim, please! It's my birthday!'

He bowed and filled her glass. 'Happy birthday!' he smiled as he returned the bottle to the ice bucket at the side of their table.

'Thank you!' She raised the glass to her lips and took a long slow drink, her blue eyes sparkling. Then putting the glass down on the table she stood up, and, grabbing hold of Peter's hand, pulled him towards the dance floor.

Peter tried to resist. When she pouted and threw back her dark head, letting her lacy shawl slip from her shoulders, he gave in and followed her, discreetly putting the shawl back into place.

The band was playing 'Night and Day' so he was able to guide her sedately around the dance floor. When they changed the tempo to the more stirring rhythm of 'Dancing on the Ceiling', Abbie began to give vent to her high spirits. She danced with abandon, pulling off the white lace shawl and throwing it carelessly over Peter's shoulder, lifting up her long skirt and making such a show of herself that people were gasping.

Peter tried to calm her, to lead her back to their table, but it made no difference at all. Stubbornly, she clung to him, keeping him in the centre of the room as she twirled like a dervish, her head thrown back and only Peter's arm preventing her from skidding full length on to the floor.

Other people moved aside to make room for them, or retired to the safety of one of the tables dotted around the edge of the dance floor. The manager appeared and ordered the band to stop playing. Then he walked over to them and laid a restraining hand on Peter's shoulder.

'If you don't mind, sir ...' He didn't bother to finish his sentence, his look said it all. Firmly, he escorted them both off the dance floor, not back to their table but towards the exit where the liveried doorman was standing with one hand already on the door handle, waiting to open it for them.

'Hold on!' Peter murmured. 'We haven't finished our drinks!'

'I'm sorry, sir. This is The Grafton and you are causing a disturbance that is unacceptable to our clientele. If you have left anything behind on your table then I will send a waiter to collect it for you.'

Peter's face was white with embarrassment and his mouth tightened into a grim line. 'Thank you, there is no need,' he said curtly.

'Thank you, sir. Goodnight, sir, goodnight, madam.' He gave a stiff little bow and signalled to the doorman to see them off the premises.

Outside on the pavement, Peter was shaking with anger. 'What the devil did you have to behave like that for, and have us thrown out,' he railed.

The cool night air cleared Abbie's woozy head like a douche of cold water. 'I was only trying to show you how well I could dance,' Abbie pouted.

'Dance! That wasn't dancing! Throwing yourself

around like a madwoman, taking your shawl off and flaunting your naked body.'

Abbie raised her eyebrows. 'You can be a right prude at times, Peter,' she said scathingly. 'Naked body! My shoulders were bare, that is all.'

'And what about when you hitched up your skirt and waved your legs in the air?'

'They weren't naked! I was wearing silk stockings.'

'You were making a spectacle of yourself. Come on, we're going home.'

'Peter! It's my seventeenth birthday. We're supposed to be celebrating!' She took his arm and looked up into his face. 'I thought you had something special you were going to say to me tonight.'

'The only thing I have to say to you tonight is come on home before you make a bigger show of yourself!'

The scorn in his eyes cut through her like a knife.

'And what if I don't want to go home?' she protested. What was wrong with him. He was acting like he had on her fifteenth birthday, trying to ruin her fun.

'Then I'll say goodnight to you here, right now,' he told her stiffly, and turned on his heel and began to walk away.

'Peter! Peter, come back! You can't leave me here to walk home all on my own,' she pleaded, running after him, her heels tapping frantically on the pavement.

He paused and turned. 'Come on, then, I'll see you home.'

'I want another drink first,' she pleaded. 'You haven't wished me a happy birthday yet, or given me my present.'

His jaw jutted. 'Are you coming?'

'No!' She tossed back the mane of black hair that framed her face, her eyes challenging. 'You'll have to come back here and make me.'

He didn't rise to her bait. Shrugging his shoulders he strode off, deaf to her shouts and protests.

She stood where he'd left her for a few minutes, then made her way across the road to the King's Tavern. She'd never been into a pub on her own before, and it took her a moment to summon up the courage to do so.

I'm no better than my mam; it must run in the blood, she thought bitterly as she elbowed her way through the smoke-filled room to the bar counter.

She groped in her purse for some money and then stood there for several minutes trying to catch the barmaid's eye so that she could buy herself a drink.

'Excuse me, you aren't Audrey Hepburn by any chance, are you?' a voice whispered in her ear.

Abbie turned quickly. A flashily dressed man, with receding slick dark hair, a Charlie Chaplin moustache and sharp green eyes, was standing beside her, looking at her appraisingly.

'I'm Edmund Styles,' he announced, holding out his hand, and Abbie caught the gleam of a diamond signet ring as she rested her hand in his.

He tipped his Brylcreemed head to one side and studied her. 'No, you are too pretty for Audrey Hepburn. It was the style of your dark hair and those big innocent eyes that fooled me. If you were on the stage alongside her, then, believe me, she'd be a past number! Can you sing?'

Abbie shook her head. 'Not really. Croak like a frog, though.'

He gave her a foxy grin. 'So what are you good at?'

'I work in a shop ... a very posh shop.'

'Ah! That accounts for the lovely dress you are wearing. Very glamorous! Can you dance?'

Abbie giggled. 'I've just been chucked out of the Grafton Ballroom because they didn't like the way I was dancing!'

Edmund Styles's dark eyebrows lifted. 'I think we should have a little drink together and talk about this,' he said, fingering his moustache thoughtfully. 'You may be just the girl I'm looking for.'

When he'd bought their drinks and found a table where they could sit down, he again broached the subject of her dancing.

'Perhaps dancing is what you should be doing for a living,' he said pointedly. He selected a fat cheroot from a gold case and lit it. 'Serving in a shop, even if it is a posh one, is hardly the sort of job a lovely-looking girl like you should be doing.'

Abbie felt flattered. 'And where would I find a job where all I had to do was dance?'

'I can offer you one!' He drew deeply on his cheroot and then let out a long stream of blue smoke. 'That's after I've seen you dance, of course.' He held up a hand as she was about to speak. 'If you've been turned out of The Grafton because of the way you dance then I'm pretty convinced you are exactly the sort of girl I'm looking for to perform at the Floral Pavilion over in New Brighton.'

'As a dancer?'

'That's right!' He took a sip of his whisky. 'If you can deliver, then the job is yours,' he told her as he replaced his glass on the table. His fingers moved up her arm and crept tenaciously round her breast. 'Perhaps we should go somewhere quiet so that you can show me what you can do?'

Abbie knew she had drunk too much and that her brain was in a spin, but she was sufficiently in control of her senses to realise that she couldn't trust Edmund Styles.

'Lemme go! Gerroff! Keep your hands to yourself,' she said angrily, pushing him away from her.

Edmund Styles's elbow caught his tumbler as he pulled back, spilling the whisky in it. He let out an oath as he thrust his chair backwards to try and avoid the residue that was running off the table and down the trouser leg of his flash suit. His chair crashed against the ankle of the man sitting behind him who let out a roar of pain and threw a punch that landed squarely on Edmund Styles's chin.

Immediately, the entire pub was in turmoil. There was uproar as fighting broke out. Chairs were pushed back, men threw indiscriminate punches and women screamed with fright.

Abbie tried to make a run for it, but the doors were already shut fast and the police whistles were sounding.

She felt a strong hand grab at her arm and spin her round, and she found herself looking into a pair of stern brown eyes, and a handsome face that she recognised immediately.

'Well, well? I seem to have had this pleasure once before,' the police constable said in a slightly amused voice. 'What have you been up to this time, Abbie Martin?'

He took her by the arm and led her to the far corner of the room, leaving his colleagues to quell the mêlée that was still going on.

Chapter Twenty-Four

'So, what are you doing here? How have you managed to break the law this time?' Bradley Fisher asked. 'Not wild dancing again, I hope?'

Abbie avoided his keen brown eyes. 'It started with dancing,' she admitted.

'What here, in this pub?'

'No, in the Grafton Ballroom. They didn't like my style of dancing so we were thrown out.'

'We?' Bradley Fisher frowned. 'Who were you with and where are they now?'

Abbie bit down on her lower lip. 'I was with my friend, Peter Ryan. He was upset because we got chucked out, we had a few words and then he stalked off and I came in here.'

'On your own!'

She nodded. 'I know, stupid, wasn't it,' she admitted, giving him a tremulous smile.

'Extremely!'

'Then this chap started chatting me up.'

'A stranger?'

'Yes!' She giggled nervously. 'He said he thought I was Audrey Hepburn and he offered me a job as a dancer over at the Floral Pavilion in New Brighton.'

Bradley's frown deepened. 'That wouldn't have been a man called Edmund Styles, would it?'

Abbie's eyes opened wide in surprise. 'Do you know everyone?' she asked.

'Only those with a dubious reputation.'

She bit her lip. 'Does that include him?'

'I'm afraid it does. Especially where pretty young girls are concerned. I hope you turned him down.'

'I was going to accept his offer, but then he started getting a bit fresh. When I tried to stop him pawing me he knocked his drink over. That was what started all the hullabaloo.'

Bradley Fisher shook his head despairingly. 'You really are trouble; you shouldn't be allowed out! Come on,' he took her firmly by the elbow.

'You're not going to arrest me, are you?' she protested. 'I wasn't involved in the fight. I was about to go home, but the landlord shut the doors the minute you arrived.'

'That's to make sure that criminals like you get their just deserts and don't go anywhere else and disturb the peace,' he told her severely.

Abbie tried to pull her arm free. 'You're not going to arrest me, surely!'

'Not this time, but I am going to make sure that you go straight home and that you arrive there safely. Once these doors are open again there will be a mad stampede. I want you to wait over by the bar until I've finished dealing with this lot and then I'll walk you home.'

'There's no need,' Abbie told him quickly. 'I promise I'll go straight home.'

'Please yourself. Either do as I say and let me

see you home or I shall have to arrest you. I can't take the risk of abandoning you.'

Abbie wasn't sure whether he was joking or not, but it was a nice feeling to have someone so concerned about her. It made her feel warm inside, protected and safe.

'Very well,' she said meekly, 'I'll wait by the bar counter for you.'

Afterwards, as they walked towards Scotland Road, she gave him a censured version about what had happened during the earlier part of the evening.

'Celebrating your birthday again? So how old are you now?'

'Seventeen!'

'Old enough to be taken out on a date, then.'

'If the right sort of person asked me,' she teased.

He gave her a penetrating look. 'Do you think I might fit the bill?' he asked.

'I could think about it!'

He grinned. 'You do that, and if the answer is yes then be at Lime Street station next Tuesday night at seven.'

'Not on your life!' Abbie laughed. 'Hang around outside Lime Street station? You must be kidding! What do you think I am, a Mary Ellen?'

He grinned back at her. 'Not so daft after all, are you!'

'Don't think that just because you're a copper you can take the mickey out of me like that,' she snapped.

'Sorry!' He held up his hands. 'I was only having you on.'

229

Abbie's spirits sank. For one moment she'd thought he really was asking her for a date and she'd had every intention of accepting, if only to prove to Peter Ryan that he wasn't the only man in her life.

'I did mean it about taking you out, though,' Bradley Fisher went on in a more serious tone. 'Will you come out with me one evening, Abbie? We could go over to New Brighton for a walk along the prom, or do anything else you fancied.'

'Yes, I'd like that,' she said eagerly. 'I haven't been to New Brighton since St Valentine's night and it wasn't the right time of year to be walking along the prom.'

'OK,' he agreed. 'That's on, then. We'll catch the seven o'clock ferryboat from the Pier Head, go for a walk and then have a meal or go to one of the shows over there.'

'You know how to spoil a girl!'

He looked at her sharply. 'You will turn up?'

'Of course I will. Even if it's raining cats and dogs,' she promised.

'Good. I'll be waiting.'

As they reached the junction of Scotland Road and Cazneau Street, Abbie stopped and held out her hand. 'I'll say goodnight, I know my way from here,' she grinned.

'No, I'll see you to your door.'

'What, and have the neighbours think I'm in some sort of trouble being brought home by a scuffer! Me mam'd kill me!' she joked.

'All right. If that's the way you want it. I'll be in

my own clothes when we meet on Tuesday; do you think you'll be able to recognise me?'

'Probably not. Perhaps you'd better be carrying a copy of the *Echo* or something because if I'm accosted by a stranger I might scream for a policeman!'

'Right, I'll remember that. And you remember it's the seven o'clock boat we're going on and don't be late.'

Abbie found herself looking forward to her date with Bradley Fisher, especially when she didn't hear a word from Peter.

She'd felt quite flattered that Bradley had remembered her name from the incident on the steps of St George's Hall. And she'd been even more impressed when he'd told her that he hadn't been able to put her out of his mind ever since then.

She'd thought about him once or twice. He was good-looking with his brown eyes, short dark hair and fresh face, and he looked very impressive in his navy blue police uniform. He had a nice friendly manner and was so easy to talk to. He didn't seem threatening or a bully like so many policemen were.

What she liked most of all was that even though he barely knew her, he seemed genuinely interested in her and what she had to say. When she told Peter things although he listened to her he either lectured her on what she should have done or ought to do, or else he dismissed what she'd told him as being of no consequence.

Bradley Fisher wasn't like that. He asked questions or made comments that made her feel important and interesting.

She hadn't intended to say anything to her mam or Billy about what had happened, but when Sam called round he let slip that he'd heard that Peter had arrived home on his own from The Grafton, and that he'd been in a very bad mood.

'Said you'd showed him up doing some fancy dance or the other,' he grinned. 'You should have known better, you know Peter's become a bit of a stuffed shirt now he's got his promotion.'

Abbie shrugged. 'There's plenty more fish in the sea,' she said, flicking her hair back behind her ears.

'I've been telling you that for ages,' her mother cackled. 'I never could fathom out why you stuck to him like glue, or why you even bothered going around with him at all. Look at you! Sandra's getting wed and having a kid and she's no older than you, and now you've fallen out with Peter Ryan you've got no fella at all!'

'That's where you're wrong,' Abbie told her. 'I'm going out on a date on Tuesday night.'

'Who with?' Ellen asked nosily. 'That Jamie from work, or one of that crowd you work with that you're always on about?'

'No. With someone else. He's quite special. Tall, dark and handsome,' she grinned and then added quickly, 'you don't know him.'

'What's his name? Anyone I know?' Sam asked.

'Bradley Fisher.'

Billy pricked up his ears. 'I've heard that

232

moniker somewhere,' he said suspiciously. 'What's this geezer do for a living? Does he work down the docks?'

Abbie tapped her nose. 'None of your business,' she told him. 'He's my date, not yours!'

She left the room quickly, before Billy could remember where he'd heard Bradley's name from and started asking her any more questions about him. She knew Billy would be livid if he discovered that she was going out on a date with a policeman.

Billy had had so many run-ins with the law that the sight of a policeman walking down Scotland Road was enough to make him quake in his shoes for all his bluster.

Her mam felt much the same way, so the less they knew about her friendship with Bradley Fisher, the better it would be.

The less he knew about her family for the moment, the better it would be as well, which was why she hadn't let him walk her all the way home.

He knew she lived somewhere off Scotland Road and that was bad enough. If he found out that she lived in the slummiest house in Bostock Street he might drop her like a hot brick.

Time enough for him to know those sort of details if they started becoming serious about each other and then she'd have to tell him about her family.

For the moment it was simply a matter of having a night out in New Brighton and a chance for them to get to know each other a bit better.

Chapter Twenty-Five

The sky hung like a thunderous black curtain over the Mersey. Ships' klaxons and foghorns sounded continuously. It was raining so hard that it was blowing in through the open doors of the cotton sheds, where that morning dozens of damaged bales had been unloaded and swung inside the shed from the ship docked alongside.

The noise of the rain drumming down outside almost drowned the voices of the women working in there.

'If they don't turn the bloody tap off before knockin' off time we'll be like drowned rats by the time we get to the top of the floating roadway,' one of them commented loudly.

'Sooner get bleedin' soaked than hang on here any longer. Getting back to me own fireside is all I give a damn about. What's a drop of rain, anyway, only cold water,' another piped up.

'It's only a summer storm; there's another hour to go yet, so with any luck it'll have eased off by then. At least we're working inside so we're out of it. Think of the poor buggers working out on the dockside, they must be like drowned rats!' Ellen Martin shouted back, pulling her black shawl more firmly round her shoulders.

'See for yourself, here's your Billy. Look at the state he's in!'

Ellen looked up as Billy, soaked to the skin, water skidding off the peak of his greasy cap, walked across to the corner of the warehouse where she was working.

She put down her sharp, curved knife and held out her hand. 'Orright' then?'

He nodded, shoving a tin box into her outstretched hand, pulling a face and turning his jacket collar up around his ears all at the same time.

'See you at home later, then.'

Billy grunted and turned away.

'Why the hell does he have to bring his snack tin over here, Ellen, for you to carry home for him?' Ruby Stacey asked. 'Lazy bugger!'

'Have to wait on him 'and and foot at home as well, do yer?' another laughed.

Ellen didn't answer. She put the tin Billy had brought underneath her own, and taking off her black shawl wrapped them firmly together in a bundle. Then picking up her curved knife she returned to hacking out a wad of the iron-hard, salt-damaged cotton, ready for teasing.

Her fingers itched to look inside Billy's tin, but she knew better than to even show a flicker of interest about what was in it. There were too many curious eyes, too many loose tongues, and too many women who would be more than ready to land her in trouble if she gave them the slightest chance.

The women who worked in the cotton sheds

235

were the roughest of the rough. Most of them lived in the dingy courts that were built around the Scotland Road area. Very few of them could read or write, but they were streetwise and hard, and they had an inborn craftiness that got them through life.

Many of them were married to men who were casual labourers on the docks, or men who were on the bottom rung when it came to jobs. Burly men who were rough and ready, and quick with their fists at work as well as at home.

Even though most of the women she worked alongside were well able to stand up to their menfolk, they regularly appeared with black eyes, cut lips and bruises. She knew only too well that they would have no compunction about throwing a punch her way if they knew the contents of Billy's snack tin.

Ellen grinned to herself. They thought themselves smart, but they were no match for her and Billy. When the pair of them worked as a team the rewards were always well worth the risks they took.

It was still raining when the hooter sounded, but Ellen barely noticed. All she wanted to do was get home and see what was in Billy's tin.

As the other women dithered about going out in the rain, she made to leave.

'You can't go out in that lot, you'll be half-drowned long before you can reach the tram stop,' Ruby Stacey yelled.

'Gerroff! I won't melt! A drop of rain never did anyone any harm,' Ellen argued. Angrily she shook Ruby's hand away from her arm and elbowed her way past the others.

'Well, at least put your shawl up over your head, you silly bitch,' one of the women at the front advised. She made a grab for the black shawl that Ellen had tucked underneath her arm. There was a scuffle and a tussle and the shawl was dragged free, spilling its contents. The lid on the tin Billy had entrusted to her flew open.

'Flippin' 'eck! Wha's all that, then?' one of the women exclaimed, as a man's silver watch and a handful of mixed silver lay scattered on the warehouse floor.

They pushed and shoved to pick the pieces up and then slowly handed them back to Ellen.

She took them without a word of thanks and thrust them as fast as she could into the deep pocket of her black skirt.

'Hang on a minute. Let's have a gander at that watch,' one of the women demanded.

Ellen pushed her aside. 'Sling your 'ook and mind your own bleedin' business, Florrie Smith.'

The woman was taller than Ellen, with a pock-marked face and brawny arms. She stood with them akimbo, as she glared suspiciously at Ellen.

'I think it is my bloody business, Ellen Martin,' she said menacingly. 'That's my old man's watch you got there.'

'Don't talk so bleedin' wet,' Ellen blustered. 'How the hell would I have your old man's watch?'

'That's something I'd like to know,' Florrie Smith told her. 'It was in that tin your Billy brought over and we all know what a right tea-leaf he is! It doesn't take a barrack-room lawyer to work out what's going on!'

Ellen tried to push Florrie to one side. 'Out of me way, I haven't got time to stand here argy-bargying with you. I got a home to go to, even if you haven't!'

'Oh no you don't!' Florrie grabbed her by the hair and spun her round. 'You ain't tear-arsing off nowhere, not wi' my old man's watch in your pocket, so hand it over.'

'And who's going to make me?'

'Me and me mates are!' Florrie Smith told her aggressively.

Ellen looked round at the rest of the women, trying to gauge who was on her side and who would be likely to support Florrie.

'What makes you think it's your old man's, anyway?' Ellen parried.

'Turn yer pocket out and let's take a dekko. If it's my Jack's watch it's solid silver and as sound as Big Ben, and it's got J. S. engraved on the back of it.'

'Give over, you barmy sod! It's only a bit of tat,' Ellen told her. 'Probably given away with a pound of tea or else it came out of a Chrissy cracker or from Paddy's Market,' she added derisively.

Florrie's face reddened. 'I think it's time to stop jangling and take a dekko,' she demanded nastily.

There was a murmur of agreement from the other women, and before Ellen could avoid it she was surrounded and her black skirt almost torn off as hands dived for the pocket where she had secreted the watch and money.

Polly Hicks, the forewoman, screamed for help. The warehouseman came running to see what all the commotion was about. He took one look at the milling mound of women, all clawing and fighting, and then yelled at the top of his voice for someone to call the scuffers.

Within seconds, police whistles were sounding the alarm and there was the dull thud of pounding feet as three policemen who had been on the dockside invaded the shed, batons at the ready.

It took the three of them ten minutes to separate all the women and find out what the fuss was about. They confiscated all of Ellen's loot. One of the policemen took out his notebook and asked her for her name and address, but she refused to give it.

'Helen. Mury Helen!' one of the other women cackled. 'Can't you see she's a scruffy Mury Helen from her shawl and black skirt?'

'That'll be enough,' the sergeant in charge snapped. Along with another officer he marched her away to the police station, leaving the younger policeman to pacify the rest of the women.

'So when're you going to let my old man have his watch back?' Florrie demanded.

The young police officer shrugged. 'You'd better ask down at the station. They may need to hang on to it as evidence. Depends if they charge her or not.'

'Wouldn't mind bettin' that if my old man's realised it's gone then him and his mates are

239

looking everywhere down on the docks for it,' Florrie babbled.

'You'd better tell him to report his loss, then, and we'll see if he can prove it's his.'

'Yer wants to track down her son, Billy. He's the real villain, not her. He's the one what stole the watch. He brought it over here and gave it her to carry home for him,' Florrie went on.

'Right, I'll do that. What's his full name and where does he live?'

'Bostock Street, off Scotland Road.'

'The number?'

'Gawd, how should I know that. You wanting me to do your job for you!' she sneered in mocking tones. 'Look for the scruffiest house in the road, dirty doorstep and dirty ragged curtains at the window, that'll be it.'

He nodded.

'What's yer name, so that I can tell me old man who it was said he was to come to the station and ask for his watch?'

'Constable Fisher.'

'Well, you damn well make sure you nab that Billy, Constable Fisher,' Florrie called after him as he walked away.

It wasn't until he reached Scotland Road and was looking out for Bostock Street, that Bradley Fisher realised he hadn't made a note of the accused woman's surname before his colleagues had marched her off, so he didn't know Billy's name, either.

He debated whether to go to the station first and find out, or whether, since he was virtually on the doorstep, he should follow Florrie Smith's directions and look for the scruffiest house in the road.

It stood out like a sore thumb! Even in a road of slummy houses, this house had the edge. The front step looked as though it hadn't seen a pumice stone in years. There was a cracked pane of glass in the front window and the grimy curtains were in tatters. As he hammered with his fist on the front door he noticed it was chipped and scarred, as though it had been kicked in a few times.

There was no reply. He knocked again, then put his shoulder to it and gave it a firm push. A dank, sour smell came from inside as he stepped into the dark passage.

'Anyone at home?'

His voice echoed. In the living room, ashes spewed from the grate into the hearth. Mugs and dirty plates with leftover food on them cluttered the rickety table and sideboard. He went to the bottom of the stairs and shouted out again, but there was still no answer. He made his way up to the landing and looked into the bedrooms. Two of them were in a state of complete disorder, the beds unmade, clothes dropped on the floor. The smaller of the bedrooms, however, was neat and tidy, but the thing that caught his attention was the full-length turquoise frock hanging from a nail on one wall.

He walked across the room and fingered it, momentarily unable to believe it was the same dress, hoping he was mistaken.

'What do you think you are doing!'

He had been so engrossed in the dress that he hadn't heard anyone come in, and he turned around startled to face Abbie.

'Bradley, what are you doing in my bedroom?' she gasped in astonishment.

'Your bedroom? This is where you live? Billy is your brother? Your mother's name is Ellen?'

She nodded, the colour draining from her face. 'Why all the questions? Is something wrong?' she asked anxiously.

He shook his head, unable to believe Ellen was Abbie's mother, wondering how to tell her what had happened.

'Has there been an accident? Are they hurt?' she persisted, her voice quivering.

Again, he shook his head. 'No, there's not been an accident,' he said hesitantly.

'What, then?'

'There was an incident at the cotton sheds and your mother has been arrested for possessing stolen goods.'

Abbie stared at him, chewing on her lower lip.

'She's been taken to Atholl Street police station,' Bradley added, almost apologetically.

'You arrested my mam!'

He squared his broad shoulders. 'Yes, I arrested her, but I didn't know she was your mother,' he said stubbornly.

'So why are you here, turning the place upside down?'

'I'm looking for your brother, Billy. According to information received, he is the real culprit and your mother was his accomplice,' he told her stiffly.

Chapter Twenty-Six

After Bradley Fisher left the house, Abbie lay on her bed, dry-eyed, staring up unseeingly at the cracked, dirty ceiling. She felt as if the bottom had dropped out of her world. She couldn't believe that Fate had dealt her such a cruel blow. For Bradley to find out where she lived was bad enough, but for him to have taken part in arresting her mam, and to be looking for Billy so that he could arrest him as well, was the final straw.

The look on his face when she had walked into the house and found him fingering her evening dress had sent goose-bumps chasing along her spine. When he had turned around he'd looked as if he was seeing a ghost, and she had been just as shocked as him.

The thought that what her mother had done might ruin their friendship made her realise how much she liked him.

Over the last few weeks, since she'd been going out with Bradley, she'd thought that at last she had found someone who was not only interested in everything she said or did, but really did like her a great deal.

For her entire life her mam and Billy had treated her as if she was of no importance. Neither of them had ever shown her any affection or love.

Her childhood closeness to Sam and Peter had now been eroded. Sam had transferred his love to Sandra; Peter seemed to have channelled all his energies into his work. Even Maggie Ryan seemed to have lost interest in her.

Meeting Bradley, and discovering someone who was not only interested in her, but who seemed to love her, had been such a wonderful experience; like starting a new life. Each kiss they'd exchanged had filled her with wonder. It had been like renewing a pledge of their love, and a promise of all the happiness that was still to come; and now those hopes were all turning to dust.

She dare not let herself dwell on what he must think of her. She wished fervently that right from the beginning she'd told him everything about herself. She should have told him where she lived, explained about her family background. She'd meant to, once they got to know each other. Then, because she was so much in love with him, she'd been afraid to do so in case it changed his feelings for her.

Looking back, she knew it would have been far better for this run-in between her mam and Bradley to have happened earlier on in their relationship, before he had come to mean so much in her life. She might have felt unhappy at losing him, but she wouldn't have been as broken-hearted as she was now. She wouldn't have known this terrible emptiness, as if someone had ripped out her heart.

When Billy arrived home and discovered his mother wasn't there he flew into a rage.

'Where the hell is she?' he demanded, barging into Abbie's bedroom and angrily kicking at the legs of her bed.

'At Atholl Street police station.'

'What! What did you say?'

'Mam's been taken to Atholl Street police station. She's been done for causing some sort of affray down at the cotton sheds.'

'How do you know?'

'The police were here when I got in from work. They're looking for you.'

'What the hell for? What's it got to do with me?'

Abbie shrugged listlessly. 'I don't know. I think Bradley said it was something to do with stealing a watch.'

'Bradley! That fella you're knocking around with? What's it got to do with him?'

'He was the one here looking for you. His lot arrested Mam.'

Billy looked at her in growing fury. 'Bradley . . . Bradley Fisher. I thought I knew that name. He's a bloody scuffer, isn't he!'

Abbie nodded.

'You've been knocking around with a bloody scuffer, opening your great gob and telling him all he wants to know about our goings-on,' Billy railed.

He caught hold of Abbie's arm and pulled her off the bed, hauling her to her feet and shaking her like a rag doll until her teeth were chattering.

'You'd better get yourself down the cop shop and find out what's going on!' he snarled, pushing her towards the door.

'Go yourself!' she muttered, pulling back from him and sitting back down on the bed.

'How the hell can I! You said that your Bradley Fisher was here looking for me! He wasn't doing that so that he could invite me to a bleedin' party.'

'So what have you been up to?'

'The less you know, the less you can mouth off to your boyfriend,' Billy snarled.

'I don't suppose there's much chance of that,' Abbie said bitterly. Her eyes filled with tears. 'Now that Bradley has found out about my family I don't suppose I'll ever see him again.'

'Lucky for you, you stupid bint. If I see you talking to him again I'll bloody well thrash you within an inch of your life!'

Abbie looked at him disdainfully. 'You'll have a job. Any minute now one of those scuffers will be back here looking for you, and when they hear what you've been up to you'll be behind bars in Walton Jail!'

Billy frowned, a desperate shifty look on his face. 'Mam won't spill the beans; she'll keep her trap shut,' he said confidently. 'All I've got to do is bugger off where that dozy-arsed copper can't find me.'

'Go on then, scarper!' Abbie said derisively. 'Be just like you, Billy, to leave our mam to fend for herself when she's charged for something you've done. What'll you care if she ends up inside?'

'They won't send an old biddy like her to the Dogs' Home,' he blustered.

Abbie shrugged. 'If they find her carrying whatever it is you've nicked, they're bound to do just that. Bradley said something about a watch,' she added, eyeing him closely.

Billy hesitated, as if trying to make his mind up about what he ought to do.

'Can you lend us some money, kiddo? I'm skint,' he said at last.

'Lend you money so that you can make a getaway and let mam take the can back for you! You must think I'm stupid.'

'Stop whingeing! Open your purse up and hand over some ackers,' Billy snarled. 'The sooner I'm away, before that bloody scuffer of yours comes back, the better. Me mam knows how to deal with the scuffers. She'll tell them that some fella she didn't know asked her to look after the ticker for 'im.'

'And you think they'll believe her?' Abby asked caustically.

'Don't see why not.' His thin lips twisted into an ugly grin. 'It's as near the truth as she can get!'

'Maybe, but the police know exactly who that mystery fella is,' Abbie pointed out. 'The women in the cotton sheds saw you hand it over to her and they've already told the police, and that's why they came here looking for you.'

Billy ran a hand over his scant brown hair. 'So what the hell am I supposed to do?'

'Own up?' Abbie said scathingly.

'If I do that they'll want the low-down on about a dozen other offences!'

'You have been busy! And has Mam been involved with those as well?'

Billy scowled. 'Some!'

'What about the bike you nicked that Peter Ryan got put away over?' Abbie said softly.

'Shut your trap! What the hell's the point of bringing up something like that after all this time. They've wiped that one off their slate years ago.'

'Only because he took the rap for it. It was you that pinched it, wasn't it, Billy,' Abbie persisted.

'Give over nagging! They'd never prove anything. Let's have some ackers and I'll be out of here, and you won't see nor hear from me ever again.'

'I'd like nothing better, but I've already told you I haven't got any money, not until I'm paid tomorrow.'

Billy's eyes narrowed. 'You get paid tomorrow. And then you'll give me enough to skedaddle?'

Abbie shook her head. 'I never said that!'

Billy grabbed hold of her. 'Say it now, then!' he ordered, twisting her arm behind her back until she was white with pain.

'What about Mam?'

'I've told you, she can take care of herself,' Billy snarled. 'Anyway, what're you so worried about her for; the pair of you hate each other's guts!'

'That's got nothing to do with it. It's not fair that someone who's innocent should be taking the rap.'

'Innocent be beggared. She's as much involved in what went on as I am. I told you before, don't worry your head about her, she knows the score and she knows how to take care of herself. She's been doing it long enough! The last thing she'll want me to do is put me own head on the block. It won't save her skin any, only give the scuffers a bloody good laugh.'

Abbie bit her lip. Billy was in an ugly mood and she was afraid of what he might do next. She didn't know what to say or do for the best. She was so frightened that she couldn't think straight. She knew she ought to turn Billy in, and she hated him, but he was her brother.

She wondered if the police would come back to the house looking for him, or if Bradley would throw them off the scent for her sake?

Even if he did manage to do that, it would only be a temporary measure. They already had her mam in custody and they knew that Billy was her accomplice and that, sooner or later, he would return home.

The sound of the front door opening startled them both. Billy let out an oath and looked round wildly for some place to hide.

'Get rid of the buggers!' he hissed as he scrabbled underneath Abbie's bed and pulled the coverlet down to hide him.

Shaking like a leaf, Abbie went out on to the landing. 'Who is it? Who is it down there?' she called out nervously.

'Who the bleedin' hell do you think it is? I lives here, don't I! Get the soddin' kettle on and let's have a decent cuppa, the muck they give you down at the cop shop is like gnats' piss.'

'Mam! Is that really you?' Abbie called as she tore down the stairs.

'It's me, so get the bloody kettle on, then!' Ellen ordered.

Rubbing away her tears with the back of her hand, Abbie did as she was asked.

'Is our Billy here?'

'Yes. He's hiding underneath my bed.'

Ellen gave a belly laugh as she flung her shawl over the back of a chair and sat down and eased her feet out of her boots.

'Crafty sod! Go on, then, call him down, tell him I'm home.'

Billy had already heard his mother's voice and was halfway down the stairs when Abbie went out into the passage.

'Is she all right?'

'Ask her yourself.'

'They let you home then, Mam!' he grinned as he sidled into the room.

'No thanks to you!'

'What's happened?' Abbie demanded. 'Are they still looking for Billy, and are they going to charge you both?'

'Charge us with what?' Ellen asked, her mouth open in surprise.

'For pinching the watch, of course,' Abbie said.

'Watch? I never pinched no watch.'

'Well, Billy did, didn't he?'

They exchanged warning glances.

'Got the wrong end of the bleedin' stick, haven't you?' Ellen snapped.

'What did they take you in for, then?' Abbie asked bewildered.

'For causing an affray. Once they got me down the station and asked some questions they realised

251

the rumpus was nothing to do with me, and so they let me go!'

Abbie looked at Billy in surprise. 'The watch. Bradley said you'd stolen it and then passed it over to Mam . . .'

'Bradley? That the name of the young scuffer who nicked me?'

'One of them.'

'Didn't take you long to find out his name, did it! Fancy him, do you?'

'She's going out with the bugger,' Billy said glumly.

'*Was* going out with him,' Abbie corrected him. 'After what has happened, and now he knows where I live and that you're my family, I doubt if I'll ever see him again,' Abbie added miserably. 'Anyway, Mam, you've still not told me the whole story about what happened.'

'There's nothing more to tell,' Ellen muttered.

'Yes there is,' Abbie persisted. 'What about the watch that Billy stole, where is it now?'

Ellen shook her head and scratched herself. 'There was a watch. It was on the floor and it was smashed to smithereens. Some woman tried to say it was her old man's, and that Billy had nicked it from him. The scuffers reckon she'd pinched it, though, and was going to flog it off.'

Abbie shook her head. 'I don't believe you,' she said flatly.

'Orright, then, here's the truth, if it will make you feel any better,' Ellen sneered. 'Billy did nick the watch, and he brought it over to the cotton sheds in his snack tin and handed it to me to bring home. The tin fell on to the floor but I managed to stuff the watch into my pocket.'

'And the police found it there?'

''Course they bloody well didn't. I made sure it was on the floor when the fight started. That's how it got smashed up. There was no evidence at all against me, except that woman's word, and, as I've just told you, the police reckoned she was the one who'd taken it from her old man and that she was going to flog it.'

Chapter Twenty-Seven

'Abbie Martin, Miss Breck wants to see you in her office right away,' Miss Webster told her officiously.

Abbie looked taken aback. 'Do you know what it's about?'

'No, but it seems to be very urgent.'

As she hurried along to the Staff Manager's office, Abbie's mind was in a whirl. Why on earth was she being summoned? As far as she knew there was no reason for Miss Breck to want to see her.

Her heart pounded. Could it be something to do with her mam or Billy, she wondered. Surely they hadn't got themselves into any more trouble and been arrested again.

'Abbie.' Miss Breck looked rather puzzled. 'There is a young man downstairs who is asking if you can go home immediately.' She hesitated. 'It is bad news, I'm afraid. Your brother's wife is seriously ill and is asking for you.'

'Sandra? She's expecting a baby any time now!' Abbie said in an anxious voice.

'I understand that is part of the problem,' Miss Breck murmured. 'Apparently there are complications. I think you had better collect your coat and run along. I will explain to Miss Webster that you have been unavoidably called away.'

'Yes, Miss Breck. Thank you.'

Feeling slightly dazed, Abbie walked to the door. As she opened it, Miss Breck said, 'We shall expect you back at work in the morning, Abbie. If it is not possible for you to come in then you must be sure to let me know.'

'Thank you, Miss Breck, I'll do that.'

Abbie's mind was still whirling as she hurried towards the entrance. Although she and Sandra had had very little to do with each other since their fall out earlier in the year, they had been friends since they were quite little and she couldn't help but feel concerned about her.

When she reached the ground floor she looked round for Sam, then drew in a sharp breath of surprise when she saw that it was Peter Ryan who was waiting for her. He looked very smart in his dark business suit and her heart missed a beat. She hadn't seen him for weeks, not since she had started going out regularly with Bradley Fisher.

The feelings she'd had for him since she was a small girl were long gone. His reserved indifference had made sure of that. He had changed so much. He was so prim, so cold, so unable to express his feelings. She occasionally wondered why she had spent so much time trying to win back the affection Peter had shown towards her when they were growing up, when he obviously no longer had any feelings for her.

Bradley was not much older than Peter, but he had been so utterly different. He'd been warm and loving, and so ready to tell her how much he cared for her that being with him had transformed her life.

Seeing Peter standing there was like turning back the calendar and reviving all the heartbreaking events of the past year that she'd been so determined to put out of her mind.

'Peter, what are you doing here? I thought it was Sam who had come to fetch me?'

He shook his head. 'That was why I didn't give a name, I thought you mightn't come down and it is very urgent, Abbie,' he said grimly. 'Come on,' he took her arm and hurried her towards the door. 'I've got a taxicab waiting.'

'Where is Sandra?' she asked over her shoulder as he followed her into the cab.

'At the Liverpool Infirmary. They rushed her in at ten o'clock this morning.'

'I didn't think the baby was due until the end of August or early September?'

'It's premature. She had it about an hour ago. The baby is fine; it's Sandra who is giving cause for concern. They don't hold out much hope for her, I'm afraid, Abbie. She was asking for you, that's why I came to fetch you.'

Abbie felt choked, but before she could ask for any more details the taxicab pulled up in front of the hospital.

After he'd paid it off, Peter hustled her inside, up two flights of stairs and along a corridor that had frosted-glass windows. He pushed open the glass-panelled door at the end of the corridor. 'Wait a moment,' he said when they were inside the ward, 'I must let the Sister know that we are here.'

The smell of disinfectant caught in Abbie's throat as they were taken to the far end of the ward, to a bed screened off with blue- and pink-striped curtains.

Sandra was so white and motionless, and there were so many tubes and drips attached to her body, that for a moment Abbie thought she had come too late. Then, as they approached the bed, Sandra turned her head and the moment she saw Abbie she seemed to rally.

Giving a weak smile she reached out and clutched at Abbie's hand, almost as if she was afraid she might walk away.

'Hello, Sandra,' Abbie said awkwardly. She felt at a loss for words yet desperate to comfort her in any way she could.

'Have you seen the baby?' Sandra's voice was a hoarse whisper.

'No!' Abbie shook her head. 'I've only just this minute got here and Peter brought me straight to see you.'

Sandra closed her eyes, fighting for breath. Then summoning up all her strength she opened her eyes again and clutched even tighter at Abbie's hand. 'It's a little boy. You will look after him, Abbie? Promise me you'll look after him,' she begged.

Stunned, Abbie stared down at Sandra, wondering if she knew what she was saying.

Sandra's ashen face contorted as she sensed Abbie's reluctance to answer.

'Please, Abbie, promise me you will,' she begged, her grey eyes pleading.

Abbie still hesitated. How could she make a promise like that? She was out at work all day. Surely Sandra's mother was the right person to be looking after the baby until Sandra was well enough to do so herself.

'Of course Abbie will look after him, Sandra,' Peter affirmed, signalling at Abbie with his eyes for her to confirm what he had said.

'Yes, don't worry, Sandra. Of course I'll do all I can,' Abbie told her. She looked round, 'Where's Sam? He should be here with you.'

Sandra turned her head restlessly from side to side and muttered something, but her voice was so faint that Abbie couldn't catch her words. She bent lower. 'I didn't hear what you said, Sandra.'

Sandra gave an enormous gulp, tears flooded from her eyes and rolled down her cheeks, her chest heaved, and then there was stillness.

'Sandra!' Abbie felt a wave of panic wash over her as the hand she was holding seemed to lose its grip on hers. 'Sandra!' she said again, her voice high and almost hysterical.

Peter whipped back the curtain and called for someone to come and help. A nurse was there in seconds, followed by the Sister.

Abbie and Peter were told to wait outside the ward as the nurses began to try and resuscitate Sandra.

Abbie stood by one of the windows, staring at the fuzzy impressions made by the frosted glass. She felt drained and frightened. She was sure

Sandra was dead, and there were so many unanswered questions in her mind that she felt utterly bewildered.

When the Sister came out into the corridor to speak to them, Abbie was aware that Peter's hand was gripping her shoulder and she braced herself, knowing her worst fears were going to be confirmed.

It was all over. They hadn't been able to save Sandra.

Abbie felt numb and in something of a daze as Peter led her away and went to find a chair so that she could sit down. She still couldn't believe what had happened.

'Would you like to see the baby?' he asked uncomfortably.

Abbie's blue eyes were pools of horror as she stared up at him. 'The baby has taken Sandra's life!' she said in a strained voice.

'You must try not to think about it like that,' he said uneasily.

She shook her head as if trying to clear her thoughts. 'Where's our Sam, why isn't he here? He should have been at Sandra's side, holding her hand, comforting her, not us!'

Peter chewed on his lower lip. 'There's something you ought to know, Abbie.'

'About Sam?' She frowned. 'He's not in any trouble, is he?'

'No, of course not.'

'Then why isn't he here?'

She stood up and began pacing backwards and forwards. She felt as if the whole world was spinning round her, as if she was going mad. Things were happening all wrong. Where was Sam, where was Mo Lewis, or even her own mam; they should all be here at a time like this.

'Abbie, listen to me and try to understand what I am telling you,' Peter said stiffly. 'Sam isn't here because he found out that the baby Sandra was carrying wasn't his.'

Abbie stared at him, bewildered. 'Not Sam's? But that was the reason why they got married, because Sandra was expecting his baby.'

'Yes, I know.' Peter ran his forefinger between his neck and his stiff white collar as if he was struggling for breath. 'I'll try and explain things if you'll give me a chance!'

Abbie shook her dark head, perplexed. She didn't want to hear what Peter had to say, she was still wrapped up in her own thoughts, in the events of the last few minutes.

'I promised Sandra that I would look after her baby! Is that why she asked me, because she knew Sam wouldn't?'

'Possibly,' Peter agreed uneasily.

Anger welled up in Abbie. 'How could she, how could Sandra make me promise such an undertaking when she knew all the time that the baby wasn't our Sam's and that she was dying.'

Peter looked uncomfortable. 'She . . . she probably wanted what she thought was best for the baby,' he said helplessly.

'Why can't her mother look after it? I know nothing at all about caring for babies. Anyway, I don't want to look after it if it isn't Sam's. If it had been Sam's then perhaps I would be feeling differently.'

Abbie held her head in her hands and rocked backwards and forwards. 'What have I done,' she moaned, 'making a promise like that to a dying woman. How can I possibly keep that promise when I hate this baby even before I see it? How could she have done something like this to Sam!'

Peter took her by the arms and tried to calm her. 'Listen to me, Abbie, you'll feel better once you have had time to get used to the idea. Why don't you come and have a look at the baby, you may feel differently towards it once you've seen it.'

She shook her head. 'I don't think so.'

'Please!' he implored. 'Come and see it.'

'They may not let me! If it isn't Sam's child then I'm not even a relation, am I,' she protested stubbornly.

Peter didn't answer. He walked back into the ward on his own and she heard the mumble of voices as he talked to the Sister, but she had no idea what they were saying to each other.

They came out of the ward together, and the Sister took them to a small annex further along the corridor and left them. Peter urged her inside and guided her across to a crib. As she looked down into it her heart almost stopped. The baby lying there appeared to be perfect in every way and completely healthy, but very tiny. Its head was covered in a thick down of fair hair, the colour Sandra's had been.

Abbie felt her heart turn over as she looked down on the baby, and when it opened its eyes and stared up at her she gasped in surprise. The baby's eyes were as blue as her own were!

There was something so familiar about the baby that she had a premonition of what Peter was about to say, even before he began speaking.

'There is something you have to know, Abbie,' he said awkwardly, 'and it may make you realise why Sandra asked for your help.'

She stared at him unflinchingly. 'Go on!'

'I was trying to tell you earlier . . .' His mouth tightened and he took a deep breath.

Abbie felt as if an ice-cold hand was grabbing her heart as he added, 'Sandra's baby isn't Sam's, it's mine!'

Chapter Twenty-Eight

They left the baby at the Liverpool infirmary until after Sandra's funeral, which had been arranged for Thursday 25th August.

Although the baby was perfectly healthy it was underweight, and there were minor feeding problems to be dealt with because it was slightly premature, before the hospital would let them take it home.

No one in authority had even asked where the baby would be going when it left hospital.

Both Maggie Ryan and Mo Lewis were too upset by what had happened to discuss the issue either with the authorities or with each other.

The baby's fate hung in the air; a spectre at Sandra's funeral, a problem for which no one had a solution.

Several times during the week Abbie had made a point of going up Brownlow Hill in order to walk past the old, smoke-grimed Workhouse building, trying to convince herself that, whatever happened, Sandra's baby mustn't end up in there.

Even the bedraggled, barefoot existence of the children who were brought up in the sun-starved courts and back streets around Scotland Road was better than being shut away inside that grim building, she told herself.

Her promise to Sandra lay heavily on her mind. Why had Sandra picked her, of all people, she kept asking herself? Perhaps she had been delirious and not really meant it like that.

Abbie wanted to talk about it, explain to Mrs Lewis that she and her husband were in a much better position to bring the baby up than she was, but Mo Lewis was so overcome with grief at losing Sandra that it was impossible to do so.

Maggie Ryan didn't seem to want to talk about it, either. She avoided her completely, and Abbie wondered how much she really knew about the situation.

Gradually, she persuaded Sam to tell her the truth about what had happened and how Peter Ryan came to be the father of Sandra's baby. When he finally broke his silence he was bitter and resentful, and he blamed Abbie!

'If you'd helped Sandra to get an abortion when we asked you to do so, then this wouldn't have happened,' he said accusingly.

She bit back her own angry retort. Sam looked so ill that, even though she smarted under the accusation, she didn't feel it was the right time to row with him. He looked so drawn and haggard and talked in such a despairing way that she was afraid he might do something foolish in an attempt to get out of the mess he found himself in.

One thing which Sam made quite clear was that he wasn't prepared to bring up the baby. The shock of finding out that Sandra had been unfaithful had broken his heart. He couldn't bear to hear her name mentioned and he didn't even want to look at the baby. As for its future, he didn't care who looked after it or brought it up, or even what happened to it.

He was bitterly angry with Abbie when he heard that she had promised Sandra she would take care of the baby.

'How could you do such a thing!' he exploded angrily.

'I didn't know she was going to die. I didn't know it wasn't your baby, either,' she snapped. 'I thought I was helping you! We've always stuck together and looked out for each other, ever since we were kids, that's why I made that promise.'

Realising she would be getting no help from Sam, Abbie tackled Peter. She had hesitated about approaching him, knowing how deep her feelings had always been for him in the past.

She felt icy cold, her emotions suspended, as he told her his side of the story.

'It happened at Christmas,' Peter said morosely. 'After my mam had had too much to drink and you had taken her home. Sam went home after that, but I stayed on at Sandra's and we ended up in bed together.'

'As simple as that?' Abbie asked sarcastically. 'I suppose you'd both had too much to drink as well and so you couldn't control yourselves?' she added caustically.

Peter bristled, his face flaming. He opened his mouth to refute what she was implying, then thought better of it. Tight-lipped, he said stiffly, 'We possibly had. I'm not used to drink, as you very well know.'

265

He chewed his lower lip. 'I bitterly regretted what happened. It haunted me afterwards.'

'Really?' Abbie looked at him contemptuously. 'So that was why you flirted with Sandra on St Valentine's night when we went to the Tower Ballroom at New Brighton?'

Peter ran a hand through his thick dark hair. 'I regretted that, too! After that I did everything I could to put things right.'

'You mean you showed some interest in me until the night you took me to the Grafton on my birthday, and then you knew that I didn't measure up to Sandra's sweet and lovely ways!'

He shook his head. 'You did disgrace us both, Abbie. I have never been thrown out of anywhere before in my life. It was most upsetting, because I do have my reputation to consider now that I am a Manager at the Royal Liver Friendly Society.'

'So how do you think they are going to react when they hear about the baby,' she asked, her blue eyes locking with his.

Peter shuddered. 'I'm afraid to even think about it,' he admitted. 'Somehow it's got to be kept from them.'

'So how will you do that? Stick the baby in the Workhouse or in an orphanage?'

Peter looked shocked. The colour drained from his lean face. 'I was hoping that Sandra's mother would bring the child up.'

Abbie gave a dry laugh. 'Mo Lewis is a control freak. She hates you to even walk into her poxy house unless you take your shoes off first. She's hardly likely to take on a young baby with its messy feeding habits and sticky fingers every-where.'

'Not even when it's her own grandchild!' Peter said in amazement.

Abbie shrugged. 'Try asking her yourself!'

'Well,' he asked desolately, 'who else is there who can look after it?' He looked at her specula-tively. 'Except you. Remember, you did promise Sandra you would look after it, so will you take it on, Abbie?'

'Me, take on a young baby! How can I afford to do that? I'm out at work all day.'

'You needn't be. I have a decently paid job now, so you could stay home.'

'Are you suggesting I should be a kept woman?' she asked scornfully.

'Not exactly!' His face brightened. 'We could get married. We'd have a home of our own.'

'And our own ready-made family? How very cosy!'

'You used to love me, Abbie.'

'I thought I did when we were growing up because you always followed me round like a faithful dog. When Sam and I tried to plan what we were going to do when we were old enough to earn money and get away from Bostock Street, you always begged to come with us. Remember?'

'So why not marry me now? We could move over the Mersey to Seacombe or New Brighton and you'd be well away from Bostock Street. A home of your own, Abbie,' he persisted.

'And a baby that is not my own! A child whose mother stole my brother's affection away from me and then treated him so shabbily that he is now almost insane. Do you think *that* is a good start for a happy family life, Peter?'

He shrugged. 'As I see it, for us to set up home together is the perfect solution.'

'Perfect solution for you, maybe. No one you work with need ever know the truth. That's what you mean, isn't it, Peter?'

'Partly. Above all, I want you back, Abbie. Since we've stopped seeing each other I realise how much I care about you.' He reached out and took her hands. 'I really do mean that, Abbie. I do love you! Being separated from you makes me feel as if I've lost part of myself. We have always been so close.'

Abbie pulled her hands away and shook her head. 'That's not true. We've grown further and further apart since you've come home.'

'Only because I found it so difficult to readjust. I was shut off from you and everything I knew for almost three years, Abbie. At that age it's a lifetime. You changed so much. I resented the fact that you never once visited me . . .'

'Only because I wasn't allowed to do so because I was still at school,' she interrupted sharply. 'I wanted to come and see you. I sent messages. Sam and I sent you comics and sweets that we bought with the money Sam earned doing deliveries.'

'I know, and I appreciated them, but what I really wanted was to see you. Then, when I did get out, you had a life of your own. You were working and you'd made new friends and you seemed to find me dull and uninteresting.'

'Only because you always had your nose in a book, studying!'

'I was doing that for you. I wanted to get on, make something of myself. To prove myself in your eyes. To get a promotion so that we could get married,' he said glibly.

'No, you wanted to get on, to justify yourself in your own eyes,' she told him. 'All that night school and studying was to make you feel good and it had nothing to do with me, or how I felt. You didn't like my new friends, you thought them shallow. I wanted some fun but you didn't. That's why we drifted apart, Peter.'

'Are you saying that you still love me?' he asked hopefully. 'That Jamie, and Bradley Fisher, and all the rest of them mean nothing to you?'

A shadow flickered over Abbie's face as he mentioned Bradley Fisher's name. That was still an unhealed sore and something she didn't want to even think about. Her feelings for him had been deep and genuine. She believed that what she had felt for him was true love, and she'd been sure that he had felt the same way about her.

She blamed the fecklessness of her mother and Billy for what had happened. Once Bradley knew the sort of family she came from, how could she expect him to go on seeing her when it might be putting his career in jeopardy.

'Please, Abbie. Say you'll marry me and make a home with me and the baby,' Peter pleaded. 'You'll never regret it. I can afford to provide you with a good home, right away from here. We can start afresh, the sort of future you promised yourself when you were growing up. I'll devote every moment of my life to you, and I know you will be a wonderful mother. If the baby grows up believing you to be its mother then it will love you as much as I do.'

Abbie shook her head doubtfully. She was very tempted. The thought of being first and foremost in someone's life was a tremendous incentive. She wanted so much to love and be loved. She still cared for Peter, she told herself, even if those feelings were nothing like as deep and as strong as the ones she had for Bradley.

Was that enough to ensure their future happiness? As for the baby, poor little mite, could she ever love him, knowing that he was Sandra's child? Her feelings were in such turmoil that she couldn't find an answer.

'Please, Abbie, I'm begging you,' Peter pleaded. 'If you don't want to get married right away then just move in with me and see how things go.' He took both her hands again, raising them to his lips.

'I need time to think about it,' she prevaricated, pulling herself free.

'Promise me you'll consider the idea,' he begged.

She nodded, too choked to speak.

'When will you give me your answer? The hospital aren't prepared to keep the baby any longer now that Sandra's funeral is over.'

Abbie took a deep, shuddering breath. He was rushing her and she was so afraid of doing the wrong thing. She needed time to talk to Sam, to talk to Mo Lewis, to her own mother, even, and eventually to Maggie Ryan. Her decision affected all of them in one way or another. The decision couldn't be hers alone.

'Soon, Peter. I'll give you my answer as quickly as possible,' she promised. 'I must talk to Sam, first. Sam and others,' she added vaguely.

Sam was still too upset about what had happened between Sandra and Peter to be able to talk reasonably about it.

'I feel cheated,' he said bitterly, running his hand through his thick brown hair. 'Sandra never told me until she went into labour. I couldn't even think straight after that. I loved her so much, Abbie, and yet I wasn't even there when she died. My life is such a mess that I can't hang around here any longer. I've found a ship and I've already signed up. I'm sailing in two days' time.'

Abbie looked shocked. 'Sam, you can't do this. The baby. What about the baby?'

He shrugged. 'It's not mine, is it,' he said flatly.

'Peter has asked me to move in with him and for us to bring the baby up. How do you feel about that, Sam?'

He stared at her, shaking his head as though he couldn't believe what he was hearing.

'It's up to you,' he said at last. 'I think you're mad to get involved. He cheated on you, remember, the same as Sandra did on me, but you do whatever you like.'

'Does Mam know you're going to sea?'

'I've told her, but she doesn't seem to care one way or the other. The only one who will miss me

271

is you, Abbie, and it looks as if your life is going to be pretty full.'

'You mean if I go ahead and do what Peter is suggesting,' she murmured dubiously.

'Don't do it unless you are sure it's what you want,' he warned.

Her mind in a whirl of indecision, Abbie went to see Mo Lewis. Despite what she had said to Peter earlier, she half hoped that once Sandra's mother heard what Peter was planning she would step in and demand the right to bring up the baby herself. She was, after all, the child's grandmother.

'No,' she told Abbie coldly, 'me and Dan have talked it over and we've decided it would be too heavy a responsibility for us to take on. Dan will be retiring in about ten years, just when the child would be at that noisy, demanding stage, wanting bikes and football and such like. You know what boys are like, and it would be more than Dan could stand,' she added dismissively.

'It is your grandson we are talking about,' Abbie reminded her.

Mo Lewis sighed. 'If it had been a little girl then I might have thought differently. It would have been like having Sandra back and she was so sweet at that age. Her daddy always called her his little princess. I always kept her looking so pretty,' she said sadly. 'And for such a thing as this to happen. I blame your Sam. He was never good enough for her.'

'She was quick enough to marry him when she found out that she was pregnant, though, wasn't she!' Abbie pointed out angrily.

Mo Lewis sighed again. 'It's such a pity she didn't tell all of us the truth about what had happened and then she could have married Peter. He is such a refined young man, he would have offered her so much more than your Sam ever did.'

'You didn't think Peter Ryan was such a nice, refined young man when he was sent off to reform school,' Abbie reminded her sharply.

Mo Lewis shrugged. 'It wasn't his fault, though, was it. He didn't steal that bike. Everyone round here knew that it was your Billy.'

Abbie bit her lip. There was no point in discussing that matter any further since it was all in the past.

'Anyway,' Mo sniffed, 'it's Peter Ryan's baby and he has a good job so it's up to him to provide for it.' She dabbed at her eyes, 'If it hadn't been for him our Sandra would still be alive today.'

Abbie wondered if she should even bother to tell Mrs Lewis about Peter's plans, then she decided that it was better that she should hear about it from her than from anyone else.

Mo looked taken aback when Abbie told her it was Peter's idea that they should move in together and bring up the baby.

'Looking for a good home for yourself, are you. I can't see Peter Ryan taking up with you again for any other reason than finding someone to look after the baby. I suppose I can't blame you!' she said scathingly. 'You Martins will cash in on anything, won't you.'

Abbie clenched her hands into fists to keep her

temper in check. 'And what is that supposed to mean?' she asked icily.

Mo Lewis shrugged her shoulders again. 'I don't want to talk about it. It won't bring my Sandra back. You do whatever you like.'

There was only one person who still needed to be told what was happening, Abbie thought wearily, and that was Maggie Ryan. She seemed to have kept very quiet about the whole affair, but, by now, the way tongues had been wagging, surely she must know that Peter was the father of Sandra's baby.

Chapter Twenty-Nine

Abbie was relieved to find that Michael and Maggie were both at home when she went round to the Ryans' house that evening.

She'd still not told her mother or Billy that she was thinking about marrying Peter and bringing up Sandra's baby. It was time enough to do that when she finally made her commitment, she decided. It wasn't as though either of them would care or even be all that interested.

The only thing that might concern her mam was the fact that if Sam was going to sea, and she was leaving home to marry Peter, then there would be less money coming in.

Maggie Ryan answered the door, but there was no warmth at all in her greeting. It touched Abbie's heart to see how much Maggie seemed to have aged over the past couple of weeks. She hoped that Maggie would feel relieved when she heard her decision and that the news would lift some of the burden from her shoulders.

Peter looked at her questioningly as she entered the room, and she felt very nervous as her eyes met his and she gave a small nod to signal her agreement to the arrangement they had discussed earlier in the day.

The look of relief on his lean, handsome face

restored her belief that she was doing the right thing. She waited nervously for him to break the news to his mother.

When he did, the reaction, not from Maggie, but from Peter's brother Michael, left her open-mouthed with astonishment.

'No!' Angrily he rose to his feet and stared round at the three of them as though trapped. 'It's completely out of the question!'

'Michael! That will do!' Agitatedly, Maggie tried to push him out of the door.

'Give over. I'm not leaving until the matter has been cleared up. I'm not letting that happen!'

'It has nothing to do with you, Michael!' his mother shouted, tears streaming down her face.

'Of course it has!' he exclaimed hopelessly. 'It's history repeating itself!'

'What are you on about?' Peter looked from his mother to his brother in bewilderment. 'Mam's right, this has nothing to do with you, Michael. Abbie and me have made our minds up that it's the best thing to do. We're going to get married and bring up the baby as our own.'

'No you are not!' Michael rubbed a hand over his face. 'It wouldn't be right,' he said dully.

'It's my baby, don't you understand that,' Peter said looking agitated. 'He's my responsibility and if Abbie is prepared to play her part then what business is it of yours or of anyone else?'

'Abbie can't do it. Nor can you.' Michael's darkly handsome face contorted with suppressed emotion. 'You two can't marry each other!'

They stared at him, waiting for an explanation, but he seemed too upset to go on.

'I'm afraid Michael's right,' Maggie Ryan said emphatically. 'The two of you mustn't marry.'

Abbie felt a frisson of unease. 'Why ever not?' she demanded. 'Surely that is for me and Peter to decide.'

Maggie shook her head. 'Are you going to tell them, Michael, or shall I?'

'You two are not getting married because I forbid it!' Michael Ryan repeated stubbornly.

'Too bad, but it's none of your business,' Peter fumed.

'Oh yes it is. I'm Abbie's father!'

'You're what?' Abbie stared at him, open-mouthed, disbelief in her eyes. 'You're my father?' She looked from him to Peter, hoping for an explanation, but Peter was as thunderstruck as she was.

'What Michael says is true,' Maggie told them ruefully.

'I don't believe it, not one word of it!' Abbie exclaimed hysterically. 'You are only saying this to stop us getting married. It's rubbish! I don't know why either of you are making such a preposterous claim!'

Michael seized her by the shoulders and turned her round to face the overmantel. 'Look in that mirror,' he ordered. 'Look at the colour of your hair and the colour of your eyes. Recognise where you have seen them before? Now look at my eyes, my hair, and then look at Peter's. Satisfied? Now do you believe me?'

277

Abbie pulled away from him, covering her face with her hands. 'Maggie, tell me it's not true,' she whispered tearfully.

'I only wish I could,' Maggie said in a low voice. 'It's the truth, Abbie. Michael is your father,' she added, her voice breaking.

Abbie uncovered her eyes and stared hopelessly at Peter. 'Did you know about this?' she asked bitterly.

He shook his head. 'I swear to you this is the first I've ever heard of it,' he assured her.

With a strangled cry, Abbie turned and made for the door, rushing out into the street in a blind panic.

She didn't believe them. She was sure they weren't telling the truth, though she couldn't understand why. There was only one person who could confirm if it was true.

'Mam! Mam!'

Her voice was a moan, an agonised cry coming from deep inside her as she burst into their house. 'Mam,' she clutched at Ellen as if she was grabbing hold of a lifebelt, 'tell me it's not true!'

Ellen shook her clinging hands away. 'What the bleedin' hell is the matter with you? What you carrying on about now?'

'Lost another of your boyfriends, have you?' Billy jibed.

'Michael Ryan ... Michael Ryan ...' She kept saying his name over and over again, unable to repeat what he had told her.

Ellen's face hardened. 'What about him?'

Finally, in a voice heavy with despair, she stuttered, 'He ... he ... says he's my dad!'

'So the bugger's owned up at long last. Better go and live with him, then, hadn't you,' Billy guffawed.

Ellen rounded on Billy, slamming her open hand hard against the side of his face. 'Shut your great trap, you stupid oaf!'

'Mam, are you saying it's true?' Abbie gasped, her cheeks hot with humiliation.

'Oh, it's true all right!'

The colour drained from Abbie's face as despair and disbelief surged through her. She stared at Ellen as if seeing her for the first time in her life.

'You mean that you're not my mam,' she whispered incredulously.

Ellen's face hardened. 'Of course I'm bloody well not!'

Abbie stared at her in disbelief. Realisation swept over her like a wave. The lack of affection from Ellen, all the times she had pushed Abbie away, slowly began to make sense. She had thought Ellen was her mam, and had never been able to understand why she didn't kiss her, make a fuss of her, love her, worry about her, even. Now she knew! Ellen wasn't her mam, that was why she had never loved her or cared for her.

So, if this bleary, scruffy woman in her long black skirt, coarse blouse and thick black shawl, whom she had always thought was her mam, wasn't really her mother, then who was?

'Are you going to tell me about it?' she pleaded in a strained voice.

Ellen scratched under her armpit and pulled her black shawl tighter. 'Hasn't Michael Ryan already done so?'

Abbie shook her head. 'All he said was that he was my dad.'

'Why did the silly bugger tell you that, then?'

'Because of Sandra's baby.'

'What the bloody hell has that got to do with this?'

Abbie looked from Ellen to Billy and back again, like a trapped animal. 'It's not our Sam's baby,' she said in a strangled whisper. 'It ... It's Peter Ryan's.'

Ellen stared at her blankly as if unable to take in the meaning of what she was saying.

'Same as before! Them bloody Ryans, there's no stoppin' the buggers,' Billy chortled loudly.

Ellen rounded on him, her face ravaged. 'Shut your gob!' she ordered.

He held up his hands as if in surrender.

'Are you going to tell me who my mother is, then?' Abbie asked.

Ellen sighed. 'Yes, I suppose it's time you knew the truth,' she said dully.

'So? Who was she?'

Ellen's haggard face softened and her eyes had a faraway look in them. 'Your real mam was Audrey! My little Audrey who died when she was thirteen.'

Abbie felt a tingling shiver run through her. 'You mean you're my grandmother!'

Ellen looked vague and didn't answer for a moment. Then she nodded.

'What happened?' Abbie persisted uneasily.

'Like I said, my little Audrey was your mam. She was only thirteen and still at school. She was a lovely girl, as pretty as a picture with curly fair hair, big brown eyes, and a smile that would melt your heart!'

She sighed heavily. 'She and Billy and Michael Ryan knocked around together all the time. The three of them were inseparable, except when they were at school.'

'Go on!'

'I'd just started working down at the cotton sheds when it happened. Left on their own all day they got into all sorts of mischief. I'd expected our Billy to keep an eye on young Audrey, but he was too busy looking after number one to see what they was up to . . .'

'Come off it, Mam,' Billy interrupted indignantly. 'I was nearly fifteen and I'd just got my first job, that's why I wasn't around to see what those two little buggers were doing. It would have happened anyway, Michael Ryan was crazy about our Aud.'

'By the time I found out that she was in the club it was too late to do anything about it. Poor little bitch, she didn't know what had happened to her, she was only a young kid herself.'

Ellen Martin paused and rubbed the back of her hand across her eyes.

'The Ryans wouldn't admit that their Michael had had anything to do with it,' she said bitterly. 'Not even after you were born and our Audrey had died. They kept well out of the soddin' picture; they always have.'

'Yeah, they left you holding the baby, eh, Mam?' Billy guffawed.

'It was up to me to take you, or for you to go into the Workhouse or some sort of home,' Ellen went on. 'They said at the hospital that all young babies had blue eyes and just fuzz on their heads, and that the colour of both would change later. I was so upset at the time about losing my own little girl that I believed them.'

'So you decided to bring me up as your daughter?'

Ellen nodded. 'I thought if you grew up looking like my Audrey then you would take her place.'

She paused and dabbed again at her eyes, this time with the corner of her shawl. 'Bloody fool, wasn't I? You were nothing like my little girl! Every day you looked more and more like the Ryans. You'd got their dark hair, as well as their blue eyes.'

'Surely the Ryans were aware of this?' Abbie said stiffly.

'They didn't want to see it, did they! That Michael was sent back to Ireland for a couple of years, out of the bloody way, and never a word was said against him. Maggie Ryan kept herself to herself and no one twigged what had happened. Instead, everybody blamed my little Audrey,' Ellen said bitterly.

'They accused her of being fast and feckless,' she went on. 'Blamed me because of the way she'd been brought up.

'Her father couldn't take all the evil gossip, so what with that, and a baby that cried night and day, and his despair at losing his precious little angel, he buggered off.'

'So he didn't go into the Army?'

Ellen shrugged. 'How the hell should I know. He left me to face all the wagging tongues in Bostock Street and bring the lot of you up single-handed. Billy was working and earning a few bob a week, but it wasn't enough to keep body and soul together. Sam was only a toddler, only a year or so older than you were.'

Ellen sighed. 'Many's the times I walked up Brownlow Hill, past the Workhouse, carrying you in my arms, and wondered about dumping you on their doorstep. It was only the fact that you were my little Audrey's kid that stopped me from doing so.'

Ellen wrapped her arms around her body and rocked to and fro. 'I didn't love you then and I've never loved you since. God knows, I've tried, for Audrey's sake, but all I can think about every time I look at you is that you killed my lovely little girl. That, and the fact that you look just like the Ryans!'

Chapter Thirty

'How can I possibly marry you, Peter,' Abbie exclaimed exasperatedly. 'If Michael is my father then you're my uncle!'

'We could live together, even if we don't get married,' Peter argued. 'If we move over to Seacombe or Liscard no one there need ever know.'

She shook her head. 'I couldn't bring myself to do that.'

'There's the baby to think about, Abbie,' Peter Ryan protested sulkily.

Abbie looked at his dark, brooding face, the selfish gleam in his blue eyes and the petulant twist of his mouth, and wondered how she could have ever thought herself to be in love with him.

'The baby is your problem, Peter, not mine,' she told him defensively. 'Ask your mother to help! Even though she didn't take any responsibility for your brother's child she might help you with yours,' she added scathingly.

She turned away, tears streaming down her cheeks as she remembered how many times as a small child she had run to Maggie for comfort when Ellen and Billy were rip-roaring drunk and fighting like cat and dog. The Ryans' home had been an oasis of safety when Ellen and Billy were smashing up the furniture or threatening her and Sam with a good thrashing.

All her life she had thought Maggie was so kind and wonderful, even longed to be one of her family. And all the time she was. She was Maggie's grandchild as much as she was Ellen Martin's.

The constant rows and drunken brawls she'd witnessed as she'd been growing up began to make some sort of sense to her.

Instead of talking matters over with the Ryans and reaching some sort of agreement with them to share the responsibility, Ellen had shouldered the extra burden. Ellen had been bitter over losing her own daughter and resentful about having to bring up a child that had been fathered by Michael Ryan, and that was why she'd turned to drink and vented her pent-up feelings by fighting with Billy.

She wondered why Billy had stood for it all these years, why he hadn't left home and made an independent life for himself. The only reason she could find was that he knew his mother blamed him for not protecting Audrey. In addition, she depended on his wages to help support herself and Sam. And to support Abbie!

I have been a burden round her neck all these years, Abbie thought guiltily. No wonder she dislikes me so much and can't bear to touch me. How she must have hated it when I tried to hug her and kiss her. No wonder she always pushed me away.

The thought that she might feel the same sort of

terrible rejection for Sandra's little boy helped her to harden her heart to Peter's pleadings.

They could never marry, and if they should set up home together what sort of life would that be for the child, she asked herself. In time, she was bound to resent the situation she found herself in, and then, heaven forbid, she might start taking her resentment out on the child like Ellen had done on her.

It wasn't as if there was no one else to bring him up. Maggie wasn't all that old, she could still cope with a baby, and it was up to Peter to help her. Perhaps someday in the future he would marry, and then he could make a proper home for his son.

Abbie kept telling herself that to go and live with him merely for the sake of the child would only be building up more unhappiness. As it was, because of Peter's action, she'd lost her best friend, Sandra. She was also about to lose Sam, the brother she'd been so close to for most of her life, if he went to sea as he claimed he was going to do.

She pulled herself up short. Sam wasn't her brother! Sam was her uncle, the same as Peter was!

The realisation shook the very foundations of Abbie's world. She didn't know who she was any more. Had she ever known who she was, she wondered bitterly?

The only place where she felt confident and sure of her identity was at Frisby Dyke's. There, surrounded by people she had come to know and like and respect, she felt reassured. No one there knew her secret. To them she was Abbie Martin, the same person as they had always known.

Those in the department where she worked knew she had lost her sister-in-law in childbirth and they had offered their condolences, but they were ignorant of the details.

She had never talked about her family, not since the first day she'd been there. She'd been quick to notice Miss Breck's hesitation when she had mentioned that Bostock Street was off Scotland Road, and knew instinctively that her background was different from most of the others who worked there, but she hadn't let it depress her.

Instead, she'd made sure that no one ever found out where she lived or that her mam was a shawlie who worked in the cotton sheds.

There had been one or two close shaves when she'd first become friendly with Jamie, and after a night in town he had wanted to see her home. Fortunately, because he lived in Wallasey, he was always worried about what would happen if he missed the last ferryboat, so she always had a wonderful excuse about why he shouldn't see her home.

When they all went out as a crowd, the problem never seemed to arise. They were all too intent on having a good time to worry about how the evening was going to end. When it was time to go home there was always a mad dash to catch a late Green Goddess, or, in some cases, a boat, and in the ensuing mêlée she'd always managed to slip away more or less unnoticed.

Her early background might have been rough

and ready but she had been quick to learn. She aped the manners of those around her and mimicked their accents, so that within a few weeks it had been hard to tell her apart from the others.

Billy had scoffed at her lah-di-dah ways, but that hadn't worried her. Knowing what she did now she felt that everything she'd done had been justified.

Deep inside her, she'd known she was different to him, better than him, even. He might have been her real mam's brother, but he was a slummy born and bred. He'd never tried to better himself. The guilt he carried about what had happened to his sister Audrey seemed to have tainted his outlook on life, which was why his mother could dominate him like she did.

At least she had the satisfaction, now, of knowing that he wasn't her brother, Abbie thought smugly. He might be her uncle, but that was nowhere near the same thing. The blood ties were so much looser that she felt she could dismiss him completely from her life. And she would, she told herself firmly. She intended to walk away from all of them as soon as it was possible to do so.

The only thing that was holding her back was the fact that she didn't earn enough money to live independently.

She could move in with Peter, she reminded herself. He had made the offer. He would always hold down a good job and earn reasonable money, so financially she would never have any worries.

Was that enough to satisfy her need to be loved and wanted, she asked herself? The baby would love her, probably think of her as his mother. He would be dependent on her, so surely she would have all the affection she wanted.

She refused to think about it during the day while she was working, but the moment she went to bed all the problems churned over and over in her head. Even when she slept, the voices of Ellen and Billy and Maggie and Michael, all arguing for and against her and Peter setting up home together, dominated her dreams.

Mo Lewis kept her own counsel. She avoided Abbie as much as possible and refused to even look at the baby.

To friends and neighbours she declared, 'I'm too heartbroken over losing my Sandra to do anything to help with the child. I've never been any good with little boys. If it had been a baby girl, to replace my Sandra, then I might have taken it on. As things stand it's the Ryans' responsibility.'

She was the first to exclaim in shocked tones, 'History repeating itself!' when news leaked out that Michael Ryan was Abbie's real father.

'They've broken up the Martin family and come between Ellen and Abbie, but they're not coming between me and my Dan,' she declared stoutly.

When pressed for her opinion about Abbie moving in with Peter and the pair of them bringing up the baby, she merely shrugged her plump shoulders.

'If that's what Abbie wants to do then good luck to her, it's nothing to do with me,' she said primly.

Abbie eventually decided it wasn't something she could bring herself to do. Any feelings she'd had for Peter were long gone. He was nothing more to her, now, than any other neighbour in Bostock Street. Even the closeness she'd had with Maggie had been eroded when she'd discovered that Maggie was her grandmother, and realised that never once had she spoken out or given any indication of how closely they were related.

Looking back, Abbie felt that the kisses and cuddles and other displays of affection Maggie had shown her when she'd been small had been to fulfil Maggie's needs. Or to allay her own conscience because she felt guilty about the way Ellen and Billy treated me, Abbie told herself sadly.

Michael's rejection rankled, however. She had always been aware of the way he watched her whenever she was in their house, and of the fact that he rarely spoke to her. Now that she knew the true reason she felt resentful. If he had shouldered some of his obligations she could have had a much happier childhood.

Peter was devastated when she told him she had decided that she wasn't prepared to move in with him and take care of the baby.

'I was relying on you, Abbie. I thought you cared for me?'

She shook her head. 'I used to, Peter. I treasured every word you said, followed you about, thought of you as my hero. I dreamed of the day when you would ask me to marry you.'

'So what's happened to change that?'

'We've both grown up! You were so changed when you came home from reform school that you had no time for me. I ached for you to notice me, to show me some affection.'

'No, you were the one who had changed, Abbie,' he told her angrily. 'You had your job and all your new friends. You didn't want to be with me, you wanted to be with Jamie and his crowd.'

'I wanted you to come along as well whenever we went out!'

'They weren't the sort of friends I wanted.'

'You didn't have any others,' she pointed out. 'Except Sam and Sandra,' she added bitterly, 'and look what happened there!'

'It wouldn't have done, if you hadn't behaved the way you did. You showed me up whenever we went out, that was when the rot set in. Sandra tried to make amends, to comfort me when she saw how upset I was.'

'Oh, she did that all right!' Abbie said sarcastically, 'and look where it left our Sam.'

'Sam was only concerned about you . . .'

'Oh, stop repeating yourself, Peter! You've said all this before. It was my fault, Sam's fault, but never your fault. You think you've been hard done by, but think about what your brother Michael did. That's the trouble with you Ryans,' she said angrily, 'you think you can do as you like, sin as much as you want to, and then go to confession and wipe the slate clean again. Well, it doesn't work like that. You've fathered a child, the same as your brother did, but the only difference is that this time you are going to have to face the music and be responsible for bringing it up.'

'I can't do that, Abbie. Not without someone to help me.'

'Then ask your mother to help you. It will give her a chance to atone for her sins of omission as my grandmother!'

'You can't leave things like this, Abbie,' Peter blustered. 'I want you – I need you! Not only because of the baby, but because I love you, I always have!'

'You may have done so at one time, but not since you came home,' she said wistfully. 'Be honest; I embarrass you.'

'Only when you behave outrageously; like a tart.'

'How dare you!' Her face flaming, Abbie turned on her heel to leave.

Peter grabbed her by the arm, spinning her round and savagely pushing her up against the wall, his mouth trying to find hers.

Abbie fought to free herself from his embrace, but he was far too strong for her. Overpowering her, he pinioned her arms behind her and began tearing at her clothes. Twisting her face away from his she gulped in a lungful of air and then screamed again and again and again.

Pushing her down on the floor he straddled her, pushing her skirt up to her waist, trying to force her legs apart.

Fear and outrage lent power to her lungs. Her screams were blood-curdling, alarming passers-by in the street outside.

Maggie came rushing out of the kitchen and

then stopped in the doorway, aghast at what she was witnessing.

Someone had called the police. There was a hammering on the front door, a loud crash as a shoulder was applied to it, then the thud of heavy boots and warning shouts before a hand caught hold of Peter's collar, dragging him away from Abbie and throwing him to one side.

As she was gently pulled to her feet by strong arms she gave a deep shudder, even though she knew she was safe. She heard the policeman who was holding her call out to his fellow officer, 'Can you manage on your own?' and an answering response.

Then the one holding her exclaimed, 'My God! Abbie!'

She had already recognised his voice, but she had been afraid it was simply a delusion because she was so upset.

'Abbie!' The voice was soothing, the hands that held her were strong yet gentle. 'You're safe now.'

She waited for him to speak again, unsure whether she was hallucinating or if it really was Bradley Fisher who was holding her in his arms.

Tears of self-pity began rolling down her cheeks, even though she kept her eyes tight shut. She mustn't attach any importance to him being here, she told herself. He was only doing his duty. The minute he saw she was recovered he would walk out of the door and she would never see him again.

'Abbie! Open your eyes. Please! Speak! Tell me you aren't hurt.'

The concern in Bradley Fisher's voice sent shivers of longing surging through her. Could it mean that he still cared! After all that had happened, and despite what he knew about her family and her background? Was it possible that he still had feelings for her?

Tentatively, she blinked and found herself looking straight into his warm brown eyes, and there was no mistaking the love and concern in their depths.

The pressure of his arms around her body increased. The nightmare encounter with Peter was wiped from her mind. All she could think about was that she was in Bradley's arms and he still loved her.

'Can you tell me what happened?' he asked solicitously.

Abbie shook her head. 'I don't want to talk about it,' she whispered. 'I'd like to go home.'

'This will have to be reported.'

'No!' She shook her head firmly. 'It's a family matter. It's all over now. There's nothing more to be said or done.'

'You're not going to press charges against your attacker?'

Abbie shuddered as she looked across the room to where Peter was sitting on a chair, a policeman at his side. Peter was resting his elbows on his knees, supporting his head between his hands. Maggie was standing near him, ill at ease, her face stark with concern. 'No!' she said tightly, 'I don't want it to go any further. I'm not hurt ... only frightened.'

Bradley Fisher exchanged an understanding glance with the other policeman who slowly put his notebook away.

'Come on, then,' Bradley took her arm. 'I'll see you safely home.'

As they walked along Bostock Street to her own home, Abbie felt tongue-tied. Now that he knew she was all right, would he simply walk away and she'd never see him again, she wondered?

'I'd better leave you here,' he said as they reached her front door. 'I don't think either your mother or your brother would welcome my presence.'

She nodded. 'I'm sorry about what happened before, it wasn't your fault. You didn't know who my mother was.'

'So why have you avoided me ever since? I've missed you a great deal, Abbie.'

She stared at him, a startled look in her blue eyes. 'I thought that would be what you wanted. I didn't think you would wish to see me again when you knew the sort of reputation my family had.'

'I'm interested in you, not them,' he stated. 'My feelings for you, Abbie, are as strong as they ever were, so when am I going to see you again?'

Her heart thundered crazily. She grinned weakly. 'Whenever you like.'

'I'm talking about a proper date, not rescuing you from some trouble you've managed to get yourself into,' he told her with mock severity.

'So am I,' she agreed.

'Would tonight be too soon?'

'No,' she smiled happily. 'That would be wonderful.'

He looked at his watch. 'Can you meet me in an hour? I'll take you to the State Restaurant in Dale Street for a meal, and we can talk about our future.'

Chapter Thirty-One

Bradley Fisher felt in an optimistic mood as he
walked away from Bostock Street. Everything was
finally coming together and at last there was a real
purpose to his life.

He had felt most uncomfortable about arresting
Ellen Martin, as he had had no idea that she was
Abbie's mother. They were so utterly different
that he wouldn't ever have guessed, even if Ellen
had told him her surname.

As events turned out, arresting Ellen Martin had
given his career the boost he had needed. Within a
few days he had been told he was to be promoted
to Sergeant.

His mother had been delighted. 'You'll end up
as the youngest Inspector in your division, the
same as your father did,' she beamed proudly.

Even that had not lifted his spirits, because he
knew that he had upset Abbie; indeed, more than
that he had antagonised her so much that he might
never see her again.

Yet it seemed that their paths were fated to
cross, he told himself as he hurried back to the
station to file his report and sign off duty. They
had met again, and once more he had the opportunity to put things right between them.

This time he'd make sure that he did. He'd

never felt like this about any other girl. He hoped that Abbie felt the same way about him, as he did about her, because tonight, given the opportunity, he intended to ask her if she would marry him.

He felt a little nervous about what his mother's reaction would be, but surely, he told himself, she didn't expect him to stay at home for the rest of his life!

His father had died when he was fourteen, and ever since then his mother had expected him to be the man of the house.

When he'd been younger he'd been flattered that she consulted him over most things and had taken an intense pride in the fact that he was 'in charge'. Lately, though, when he'd suspected she was using her dependence on him as a ploy to stop him from leaving home, he had grown to resent it.

When he had said he wanted to move out and have a life of his own she'd been quick to offer an alternative arrangement.

'Marry a nice girl and I'll convert this place into two separate flats,' she told him. 'It's really far too big for me, now that your father is gone, and I don't entertain on anywhere near the same scale.'

'Why don't you find somewhere smaller, then, if it's too much for you to cope with?'

'It's our home, Bradley, yours and mine! I'm being sentimental, I suppose, but we've had so many happy years here that I couldn't bear to move. It would make two delightful flats. There are four bedrooms, and with three reception rooms downstairs as well as the kitchen we would be able to have it converted properly. We'll call in an architect and see if he thinks it's possible to even have separate entrances so that we would be completely independent, if that means so much to you.'

He'd looked round the room they were sitting in and his heart had sunk as he compared the middle-class luxury he took for granted with the room he had seen at Abbie's home.

In this room there were polished wood-block floors, a magnificent Persian carpet, a huge three-piece suite upholstered in dark red velvet, and matching wing-backed armchairs. There were occasional tables, a glass cabinet, and a bookcase that spanned most of one wall and reached almost to the ceiling.

The dining room across the hallway was fitted wall to wall with celadon green Wilton, and there was an impressive, highly polished mahogany table that could seat ten people. There was also a matching sideboard and a side table for serving, and a huge bow-fronted cabinet filled with cream Spode china and elegant glassware.

All the windows at the front of the house were screened with identical Nottingham-lace curtains in addition to the heavy velvet drapes with their matching pelmets.

His mother's bedroom was enormous, with a fitted walk-in wardrobe and a canopied bed. Even his own bedroom was probably larger than the whole of the ground floor at Abbie's place.

He knew, though, that the difference in their

living accommodation wouldn't be the only reason that his mother wouldn't approve of Abbie as her future daughter-in-law. Once she found out about Abbie's family background she would be mortified.

Leonora Fisher was in her mid-fifties. She was smartly dressed and very house-proud. Her husband, Robert, Bradley's father, had been much older than her. He had been an Inspector in the Wallasey police force so they had been able to afford to live in Seabank Road, which was within walking distance of Manor Road Police Headquarters and was one of the most respectable areas in Wallasey.

Leonora was a stickler for routine. Always on a Friday morning, while a woman came in to clean the house, she had a regular appointment with her hairdresser where she had her mousy-blonde hair shampooed and was given a henna tint and a marcel wave.

Ever since her husband had died, Leonora had received a pension that was adequate for her to go on living in the same house and in the same style.

Robert had always told Bradley that he wanted him to go to University, but after he died Leonora was quick to point out that this was no longer possible unless she made stringent economies.

'Your father,' she told Bradley proudly, 'was the youngest Inspector in the Wallasey police force at the time of his promotion. He managed that without going to University, and I am sure you can be as successful as he was if you put your mind to it.'

Young, and easily flattered, he had believed her and set that as his goal in life. The moment he was old enough to do so he had applied to enter the force. His mother had been unable to understand why he had joined the Liverpool police and not the Wallasey force.

'Everyone at Manor Road knew your father and would be only too willing to help you in your career,' she pointed out. 'The Chief Constable there was a special friend of your father's, they played golf together and they were both in the Masons.'

'It's for those very reasons that I've joined a different force,' Bradley told her. 'I want to succeed because of my own achievements, not because everyone knew my father.'

His mother was very put out at the time, but later, once he began to succeed by his own efforts, she became inordinately proud of his achievements.

When he had been told he was to be made Sergeant, she threw a party to celebrate. She invited half a dozen girls of his own age who were the daughters of her closest friends.

They were all nice girls in their twenties, wearing the very latest style of silk party dresses and high-heeled shoes. All of them were eager to be married and have a home of their own and they'd been primed in advance by their own mothers about how suitable a catch Bradley would be.

They could see for themselves that he was very

tall, with broad shoulders and slim hips. He was clean-shaven and extremely handsome.

Those who flirted with him found he had a pleasing personality. He looked boyishly attractive in his blue uniform, and most of them thought he would look positively terrific when he was finally wearing his Inspector's uniform.

For his mother's sake he played the part she'd allocated to him. He charmed them all, but he didn't lose his head or his heart over any of them.

He'd already lost his heart to black-haired, blue-eyed Abbie, even though he knew his mother would consider her to be totally unsuitable.

Abbie's only redeeming asset was that she worked in Frisby Dyke's. On the face of it that might make her acceptable, but the moment his mother heard a whisper about her background then she'd have an attack of the vapours and have him running for her smelling salts.

This particular frailty was her favourite ploy when he upset her in any way. When he had been much younger it used to leave him cowering under the bedclothes, scared that she might die. As the years passed and her attacks not only never proved fatal, but usually only lasted for about an hour, he stopped taking them seriously.

This time, however, it was a more sombre matter. He wanted his mother and Abbie to meet. Above all, he wanted them to like each other, since, if Abbie accepted his proposal and agreed to marry him, then they would be the two most important people in his life.

*

Abbie found it hard to believe that she had met Bradley Fisher again, and that he had asked her out.

She'd dreamed about it happening countless times, but she'd never really thought it would come true.

What was more, there had been something excitingly significant in the tone of his voice and in his dark brown eyes, as well as the way he had cradled her so tenderly in his arms.

She was confident that his concern about what had happened to her had been far greater than he normally showed to people who had been attacked.

She smiled to herself, her heart singing because he'd asked her out to dinner so that they could talk things over.

She wondered if he had missed her as much as she had missed him. Her spirits soared as she remembered the anxiety in his voice. There had been so much more than mere concern for her safety. He had been so tender, so anxious about her, and she was sure that what she had seen in his dark brown eyes was love.

What had happened before hadn't been entirely his fault or his mistake, she told herself. After all, he had only been doing his job, and since Ellen hadn't given him her full name how was he to know who she really was?

Would it have made any difference if he'd known that, she asked herself? Probably not! He had been doing his job. They were the ones who had been in the wrong.

Yet, knowing this, fully aware that they were villains, he still wanted to see her. Or was she building up false hopes? Was he going to try to explain why he couldn't see her again?

Her thoughts went back to the moment when he and another policeman had burst into the house and found Peter attacking her. Once again she recalled the timbre of his voice and the look in his eyes, and she was overcome by a crazy gladness because she knew she loved him, and instinctively, from deep in her heart, she was sure that he loved her.

Chapter Thirty-Two

It was the first time Abbie had ever been to the State Restaurant in Dale Street and she felt extremely nervous. She wasn't used to eating out in such places. Even though she was wearing a new dress, a pretty floral voile one that she'd bought in the summer sales, and knew she was looking very attractive, she still felt on edge.

When she arrived and found that Bradley wasn't outside waiting for her, all sorts of doubts began crowding her head. Had he changed his mind? Was she too early? Had something prevented him from being there? Had she made a mistake about the time he had said to meet him?

She paced up and down the pavement for another few minutes, looking hopefully at every tram that trundled past, hoping that Bradley might be on it. She checked the time with the great clock-face on the Liver Buildings, and then decided she was either quarter of an hour early or over a quarter of an hour late.

It had started to rain. What started as a fine sea mist quickly turned to a steady drizzle, turning the cobbled road into shiny black glass. Not only was her hair getting wet, but if she stayed out in it any longer, even though she was wearing a coat, her dress would be ruined, so she took shelter in a shop doorway.

The minutes ticked by and she started wondering if Bradley had already arrived and was waiting for her inside the restaurant. She tried to remember what his exact words had been, but she'd been so excited at seeing him again and finding he wanted to take her out that her mind had been in a whirl.

It was ridiculous hanging about outside in the rain, she told herself, so taking a deep breath she ventured into the restaurant.

The moment she entered the doors she felt overcome by fright, as a tall pompous man wearing black evening dress and a stiff-fronted white shirt bustled forward with a clipboard in his hand and asked if she had reserved a table.

Unable to speak, her mouth so dry that her tongue was sticking to her teeth, she could only gulp and shake her head as she turned to leave.

Then she heard her name called, and Bradley appeared as if from nowhere, his coat collar turned up, his brown hair almost black with rain.

'Abbie! I'd given you up!'

'I'd given you up!'

'I've been sheltering in one of the doorways!'

They spoke in unison, then stood there holding hands and grinning at each other like two school kids.

Suddenly aware that the head waiter was still waiting patiently to know if they had reserved a table, Bradley let go of Abbie's hands and gave him the necessary information.

'Do you want to go to the Ladies' room,' he asked, as they were shown to their table and he took her coat and handed it over to a waiter who was hovering solicitously.

Abbie shook her head. She didn't want to let Bradley out of her sight for one minute in case she lost track of him again.

The waiter pulled out her chair and she sat stiffly on the edge of it, waiting nervously until Bradley had taken his place opposite her before she could relax.

Waves of noise ebbed and flowed all around as people laughed and chattered; the sound swelled like some strange music, making her feel dizzy.

She looked at the beautifully laid table, the crisp white damask cloth and napkins, the single flower in an elegant cut-glass vase in the centre of the table, and at the gleaming array of silverware and glasses, and wondered if she was going to be able to cope with it all.

Until now, her eating out had consisted of visits to Lyons Corner House, the Kardomah, or a milk bar. The nearest she had got to this sort of setting was when Peter had taken her to the Grafton Ballroom and they had sat with their drinks at one of the little tables that circled the dance floor.

She'd drunk rather too much wine that night and had made a complete fool of herself, she remembered ruefully. She must be very careful not to repeat that mistake tonight, she reminded herself.

A new feeling of panic surged through her as the waiter handed them both a large, leather-bound menu. She tried to read what was on it, but her eyes became blurred with embarrassment when she realised that she didn't understand half of what was written there. Some of the words describing the dishes were in French, and even those dishes that were in English had names which she didn't recognise.

'Would you like me to order for you?' Bradley asked quietly.

She nodded.

She watched his dark brows knit together in a frown as he perused the list in front of him. Then, in a firm, crisp voice, he placed their order. Before she could sit back with a sigh of relief that the ordeal was over, the wine waiter appeared at his side and once more his attention was diverted.

'Right! Now that's all done we can talk,' he grinned.

He put her at ease, admiring her new dress and talking of trivial everyday matters until she was completely relaxed, and laughing with him over something he described to her.

She was grateful that he hadn't mentioned her family or any of the other events that had caused so much friction and trauma between them. She knew these had to be talked about, but she was thankful that he was leaving that part of their reunion for the moment. Coping with the meal was going to be nerve-wracking enough for her.

The food was delicious. Skilfully, Bradley guided her through the minefield of cutlery and glasses. He didn't press her when she refused a second glass of wine although he refilled his own glass to the brim.

At the end of their meal, as they sat drinking rich, dark coffee from delicate little cups and nibbling tiny, minted chocolate-covered biscuits, she felt she had never experienced an evening like it in her entire life.

There was more to her enjoyment than the appetising food and the wonderful wine, delicious though those had been. It was being with Bradley, knowing how much he cared, how serious he was about their friendship and the fact that he was so anxious to go on seeing her in the future.

By the time they left the State Restaurant the rain had cleared. The warmth of a balmy, late September evening lay over Liverpool. In the velvety dark sky above there was a sprinkling of stars, and a crescent of moon hung like a bright yellow pennant over the Liver Building.

Bradley walked as far as the junction of Scotland Road and Bostock Street with Abbie. She felt uneasy, knowing that the right thing to do was to take him back to her home, but if Billy and his mam were there she wasn't sure what sort of a reception they would give him.

As if reading her thoughts, Bradley stopped and pulled her into his arms. 'I'm going to say goodnight to you here, Abbie,' he said softly.

Gently, he kissed her on the lips, and then, as she clung to him, his kisses became more intense. With tremendous willpower he pulled back.

'Can I see you at the weekend?' he asked. 'If

you are free on Sunday I'd like to take you to Wallasey to meet my mother.'

Abbie caught her breath in alarm. 'Your mother?' Her eyes were wide with shock. The idea scared her stiff.

'Why not? You're the two most important people in my life and you've got to meet sometime. The sooner the better, surely?'

'She mightn't like me!'

'Like you? She'll love you, the same as I do,' he told her confidently. 'We'll catch the two o'clock ferry over to Wallasey on Sunday afternoon and go and have tea with her.'

'I'm not sure. Perhaps we should leave it for a while.'

Bradley shook his head. 'I'm off duty this Sunday and I won't have another weekend free for almost two months.'

Abbie looked relieved. 'Let's leave it until then, shall we?'

Bradley shook his head. 'No,' he said firmly. 'This Sunday. Now do you want me to come to your house and collect you or would you rather meet me at the Pier Head?'

'I'll meet you at the Pier Head,' she told him quickly.

She didn't want him coming to Bostock Street. That could well spoil things between them, even though he had already been there and knew what it was like. On Sunday, both Ellen and Billy would have been out drinking until the early hours of the morning so they would have hangovers and one or the other of them would probably have been sick. The house would smell vile, and there would be dirty clothes strewn everywhere and unwashed dishes piled up on the table and in the sink.

The only place in the entire house that was ever tidy was her own room. Even if she cleaned the house up before Bradley arrived the unpleasant smells would still be there.

She wasn't sure where he lived, except that it was in Wallasey, but she had no doubt that it was far better than her home. He had mentioned his mother several times in conversation during their meal and he had told her that his father had died while he was still at school. Apart from that, though, he had said very little about his family background.

She tried to tell herself that she was being silly to make such a fuss about meeting his mother. He was only a policeman, after all, not a doctor or anyone of any great importance. Well, she smiled to herself, he had been promoted to Sergeant, she mustn't forget that fact. He seemed very proud of his new rank and she felt sure his mother was equally delighted by his achievement.

'Right, I'll meet you on Sunday at the Pier Head in time for us to catch the two o'clock boat,' she promised.

'Don't be late,' he warned. 'The ferry to Seacombe only operates hourly on a Sunday.'

She hesitated, still wishing she could persuade him to postpone the visit to meet his mother. Being back together was still so new. So much had happened in her life since she'd last seen him that she still hadn't told him about.

She should have told him about Sam and Sandra and the baby, and explained why Peter had attacked her.

What was even more important was that she wanted to share with him all the information she now had concerning who her mother and father really were, because she was sure it would make a difference in his eyes.

She felt it was terribly important that she explained all these things, especially the fact that she was not as closely related to Ellen and Billy as he thought she was.

She would have preferred to do this and clear the air properly, so that there were no secrets and no misunderstandings between them, before she became involved with his family.

Chapter Thirty-Three

Abbie was up early on Sunday morning and off across town to the public baths in Cordwallis Street, anxious to be there before a queue formed.

Usually she had a bath on a Saturday night when she knew that Billy was at the pub and wouldn't be back until after midnight. She dragged in the tin bath that hung on the wall outside their back door and boiled up as much hot water as she could, but this was a special occasion.

Lying back in the deep soapy water, after first shampooing and rinsing her hair, Abbie let her mind go over all her preparations for the coming visit to meet Bradley's mother.

She still felt terribly nervous, but at least she'd know she was clean from top to toe, she thought wryly, as she wriggled down deeper so that only her nose was above the water line.

She wished Bradley had been willing to wait a little longer before putting her through such an ordeal. She would have liked to enjoy whatever time they could spend together, just the two of them, getting to know each other better.

There was so much about her and her family that he still didn't know, and she wanted to be able to tell him every detail before he heard it from someone else.

Bradley being in the police force didn't help matters, not when Ellen and Billy were such well-known scoundrels. She supposed it proved how strong his feelings were for her, she reflected, that he still wanted to see her even though he believed a disreputable old shawlie like Ellen was her mother.

Abbie's name wasn't really Martin, though, she'd been given her mother's family name, not her father's. If Michael Ryan was her father then she should be called Abbie Ryan, not Abbie Martin. She wondered how Bradley would feel about this. Would it make her seem any more respectable? Unlike the Martin family, as far as she knew the Ryans had never been in any real trouble with the police. Apart from Peter being wrongly acccused of stealing the bike and being sent to reform school.

It was funny, she reflected, looking back and remembering how all the time she had been growing up she had craved Ellen's love and had always been rejected. She had done everything in her power to win approval from her, yet Ellen would never throw a kind word, let alone praise, her way. Even when she'd been only a toddler she had sensed that there was love for Sam but not for her and she had resented always being pushed away!

Now, to some degree, she could understand the reason for this. Ellen had lost Audrey, the daughter she had adored, when Audrey had been little more than a child herself; and she blamed me for that, Abbie thought sadly. It wasn't my fault, though, so she shouldn't have punished me as she did.

Yet, she asked herself, had Maggie Ryan behaved any better? Maggie had kissed and cuddled her and shown her kindness, but she had never taken her into her home and brought her up as she could have done. After all, if Michael Ryan was her father then surely Maggie, who was also her grandmother, was as responsible as Ellen Martin was for looking after Abbie.

She was better placed to do so as well. Paddy Ryan had a good job and sent money home regularly. Maggie also had a job. In fact, Abbie was at a loss to understand why the Ryans had gone on living in Bostock Street when they could have afforded to move to a much better place.

Was it because of me, she wondered? Was there a guilt factor that kept Maggie there so that she could keep an eye on me and see I was all right?

If that was the case, then why didn't she bring me up? Unless, Abbie reasoned, Ellen Martin refused to allow her to do so. Or had Paddy Ryan been against it, she wondered, remembering his reaction on the day she'd walked into the Ryans' house unaware that he was home from sea.

Perhaps that was the reason, she mused, as she remembered the rows whenever Ellen discovered that she and Sam had taken refuge at the Ryans' house when Ellen and Billy had been fighting. She never created like that if she knew they had been at Sandra's house. Yet she never stopped them from going to the Ryans'.

There were so many questions to which she

would probably never know the answers. Even so, she would have liked to have had the chance to talk them over with Bradley before she met any of his family.

A loud banging on the cubicle door and a raucous voice declaring, 'You've had more than your time, missy, there's a load of others waiting to get in there,' brought Abbie out of her reverie.

The water is cold anyway, she told herself, as, scowling at being so abruptly disturbed, she drained the bath, dried herself, and put her old clothes back on.

Someday, if she was lucky enough to marry Bradley Fisher, she might have a bathroom of her own. Then she would not only be able to take a bath whenever she felt like it, but she would be able to lie in it, soaking away her problems and indulging in her daydreams for as long as she liked.

Ellen was still in bed when she reached home, and Billy, snoring loudly, was sprawled in an armchair where he had been all night.

She was dying for a drink and debated whether or not to make a cup of tea. She was afraid that it might disturb Billy if she started clattering cups, and it was more peaceful to leave him sleeping, so she crept past him and went up to her room.

There was plenty she wanted to do before either of them woke up and started ordering her round and demanding something to eat.

Before she left the house she had hung the dress she intended to wear on a nail on the back of her bedroom door, and she'd also laid out her clean underwear on the bed.

She studied it all carefully, not sure if she had made the right choice or not. She wished she knew a little bit more about Bradley's mother. She didn't want to turn up looking dowdy, but neither did she want to turn up looking overdressed and give Mrs Fisher the wrong impression.

She had thought about asking Bradley what she should wear, but she knew this would be a waste of time because his answer would be, 'You look lovely no matter what you are wearing.'

That was the trouble with men, they didn't seem to realise that knowing you were dressed right helped you to feel confident, she thought worriedly.

She wondered if he had warned his mother that he was bringing her over for tea, and if his mother was fretting about their forthcoming meeting the same as she was doing.

The idea of someone of Mrs Fisher's standing worrying about what she should wear to meet her son's girlfriend brought a smile to Abbie's lips. She probably regards it as something of a nuisance, having her routine upset by having me to tea. She'd probably much sooner have Bradley all to herself, Abbie mused.

From what little she had gleaned from Bradley's conversation, his mother regarded him as the man of the house and relied on him for advice and companionship. Perhaps this was why he didn't appear to have ever had a steady girlfriend.

A frown clouded Abbie's face. If his mother was

so anxious to keep him all to herself then did she discourage him from having girlfriends? If this was the case then how was she going to react when they met, she wondered apprehensively.

'Stop looking for trouble!' she told herself out loud. Mrs Fisher was probably a very nice woman. Bradley is a good son who's happy to shoulder his responsibilities and help her as much as he can since his father is dead, and that is all there is to it.

Plenty of middle-aged women of her type came shopping at Frisby Dyke's. They were usually well fed, contented, stylishly dressed and able to afford to indulge themselves. Their idea of having a good time was going to the pictures, taking tea in town with their friends or visiting each other in their homes.

For all I know I may be just one of a long string of girls that Bradley has taken home to meet her, she told herself sternly. Probably after they've left she points out how unsuitable they are and that is the end of that. He is probably far too comfortable and too well looked after by his mother to ever seriously think about leaving home.

Nevertheless, it still didn't stop Abbie from wanting to look her very best. She spent the next hour and a half drying and styling her hair and trying on everything she had in her wardrobe in case it looked more suitable than the pale green dress with a pleated skirt that she had already chosen.

By then, Ellen was awake and calling out that she wanted something to take away the pain in her head, and Billy was complaining that he had a mouth like the bottom of a birdcage. Slipping her old clothes back on again, Abbie went down to make them a pot of tea and see if they wanted anything to eat.

'Not yet, I've only just come to my senses,' Ellen scowled, holding her head in her hands. 'You can cook us something later on. I'm off back to my bed for an hour or two.'

'I'm going out before two,' Abbie told her.

'Out? Where are you going? Not round to that Maggie Ryan's place to help with that baby, I hope!'

'No, I'm going with a friend to New Brighton,' she said vaguely.

'Sod that! We need you to get us a meal.'

'Then I'll get it ready for you now and leave it in the oven to keep warm.'

'Bloody well do it later, like our Mam said,' Billy muttered. 'I don't want scoff that's all dried up!'

'No, I can't! I've already told you I'm going out.'

'Answer me back an' you'll bloody well be going out with a black eye,' Billy snarled.

As Abbie turned on her heel to go back upstairs, Billy reached out and grabbed her by the arm, jerking her towards him so violently that she screamed out in pain.

'You bloody deaf or something? We want a proper meal, but we want it cooked later on. Mam and me have both got bad heads and we don't want you clattering bloody dishes right now. Understand?'

'Let go of me!' Abbie shook herself free. 'If you

must know, I'm going back upstairs to finish doing my hair, if that is all right with you?' she added sarcastically.

'Less of your bleedin' lip! I heard you sneaking out earlier on. Gone for a couple of hours or more. So where were you, then? Round at the Ryans'? Helping with that soddin' baby?'

'I haven't seen the baby since last week sometime, not that it's any concern of yours.'

Billy belched loudly and sprawled deeper into his chair and closed his eyes.

Abbie waited until he started snoring again and then she made her way upstairs. It was really too early to leave yet, but it was obvious that Ellen and Billy had both had a skinful the night before and were now feeling the ill-effects, so it would be better if she was out of the house before either of them turned nasty.

The sun was shining so she would walk down to the Pier Head. She could always sit on a bench there until Bradley showed up.

Quickly she changed into her dress and combed her hair so that it framed her face. As she was carefully outlining her mouth with lipstick she heard Billy moving about downstairs. Her heart thumped rapidly as she heard his footsteps on the stairs.

Swiftly she moved behind her bedroom door and stood there, holding her breath, praying he wouldn't come in and see that she was all ready to leave.

She heard him pause outside the door and hoped he couldn't see her and that he hadn't noticed her coat and bag lying across the foot of her bed. As his steps moved away and she heard him go into his own room she snatched up her coat and handbag and cautiously tiptoed out of the room and down the stairs.

Ellen was still sitting at the table, her head in her hands, her eyes closed. Biting her lip as she concentrated on not making a sound, Abbie made her way to the backdoor, opened it, and was out into the back jowler before Ellen could look up.

Abbie waited until she reached Scotland Road before she stopped to put on her coat. By then she was so breathless from running that she had a stitch in her side and was gasping for air.

Chapter Thirty-Four

Abbie and Bradley caught the Royal Iris ferryboat, which sailed promptly at two o'clock. Although it was September the weather was mild and the Mersey was like a millpond with gulls dipping and skimming over the surface. Abbie enjoyed every moment of the journey across to Seacombe.

They went up on to the top deck and leaned over the rail, admiring the two giant liners berthed at the dockside, and trying to identify some of the many cargo boats also moored there. They passed the Isle of Man boat coming into the landing stage and the ferryboat Royal Daffodil travelling in the opposite direction to them, heading for Liverpool Pier Head.

It wasn't until they were on one of the bright yellow double-decker Wallasey buses, and already on their way up King Street towards Seabank Road, that Abbie allowed herself to think about the real purpose of their trip. Immediately some of the sunshine went out of the day for her.

Before she could voice her fears to Bradley he was standing up and taking her by the arm. 'Come on, the next stop is ours.'

Abbie looked around her with increasing trepidation as they alighted from the bus. Seabank Road looked so imposing that it took her breath away. The road seemed to go on forever. On the left-hand side there were very large, detached red-brick houses with well-kept front gardens. On the right, row after row of big terraced houses running in parallel lines right down to Egremont promenade.

The whole area spoke of well-off middle-class living and contrasted so sharply with her own background in Bostock Street that Abbie wanted to turn tail and run.

'Here we are!' Bradley pushed open a low wrought-iron gate that led on to a paved pathway, bordered by a wall on one side and a large round flowerbed on the other.

As he slipped his key into the door, Abbie was sure that the lace curtain in the huge bay window stirred just a fraction, and she had the feeling that they were being watched.

Leonora Fisher came into the hallway to greet them. She was smartly dressed, in a dark blue silk dress with a lace-edged modesty vest at the 'V' neckline. Her hennaed hair had been given a marcel wave and she looked much younger than Abbie had expected.

Mentally, Abbie compared her with Ellen. They must be about the same age, she reasoned, yet Ellen, with her raddled face, bleary eyes and stringy unwashed hair, looked twenty years older. She tried to imagine what Ellen would look like if she was dressed as elegantly as Bradley's mother, instead of in her coarse black skirt, flannel blouse and black shawl.

If she had clothes like Leonora Fisher the first

thing she would do would be to take them down to Old Solly's and pawn them, and spend the money in the nearest boozer, Abbie thought bitterly.

'As it's such a lovely day I thought we'd take tea in the conservatory,' Mrs Fisher announced. 'Do take your little friend through, Bradley, and I'll bring in the tea things, I have everything ready.'

Bradley guided Abbie down the length of the dining room to the far end, where French doors opened into a sun-filled room that had glass on all three sides. The floor was a mosaic of blue, green, yellow, white and black tiles. The room itself was furnished with cane chairs and settees upholstered in flowered chintz. In the centre of the room was a round, glass-topped cane table. The double door at the far end of the conservatory was fastened back so that the long garden outside seemed to be an extension of the room.

To Abbie it was so breathtakingly beautiful that she couldn't speak. She perched uneasily on one of the settees next to Bradley, wondering how she was going to cope with the ordeal of drinking tea in such an atmosphere.

As Mrs Fisher appeared in the doorway, pushing a loaded tea trolley, Bradley jumped to his feet to assist her. Abbie watched in dismay as she saw the array of dainty, crustless sandwiches, the elaborate chocolate cake and the cream sponge cake. They all looked delicious, but how on earth would she be able to eat any of them and balance a teacup at the same time!

Before he sat down again, Bradley moved the

glass top table so that it was immediately in front of the settee and laid out plates and serviettes and tiny pastry forks.

'Do you take milk, Abbie?' Mrs Fisher asked as she poured out the tea from an elaborate china teapot into matching cups.

'Of course she does!' Bradley smiled. 'And sugar!'

'Put the sugar bowl on the table, then, Bradley, so that she can help herself,' his mother instructed.

Conversation was stilted. Abbie took a mouthful of her tea and almost choked it was so hot. Blinking back her tears she accepted one of the cucumber sandwiches, grateful for the cool filling. Gaining confidence, she also accepted a slice of chocolate cake and then wished she hadn't because she found that the icing was so sticky that it clung to her fork.

The ordeal of tea over, Abbie wondered if she was expected to help clear away. When Mrs Fisher wheeled the trolley out of the room she asked Bradley in a whisper whether she should offer to help to wash up.

'No! Don't worry about that. Mother will leave everything on the trolley and the woman who comes in to do the cleaning will see to them.'

Abbie felt shocked. No wonder the house looked so perfect, almost as though no one ever used it, she thought. A woman to come in to clean when there was only two of them living there. It seemed to her to be an outrageous extravagance.

To Abbie's relief, when their meal was over, Bradley suggested that the two of them should take a walk as far as New Brighton. 'We can walk along Seabank Road to Rowson Street, then down Victoria Road to the prom. We can catch the ferry back to Liverpool from there or take a bus to Seacombe and get a boat there.'

'Oh dear, I didn't think you'd be planning on leaving so soon!' Mrs Fisher sighed. 'This is a flying visit, isn't it! I've seen hardly anything of you this weekend, Bradley.'

Her voice was so reproachful that it made Abbie feel guilty. She wondered if she was expected to suggest that Bradley should stay with his mother and that she would make her own way home.

Bradley's chuckle as he took Abbie's arm was reassuring. 'I'll be home later this evening if you want to sit up and wait for me,' he told his mother.

'There, that wasn't such an ordeal, now, was it?' Bradley grinned as he took her arm while they walked along Seabank Road.

Abbie frowned worriedly. 'It was all right, but I'm wondering what sort of impression I have made on your mother.'

'She thinks you're lovely, and so do I!' he reassured her, giving her arm a squeeze to emphasise his words.

Abbie bit her lip. She wasn't sure if he was right or not. She had a feeling that when Bradley got home again that night, no matter how late he was, he would find his mother sitting up waiting for him in order to talk about her.

There was nothing she could do about that so she pushed it firmly to the back of her mind, determined to enjoy the rest of her day with Bradley.

Even though it was Sunday, Victoria Road was packed with day-trippers making the most of the late summer weather. Because they were all in holiday mood, they were all smiling and happy, and Abbie found the atmosphere quite exciting.

She'd had no idea there were so many things to see and do in New Brighton. They considered the idea of going to the Floral Pavilion to see a show, but there were no seats left.

'We could go to the Trocadero Cinema,' Bradley suggested. 'Shall we see what's showing?'

Abbie looked doubtful. 'It's such a lovely day that I'd rather stroll along the prom or go for a walk on the pier,' she told him.

They did both, and by then it was getting towards dusk so they decided to catch the next boat back to Liverpool.

Abbie felt it had been the most perfect day of her whole life as she sat next to Bradley on the open deck, his arm around her waist, and watched the receding lights of New Brighton and the myriad of approaching lights from Liverpool.

She wished they could go on drifting forever, locked in each other's arms, just the two of them with no one else to worry about.

'Do you want to stay on this boat for the return journey?' Abbie asked, as they bumped into position alongside the floating roadway and there was a grating sound as the vessel was secured.

'I'm seeing you home first!' he told her. 'You

don't think I'd let you make your own way home at this time of night, do you?'

It was quite dark as they reached Scotland Road. Dark and drab and sour smelling, Abbie thought, wrinkling her nose in disgust. What must Bradley think, bringing her back to this squalor after showing her the lovely area where he lived?

'I can find my own way from here,' she said abruptly, stopping on the corner of Scotland Road and Bostock Street.

'I'm seeing you right to your door,' he told her firmly. 'Don't worry, I'm not expecting you to ask me in, but I do want to make sure you reach home safely.'

As they left the bright lights of Scotland Road and turned into Bostock Street, an ambulance turned the corner at the same time, its headlights splitting the gloom like a searchlight.

'That's not going to your house I hope!' Bradley murmured.

'No, but it has stopped outside the Ryans' house,' Abbie said worriedly. 'I wonder what's happened?'

Bradley frowned. 'That's where Peter Ryan, the chap who attacked you, lives.'

Abbie nodded. 'I wonder what's wrong?' She let go of Bradley's arm and started to run towards the house where several people were already gathered.

Bradley grabbed her arm, pulling her to a standstill. 'Keep away,' he warned, 'I don't want you getting into any more trouble!'

She wriggled free. 'You don't understand, it

might be Maggie who is in trouble,' she called back over her shoulder.

As she reached the Ryans' door, Maggie came out of the house, following one of the ambulance men who was carrying the baby wrapped in a shawl.

'What's going on, Maggie? What's happened?' Abbie called out.

Maggie Ryan shook her head as if dazed. 'I don't know, Abbie. I'm not sure what happened. I asked Peter to keep an eye on the baby while I went to church. When I got back I found him asleep in the chair so I went to check the baby was all right, and he wasn't breathing.'

'We've already told you, missus, that it looks as though the child has been smothered,' one of the ambulance men muttered.

'I've been trying to tell them it must have been some sort of an accident,' Maggie said agitatedly, 'but they won't believe me.'

'Come on, missus, we're wasting precious minutes hanging around here. Get in the ambulance if you are going to and let's get the kid to the hospital and see if they can do anything for him there.'

'Maggie, do you want me to come with you?' Abbie offered, as Maggie clambered up into the back of the ambulance.

'No, luv, no don't do that. Stay here and make sure that Peter's all right. He's still in the house and he's in a terrible state because someone has sent for the police and he thinks they are coming to arrest him!'

Chapter Thirty-Five

Bradley laid a restraining hand on Abbie's arm. 'Come on, let's go. We can go to the hospital, if you wish.'

She shook her head. 'Maggie asked me to see that Peter was all right. I must stay with him.'

'You're not to go in that house. Peter Ryan attacked you, remember,' Bradley said, his voice edged with anger.

'I know that, but I promised Maggie,' Abbie said helplessly.

Bradley's jaw tightened. 'No!'

She was startled by the resentment in his voice. For a brief second she hesitated, then, as she saw the two uniformed figures approaching, she pushed her way through the crowd towards the house and took up a defiant stance on the Ryans' doorstep.

'There's no need for you to get involved, miss,' one of the policemen told her curtly, elbowing her aside.

'Hold it! What's going on?' Bradley demanded.

'Who's asking?' one of the policeman snapped, then as he recognised Bradley he gaped in surprise.

'Well?' Bradley's tone was so authoritative that the policeman responded automatically.

'We're here to take a suspect in for questioning, Sarge. A young baby left in his care appears to have died in suspicious circumstances.'

'Died! I thought they were taking it to the hospital and that it would be all right!' Abbie gasped. 'And what do you mean "in suspicious circumstances"?' she gabbled. 'He wouldn't hurt it, he was its father!'

'Sorry, miss. We have our orders. If you'd just stand aside, please.'

'At least let me go in first and warn him,' she begged.

Before they could stop her she had slipped past them and into the house, calling out Peter's name as she went.

Bradley strode after her. 'Wait, Abbie! Don't be foolish. He's attacked you before . . .'

A sudden piercing scream from Abbie drowned out the rest of his warning. Bradley and the two policemen rushed inside.

Abbie was at the foot of the stairs, screaming and sobbing, and pointing at the dark shape dangling from the stairwell in front of their eyes.

'Christ! He's topped himself,' one of the policemen exclaimed in horror. 'Here,' he addressed his colleague, 'grab his legs and try and take his weight while I cut him down, we may still manage to save him.'

Bradley pulled Abbie into his arms, holding her close, shielding her from the gruesome sight, whispering words of comfort as he tried to calm her.

Her screaming startled the people who were

gathered on the pavement outside the front door and had now been joined by others who had seen the police arrive. All of them were speculating about what had happened.

Once again the ambulance was called to the Ryans' house, although it was quite obvious that Peter was dead and nothing could be done to save him.

After Peter's body had been taken away, Abbie couldn't rid herself of guilt. She felt what had happened was as much her fault as anyone else's. Maggie had asked her if she would look after the baby on Sunday evening while she went to church. Her mind had been so full of her invitation from Bradley, and the thought that she was going to meet his mother for the very first time, that she had forgotten all about it.

When she tried to explain all this to Bradley he merely shrugged.

'Really! Well, it isn't your fault. You're no relation, only a friend, so it was up to Mrs Ryan to make other arrangements when you didn't get back to her. Anyway, even if you had, she couldn't expect you to alter plans you'd already made.'

'It isn't quite as simple as that,' Abbie said hesitantly. 'I meant to tell you long before this, but there is something else that you don't know.'

Bradley's face hardened. 'You're not going to tell me that it was your baby – yours and Peter Ryan's!'

'How dare you! If that's what you think of me

then let's end it here and now!' Abbie flared angrily, her face flaming, her blue eyes icy.

'I'm sorry!' He caught hold of her arm, turning her round to face him, pulling her into his arms and burying his face in her smooth black hair.

She struggled free, placing both her hands on his shoulders and pushing him away from her.

'I think it might be best if you listened to what I have to tell you,' she said forcefully.

Bradley was conscious that the groups of people who had come out of their homes to see what was going on were listening with avid interest to their exchange.

'All right,' he agreed. 'Let's find somewhere quiet.' He tucked her arm into the crook of his elbow and walked back towards Scotland Road. 'There might be a milk bar still open, if not we'll go into one of the pubs and find a quiet corner. By the look of you a drink wouldn't go amiss. I really do understand that you've had a terrible shock, Abbie.'

She waited until they had found a quiet spot in the Newsham Arms and the two brandies that Bradley had ordered were on the table in front of them.

She took a sip from her glass and shuddered as its potency hit the back of her throat. Then she sat up straight and stared at him, almost as if he was a stranger.

'To start with, my name is not really Abbie Martin, but Abbie Ryan.'

Bradley frowned. 'Ryan?' He looked bemused. 'So why all the fuss when I arrested Ellen Martin?'

'At that time I thought she was my mother,' Abbie explained. 'In actual fact, she is my grandmother. My mother was her daughter, Audrey, and she died when I was born. She was only thirteen.'

Bradley let out a low whistle. 'My God, Abbie, what are you saying? Do you mean that Peter Ryan ... ' he stopped and frowned. 'He can't be your father, he's too young, he's only about your age.'

'No, Peter is my uncle. My father, it seems, is his elder brother, Michael Ryan.'

'So Mrs Ryan is your grandmother as well as Ellen Martin?'

'That's right.'

Bradley looked confused. 'And the baby, the one that's just been found dead. In what way is that related to you?'

Abbie shrugged. 'Well, I suppose it's my cousin or something.' She shook her head as if mystified. 'It's very complicated. Sandra, the baby's mother, was married to my brother, Sam.'

She stopped and shook her head. 'Well, that's not quite right, either. I know now that Sam is not really my brother, but my uncle.'

'Sam is the baby's father?'

Abbie shook her head. 'Sandra had been going out with Sam ever since we were at school and they'd not long been married. It seems she had a fling with Peter Ryan last Christmas. No one knew about it and we all assumed that the baby she was expecting was Sam's.'

'And it's not?'

Abbie shook her head. 'No, but Sandra only told Sam that it was Peter Ryan's baby, not his, just before it was born.'

Bradley looked puzzled. 'In that case, shouldn't Sandra's mother be responsible for bringing it up?'

Abbie sighed. 'Mo Lewis didn't think she could take on such a burden so in the end Peter Ryan persuaded his own mother to bring the baby up.'

She hesitated, wondering if she should tell Bradley that Peter had wanted her to either marry him or go and live with him, so that they could bring up the baby together, but she felt she had stretched his patience far enough.

'This situation becomes more complicated the more you try and explain it,' Bradley muttered. He placed a hand under her chin and raised her face so that he was looking directly into her eyes. 'I think it's a good job that you will soon be changing your name to Fisher, don't you?' he asked softly.

Abbie felt her heart thud. Her blue eyes widened in disbelief. She looked at him dubiously. 'I can't believe you still want to see me, or talk to me, even. I thought you would turn tail and walk away when you heard the whole story,' she said nervously.

'You've not got very much faith in the man who is planning to become your husband, have you!' he retorted.

She smiled, comforted by his words, but refusing to allow herself to believe that such a dream could ever happen. Life had dealt her so many unexpected blows lately that she had grown cynical and afraid to take anything for granted.

'Come on, finish your drink,' Bradley urged, 'and then I'm going to take you home.'

Abbie shivered. 'I suppose I ought to go and see if Maggie Ryan is back home and how she is. She'll know by now about Peter, poor woman. Peter and the baby. Two deaths in one night!'

'You're not visiting Maggie Ryan tonight, or anyone else in Bostock Street. When I said I was taking you home I meant you're coming home with me,' Bradley told her firmly.

'To Wallasey? To your house in Seabank Road?' Abbie looked stunned. 'I can't go there!'

He frowned. 'Why not? There's a spare bedroom. You'll be living there soon enough. In the near future it will be your permanent home.'

'You mean, if we get married we'll be living with your mother!'

'Yes, why not?'

Abbie shook her head. 'I don't think she would like that! When she knows the truth about my past she'll tell you to drop me and find a nice girl of your own sort,' Abbie told him flatly.

'Not a bit of it. I could see she liked you!'

'Tolerated me, perhaps, because she was being polite and gracious. But like me?' She shook her head, 'I don't think so!'

'Of course she did!'

'We're completely different types of people, Bradley,' Abbie persisted. 'In fact, I don't know

336

how you can possibly like both of us; we are so very different.'

He laughed and squeezed her hand. 'No more arguing. I'm on early shift tomorrow so I have to be up at five a.m. Come on, back to Wallasey and leave all your problems until the morning. You'll find they'll be much easier to deal with once you've had a good night's sleep.'

'I can't come back to Wallasey! I have to go to work tomorrow as well, you know. I need my uniform.'

He frowned, remembering the expressions he had seen on some of the faces of the people who had crowded round the Ryans' front door. He was pretty certain there were going to be unpleasant repercussions in Bostock Street before the night was out and he didn't want Abbie to become embroiled in it.

'I don't think it is advisable for you to go to your own house tonight,' he said firmly. 'Come back to Wallasey with me and you can catch the same early ferry as me first thing tomorrow morning. That will give you plenty of time to sort out your clothes and be at Frisby Dyke's before nine o'clock.'

Abbie still felt undecided. 'What will your mother think, though, if I turn up with you at this time of night?'

'She'll understand. I'll explain that there has been a spot of trouble with your neighbours and that you are rather upset, and she won't ask any questions, I promise.'

*

Mrs Fisher appeared to accept Bradley's explanation with perfect equanimity. She lent Abbie a nightdress and provided her with toiletries.

'Now you run along and have a hot bath and then pop into bed,' she told her. 'I'll bring you up a hot drink to help you sleep.'

She was as good as her word. Abbie was revelling in the comfort of being in a feather bed when there was a tap on the door and Mrs Fisher appeared with a steaming cup of Ovaltine.

'Bradley is already sound asleep. He must have dropped off the moment his head touched the pillow, so I hope this will help to do the same for you,' she told Abbie. 'Perhaps you have too much on your mind, though, to sleep easily,' she added.

The words were said kindly, but Abbie sensed the undertone and resolved to put matters right. Bradley might be right in thinking his mother liked her, and she had certainly shown her great kindness, but she didn't want Mrs Fisher to be under any illusion about who she was.

As if reading her mind, Leonora Fisher commented, 'I recognised the name, Martin, the moment Bradley introduced you this afternoon. Is it your family whose name is always appearing in the *Liverpool Echo*?'

For a moment Abbie thought of denying it, saying her name wasn't really Martin, but one look at Leonora Fisher's sharp face and she knew she would be wasting her time.

'You'd really like to learn all there is to know about me so that you can judge whether I am a suitable girlfriend for your son, wouldn't you, Mrs Fisher?' she said stonily.

Leonora Fisher nodded. 'You are a strikingly pretty girl, Abbie, and I can see why Bradley has taken such a shine to you,' she admitted grudgingly. 'He is young and easily impressed by a pretty face.'

'And you think that is all there is to it, do you, Mrs Fisher?'

Leonora avoided Abbie's direct stare. 'I think it would be best if we laid our cards on the table,' she stated firmly. 'Bradley is my only child and very important to me. As a policeman he has a great future ahead of him and I don't want him held back in any way. He is already on the first rung of the ladder, he has been made a Sergeant even though he is only twenty-four.'

When Abbie said nothing, she went on, 'My husband was highly respected in the Wallasey police force. He was an Inspector, and I am confident that one day Bradley will be his equal.'

Abbie nodded as she drained the last of her Ovaltine and set the cup down on the bedside table.

'And you don't think I am the right sort of person to be the wife of an up-and-coming Inspector?' she said tightly.

Leonora's face froze. For Bradley to have Abbie as a friend was disturbing enough, but the thought of her ever becoming Bradley's wife horrified her.

'Not when you come from a family with a criminal record like the Martins have,' she said furiously.

339

'Criminals who keep your son in work,' Abbie said caustically.

'A mother who works in the cotton sheds and gets herself into fights on the dockside; a brother who is always drunk and is frequently arrested for brawling,' Leonora Fisher contended.

'What if I told you that my real name is not Martin, that Ellen Martin is not my mother and that Billy Martin is not my brother?'

Leonora looked taken aback. 'You *are* related to them?' she blustered.

'Yes, but not in quite the same way as you have been told.'

Abbie watched the changing expressions on Leonora Fisher's face, as once again that night she gave details of her true parentage and her complicated family relationships.

'Well, perhaps things are not quite as bad as I thought they were,' Leonora Fisher admitted reluctantly. 'Even so,' she added, with grim determination in her voice, 'they're very disturbing. I certainly don't think you are the sort of girl Bradley should be going out with, or thinking of marrying. Not the right sort at all.'

Chapter Thirty-Six

'What sort of time is this to come home! You been out all bloody night with that scuffer you're knocking around with, have you,' Billy Martin sneered.

Knowing it was not yet six o'clock in the morning, Abbie had let herself in as quietly as possible and tiptoed her way across the room, hoping not to waken Billy who was sleeping in the armchair.

'Put the bleedin' kettle on then, kiddo, I've got a mouth like the bottom of a birdcage,' Billy muttered as he sat up in the chair and rubbed a hand over the stubble on his grimy jaw.

Abbie shuddered as the rasping sound hit her ears. She was feeling pretty fragile herself, although not for the same reason as Billy.

He yawned and scratched. 'So where've you been, then?'

'I spent the night at Mrs Fisher's house in Wallasey, not that it's any business of yours,' she told him quietly.

'Who the hell is Mrs Fisher. Is she that copper's mam?' he grinned.

'Yes, she's Bradley's mother.'

'Getting a bit above yourself for a feckless Judy from Scotty Road, aren't you,' he jeered. 'You should have come home, you missed all the bloody carry-on that was happening here. Flippin' 'eck it was better than a tanner's worth at the Trocadero!'

He gave a deep belly laugh, watching Abbie closely to see her reaction. 'We had the scuffers and the ambulance here twice! There's been a bloody murder and a suicide, and Farder Bunloaf was running round like a blue-arsed fly trying to stop any more silly buggers toppin' theirselves. Thought perhaps you'd heard all about it and you'd got yourself in a tizzy and slung yer 'ook.'

Abbie turned away, sickened by his sneering, taunting tone. She busied herself raking the fire back into life, putting the kettle over the red-hot coals, and washing up a couple of cups so that she could make some tea as soon as the kettle boiled.

Seeing how unresponsive she was, Billy changed his tactics.

'You know all about what happened here last night, don't you,' he accused. 'Right little bitch you are, an' all,' he scowled, 'clearing off and leaving Ma Ryan in the lurch. Reckon Farder Bunloaf was reading her the riot act and no maybe because Peter had topped himself. You were sweet on him once. Perhaps that's why he did it. Couldn't stand to see you bugger off with a scuffer!'

'Shut it, Billy!' Abbie kicked his feet out of her way as she leaned across him to lift the kettle off the fire. 'You've got a mouth on you like a barn gate and you haven't a clue what you're talking about.'

'So you do know!'

'Yes, I was here last night when Maggie found the baby. I don't know why it died. I saw her into the ambulance. Then I saw the police arrive to take Peter in for questioning. If you must know, I was the one who found him hanging there.' She glared at him, dry-eyed and stony-faced. 'Know all you want, now?'

'Whew!' He let out a long low whistle and then gave a snort of contempt. 'Hard-faced bitch, aren't you. Take it all in your stride. You must have a heart like a lump of bleedin' lead.'

'I learned early on that you needed one to survive in this house,' she told him in withering tones.

He pulled a face. 'Mam's not going to be too pleased when she hears you've spent the night shacked up with a scuffer,' he taunted.

'Trying to stir it again, are you? I wasn't shacked up with him, as you so crudely put it. I stayed at his house, but I slept in the spare bedroom, if you must know.'

He watched her through narrowed eyes as she poured the boiling water into the teapot. 'Me mam still won't like it. He arrested her once, it's not something she's likely to forget.'

'I know, and he's run you in a few times as well. So how do you think I feel about that? It doesn't do much for my reputation!'

'Your bloody reputation! Who the hell cares about that? You're a bloody bastard, don't forget! You bein' born killed my sister, and we've had

343

you, a poxy girl, lumbered on us ever since. How do you think me and Sam feel about that?'

'Sam and me were the best of friends,' she reminded him. 'Sam probably still thinks I'm his little sister.'

'Well, that's another bloody shock to add to the list for him when he comes home, isn't it!' He took the cup of tea Abbie had poured for him and spooned sugar into it and stirred it noisily. 'Bloody hell! Sam's going to find that his sister is his niece; and not only is Sandra dead but the little bastard she cuckolded him over is dead, too!' He guffawed loudly and took a loud slurp of tea. 'And that his wife's lover-boy has topped himself into the bargain!' He slapped his hand across his thigh. 'If our Sam's got any bloody sense he'll stay as far away from Scotty Road as he can!'

Abbie drained her cup. 'I'm going to see Maggie Ryan,' she told him as she picked up her coat from the back of the chair and pulled it round her shoulders.

'Sooner you than me!'

Maggie's face was so red-eyed from weeping, and drawn and haggard from lack of sleep when she opened the door, that Abbie's heart ached for her.

She reached out to put an arm round Maggie's shoulders, but Maggie shrugged her away.

'There's tea in the pot, pour it if you want a cup,' she muttered dully as she sat down again in the chair she'd drawn up to the fire.

'I've only just had one,' Abbie said quietly. 'I've not long been home. Bradley took me back to his mother's place last night,' she added by way of explanation.

'I heard you were the one who first found Peter,' Maggie said listlessly. 'Two of them gone in one night!'

Abbie kneeled by the side of Maggie's chair and once again tried to put her arm round the other woman's shoulders.

'I know how you must be feeling, Maggie. I only wish there was something I could do to help.'

Maggie's blue eyes were cloudy with sorrow as she looked at Abbie. 'Too late now, isn't it,' she said dully. 'If you'd looked after the baby for me yesterday evening like I asked you to do, then none of this would ever have happened.'

'If the baby was sick . . .'

'Sick? Who says the baby was sick? The baby died because it was left unattended. It rolled over on to its face and was smothered because there were too many covers on it. Peter must have put another shawl over it when I went out, thinking it wasn't warm enough. You would never have done something like that.'

'You don't know that was what Peter did.'

'He either did that or he smothered the baby on purpose.' Maggie shuddered. 'The police think he did it on purpose. Those smart-arsed scuffers that work with that chap you left my Peter for say he deliberately smothered it. If he hadn't hung himself then they'd have had him up on a murder charge. Do you know that?'

Abbie shook her head. 'I'm sure he wouldn't have harmed the baby. I realise we'll never know

345

the truth, but there's no cause to think the worst of Peter, is there.'

'Why are you championing him all of a sudden?' Maggie asked bitterly. 'You refusing to help him out with the baby was the start of all our troubles.'

'Oh no it wasn't! Come on, let's set the record straight. It all goes back much further than that, doesn't it. If you and Ellen Martin hadn't lied to me and to everyone else about who I really was then Peter would never have thought about me in the way he did.'

Maggie stared at her without answering.

'It's true, Maggie. If Peter had known he was my uncle he would never have gone out with me in the first place, probably never even played with me when we were kids.

'What's more, if you'd all owned up to Michael being my father, and you had brought me up instead of letting Ellen Martin do it, my life would have been so much better, wouldn't it. Why didn't you?'

Maggie shook her head. 'You don't understand what you're talking about.'

'Then tell me! Put me right. What don't I understand?'

'Paddy wouldn't let me because he didn't want anyone to know that you were Michael's child. He battered me black and blue, and half killed our Michael, when he first heard about it.'

'So you let the Martins bring me up because they didn't worry about such things?'

'Jimmy Martin scarpered almost the moment he

heard his Audrey had given birth. Couldn't see him for dust!'

'And that's when Ellen took charge?'

'Audrey was her daughter. She hadn't counted on her dying like that. She was far too young to be preggers, of course, but she was fit enough. She should have sailed through it. When she died, Ellen hung on to you and didn't want anything to do with me or mine.'

'So you left it like that!'

Maggie sighed. 'Looking back, I suppose I should have acted differently and given it more thought. I never thought about how it would affect you in the future.'

'No, all you were concerned about was that the scandal was hushed up nicely and you could all get on with your lives.'

'I tried to keep an eye out for you, especially when Ellen Martin and that Billy were smashed out of their heads. I did what I could,' Maggie said defensively.

'You were my grandmother, yet you left me living in that hovel with those two drunken, abusive tyrants,' Abbie said bitterly. 'Have you any idea what I endured?'

'I tried my best to help you,' Maggie sniffed.

'And you were content to see me getting involved with your Peter, even though you knew how closely related we were and that someday he might want to marry me?'

Maggie shook her head. 'I prayed for guidance and I never stopped worrying about what I should do if you two ever did decide you wanted to marry. It never came to that, though, did it. When Peter came home from that reform school he'd changed; all he could think about was getting on in the world.'

Abbie shook her head sadly. 'I thought you were so kind, so caring, that I envied Peter. Yet all the time you were simply protecting yourself. You weren't even a good mother to Peter. You said you knew it was Billy who'd stolen the bike, yet you did nothing about it. You kept quiet and let Peter go to reform school rather than risk the truth coming out.'

Maggie sighed. 'None of us can turn the clock back.'

'I'm beginning to think that the only true friend I've ever had in the whole of my life was Sam Martin!' Abbie said dejectedly. 'I'm not sure how he'll react once he knows that I'm his niece, not his sister!'

As she opened the door to leave, Maggie called her back.

'Are you seriously thinking of marrying Bradley Fisher, Abbie?'

Abbie stiffened, her eyes glacial. 'I hardly think, after all that has happened, that it is any of your business,' she said acidly.

'Oh, but it is Abbie. Michael has said he doesn't want a scuffer brought into the family.'

'Michael! What business is it of his?'

'Michael is your father, Abbie! He can step in and stop you marrying him.'

Abbie smiled contemptuously. 'Let him try!

Rather too late in the day for him to say he's my dad now, isn't it?'

Chapter Thirty-Seven

Abbie found it was hard trying to keep her mind on her work next day. Twice she made mistakes that entailed sending the money and bill winging back in its little metal cage to make a correction.

She knew this would be noted down and she would be taken to task for it when they closed, but it made no difference. Try as she might, the happenings of the past couple of days went round and round in her mind, making her head spin.

No one at Frisby Dyke's had actually mentioned it, but she knew there had been a report in the morning paper, the *Liverpool Post*, and there would be a longer version in the *Liverpool Echo* about what had happened in Bostock Street the night before.

Since the first edition of the *Echo* came out just after midday she was pretty sure that some of the other staff, those who took a late lunch-break, had already seen it, and she hoped they wouldn't realise the part she'd played.

She had deliberately gone to lunch late so that she could buy a copy, and she had been horrified as she read all the grisly details that had been used to embellish the story.

The reporter's description of Bostock Street made it sound like the vilest slum in Liverpool.

Peter had been painted so black that she hardly recognised him. There was, fortunately, no mention by name of the Martins, or of her own part in the debacle.

She suspected, however, that Leonora Fisher would hazard a pretty shrewd guess as to her involvement, since she already knew the truth about her background.

Before she'd come to work that morning she'd packed the best of her clothes into a canvas bag and brought them with her, together with her savings which she'd kept hidden under her mattress.

Once the whole story was out, Billy would be so enraged and blame her and Bradley and refuse to let her back into the house. Now, after having time to think matters over for herself, she knew she didn't want to go back to Bostock Street ever again.

There was no longer anyone there that she cared about. The only person she would miss was Sam and she could only hope that when he did eventually come ashore he would get in touch with her. He knew where she worked so if he wanted to see her then he knew where to look for her.

She had no idea where she was going to find a place to spend the night, or where she would live from now on. All she knew was that she had to make the effort to break free of the past and from the influence of both the Martins and the Ryans.

As the hands of the clock came ever nearer to closing time she remained resolute in her decision not to go back to Bostock Street when she left Frisby Dyke's that night.

She was overcome with relief when she found Bradley waiting for her as she came out of the staff entrance. He was wearing grey slacks, a tweed jacket and a brown tweed cap, and she felt relieved that he hadn't come to meet her while still in uniform.

'I was hoping you'd see sense and bring your things with you,' he told her as he took the bulky canvas bag from her. 'I nearly came along to the store when I came off duty at three o'clock to suggest it, but then I thought it would be better if the decision was yours.'

'Where are we going?' she asked, as he took her arm and steered her towards a Green Goddess tram that had just pulled up.

'To the Pier Head to catch the next ferry to Wallasey and then a bus to Seabank Road, and you are staying at my place,' he smiled.

She pulled back. 'Do you think that's wise?' she asked hesitantly. 'I don't intend going back to Bostock Street,' she said quickly, 'but I thought I would try and find a room somewhere.'

'At my place?' He grinned broadly. 'Where else?'

'By now your mother will have seen the *Echo* and read the whole story of what went on last night.'

He shrugged. 'You're not mentioned by name.'

Abbie shook her head. 'That makes no difference. She came up to my room last night, after you went to bed, and I told her everything.'

He frowned, looking puzzled. 'Everything? What do you mean?'

'I told her I wasn't really Abbie Martin but Abbie Ryan, and everything else there was to tell her,' she said lamely.

'Crafty old witch! She never said a word to me about it.'

'No, she's too clever to tell you outright that she doesn't approve of me.'

'Rubbish! What gives you that idea, anyway.'

'She wants you to marry one of the nice young girls you've grown up with and known all your life. She has such high hopes of the kind of future you will have, and she certainly doesn't think that someone from the Scotty Road area will make you a suitable wife.'

He gave her arm a gentle squeeze and dropped a kiss on the top of her head. 'Then we will have to prove her wrong. You do want to, don't you?'

Abbie looked puzzled. 'Prove her wrong?'

'Yes, by marrying me,' Bradley grinned.

'I want to marry you more than anything else in the world, but I'm afraid it's going to upset too many people if I agree to do so.'

'You mean my mother?'

'Your mother, the Ryans and the Martins.'

'I can talk my mother round, don't worry about her,' he said confidently. 'Do any of the others matter?'

She shook her head. 'Not to me, not any longer. I wouldn't want to cause a rift between you and your mother, though.'

'You won't. She'll accept it.'

Abbie shook her head again. 'I don't think so.'

'She's only worried that I might leave, because then she'll be all on her own.'

'I can understand that. You are her life, Bradley.'

'There's a simple way round that,' he smiled, as they got off the tram and hurried to catch the next boat to Seacombe. 'She has talked incessantly about turning the house into two self-contained flats, so that we can have separate lives, but still go on living under the same roof. Up until now I've always scoffed at the idea, but if I go along with her plans she won't raise any further objections to us getting married, I'm quite sure of that.'

'Do you think it would work, living so close to each other?' Abbie asked as they found seats on the upper deck of the ferry.

'I don't see why not. We would have separate front doors!'

'She'd have to understand right from the start that we would live independently of each other,' Abbie said reflectively.

'Don't worry. She has quite a busy social life, you know. She belongs to all sorts of clubs and associations. She's out every day of the week. It's just the idea of being completely alone that bothers her. I think she'll be pleased to know that I've settled down at last,' he grinned.

Abbie stared out at the busy Mersey as she pondered on the idea of the house in Seabank Road being divided into two flats. It was certainly possible. There was plenty of space to do that, but would Mrs Fisher want to give up her lavish accommodation and exist in a flat that was only half the size?

'It wouldn't only mean she'd have to give up half of her home, but she would have to get rid of an awful lot of her beautiful furniture and she's so house-proud,' Abbie pointed out.

'She can always give it to us if she doesn't want to sell it. You leave it to me,' Bradley grinned as the ferryboat docked at Seacombe.

'There really won't be any problem at all,' he assured Abbie as they became part of the jostling crowd making their way up the floating roadway to the bus terminus.

Abbie still felt doubtful. As the double-decker bus took them along King Street, the nearer they got to Seabank Road the more insurmountable the problems seemed to become.

'Don't say anything to your mother about us getting married . . . not yet,' she said anxiously as they reached the house and Bradley opened the wrought-iron gate.

'Why not?'

'We do come from very different backgrounds, you know. If she's read the paper then she's going to be horrified at the thought of meeting the Martins and Ryans at our wedding and having to introduce them to all her friends,' she grinned.

He frowned. 'Does she have to? Must they come?'

'No, of course not. I had no intention of inviting any of them,' Abbie said quickly. 'I never want to see any of them again. I was really thinking of the problem she would have introducing me to all those important friends of hers, all those nice girls that she had hoped you would marry one day.'

He stopped and looked at her in surprise. 'You do have a point there, Abbie. I'd not really thought about that.' He frowned. 'She certainly might find that a little tricky.'

Her face fell. Why couldn't she keep her big mouth shut, she thought miserably. Why, when everything was so wonderful and her wildest dreams were about to come true, did she have to go and ruin everything.

The fact that Bradley had seen the sense of her argument was not going to do her any favours at all. He'd listen to his mother's objections and realise that she was saying much the same thing so there must be more than a grain of truth in it. Then he was bound to come to the conclusion that he couldn't go against his mother's wishes.

She was so caught up in her own despair that at first she didn't comprehend what he was saying.

'What did you say?' she asked in bewilderment.

'I was telling you what the answer to that problem was,' he grinned.

She looked at him blankly.

'I said I agreed with you that we would say nothing to my mother about us getting married. Instead, we'll elope to Gretna Green and get married "over the anvil".'

Abbie stared at him incredulously. 'She'll disapprove even more if we do that!'

He shook his head. 'No she won't. Not when we remind her that it is fashionable in high society these days to elope. Do you remember the piece in the *Echo* a short time back about the heir to the Larrinaga Steamship Company eloping with eighteen-year-old Jessie Hands?'

'Jessie Hands?'

'Yes! All her friends called her "Midgy". She belonged to our tennis club and my mother talked about their daring exploit for months afterwards.'

Abbie looked puzzled.

'If we do the same, and if I tell her I was only copying what Midgy did, my mother will be impressed, and it will give her something to dine out on for years to come.'

Abbie looked at him in wide-eyed admiration. 'Do you think we dare do that?'

She'd never met anyone quite like Bradley before. He was forceful, confident, and so capable that he seemed to be able to achieve anything that he wanted to do.

'We're going to!' he assured her.

She frowned. 'Since I'm only seventeen I suppose I will have to get consent, but I'm sure one of my grandmothers, or perhaps even both, will sign the forms. Probably only too pleased to get me out of their lives forever.'

'Good! I'll arrange for some time off and you do the same. Keep what we intend doing a complete secret. I'll leave a note for my mother the day we leave.'

Abbie giggled. 'She probably won't let us back in the house when we come home again.'

'Oh yes she will!'

He put his arm around her shoulders, pulling her close as they stepped off the bus. 'When I tell her she either converts the place into two flats or we go and live in Liverpool or Birkenhead or somewhere like that, she'll fall in with our plans quick enough.'

'You're a devious blackmailer,' Abbie laughed, snuggling up to him. 'I can see I'm going to have my work cut out keeping up with you, or you'll be leading me a merry dance.'

Chapter Thirty-Eight

Curled up next to Bradley on the sofa in Mrs Fisher's lounge, Abbie felt wonderfully relaxed. She had never felt so happy, so safe, or so loved. She was almost unable to believe that before the year was out they would be married.

It still seemed incredible to her that someone so good-looking and so successful as Bradley could be in love with her as much as she was with him.

He was a tower of strength in so many ways. Tall and broad yet lean and imposing, whether in his policeman's uniform or out of it. Added to that he was strong-minded yet fair. She could never imagine him doing anything underhanded, or allowing any kind of injustice.

She looked down at the symbol of his love for her that glittered on the third finger of her left hand. The solitaire diamond was the most beauti-ful engagement ring she had ever seen.

They were not going to elope, romantic though that would have been. She had sensed that deep down he'd not really wanted to do that in case it upset his mother, so she had agreed when instead he had suggested that they had a very quiet wedding.

It would take place in Wallasey, and apart from his mother and the best man, who was one of his colleagues, there would only be one or two guests. To follow they were all having a celebratory meal at the Victoria Hotel in New Brighton. Afterwards, she and Bradley would leave for the Isle of Man on their honeymoon.

None of her relations would be there, neither the Martins nor the Ryans. She would have invited Sam, but he was on the high seas and she had no idea where he was, or even the name of the ship he was on.

Like her, Sam was trying to start a new life. They'd meet up again in time, she was sure of that. They'd been so close while they were growing up and she was sure that the bonds that they'd forged then were strong enough to survive the recent upheaval and tragedy.

She and Bradley would be married before Christmas and, for her, 1933 would not only be the start of a new year, but of a whole new way of life.

She wouldn't let herself think too much about the future or she became nervous and wondered if she was going to be able to live up to Bradley's expectations. His background was so different from her own. She had so much to learn.

When, tentatively, she had mentioned this to him, he had hugged her close and kissed her passionately.

'I love you exactly as you are,' he whispered, and kissed her again.

She knew he meant it, but she was also wise enough to know that at the moment he was blinded by love. She knew she had to make a lot of changes if she was to fit into her new role as Leonora Fisher's daughter-in-law.

She shuddered as she remembered the sort of area she had grown up in. There had been dirt, squalor, and the stench of poverty everywhere. Grubby, barefoot children, drunken, abusive men, women old beyond their years, their health ruined by lack of food and constant child-bearing.

The behaviour of the people she'd lived with and the way they spoke to each other would shock Mrs Fisher and her friends. She'd found it hard enough to adjust when she'd first gone to work at Frisby Dyke's.

'You managed OK when you started work there, so why not here?' Bradley had asked, lifting one of his eyebrows quizzically when she told him how worried she was.

'Yes, but that was different. I put on a posh accent in the same way as I put on my uniform. When I was wearing my black top and long black skirt then talking in a refined manner came naturally.'

Bradley thumped the heel of his hand against his forehead dramatically. 'Does that mean you are always going to have to dress in black after we're married?' he groaned.

She knew he was teasing her simply to show that it wasn't all that important to him, but it was important to her.

For the first time in her life she'd found someone who loved her and she didn't want that to change ... ever!

She never wanted the day to come when

Bradley wondered if he'd done the right thing in marrying her.

Abbie looked forward to 1933 not simply as being a whole new way of life for her, but one filled with happiness and contentment. She had always yearned for someone to love her and now that dream had come true at last.

As long as she lived she would never understand why, or even how, Ellen Martin and Maggie Ryan had kept the truth about her parentage from her for all those years.

They must have done it so that their own names and reputations wouldn't be sullied, she thought sadly. In the end, all they had done was cause her and so many other people a great deal of misery.

All she'd ever wanted was to be shown love and affection. She wouldn't have cared who her mother was, or about the scandal that had led to her birth. She was sorry about Audrey, of course, but she couldn't feel anything for her. She was just a name.

Learning about Michael Ryan being her father was different. A shudder went through her as she recalled his coldness towards her. Over and over again she asked herself how he could have been so abrupt, so disinterested in her, when he knew she was his daughter?

She'd always thought Maggie so kind, but looking back she wondered if perhaps Maggie hadn't been the most evil of them all. Ellen had made no secret of the fact that she didn't love her, didn't even like her and had no time for her. Maggie, though, had shown her affection, and turned a blind eye about her closeness to Peter even when she'd told her that she thought she was in love with him.

When she talked about this to Bradley, he hadn't seemed shocked or surprised. 'It was only natural that you were attracted to each other and that there was a closeness between you, since you were uncle and niece.'

'Yes, but I didn't know that. In my eagerness to get away from there I would have married him if he'd asked me!'

Bradley nodded understandingly. 'And what about Sam?'

'I thought the world of him, but I thought he was my brother. Even that was a lie.'

'That's all in the past and you should try and put it all behind you,' Bradley told her seriously.

'I know, but I shall never completely forget what a terrible tangle it all was.'

Abbie still felt it was incredible that, knowing so much about her, Bradley should still love her and want to marry her.

Living at his home she had never felt so safe and pampered. Now that Mrs Fisher knew that Bradley's mind was made up and that she was the girl he intended to marry, she couldn't do enough to help her.

There was still a dreamlike quality about all that had happened. She still couldn't credit that Mrs Fisher was willing to give up half of her beautiful home so that they could have a place of their own waiting for them when they came back from their honeymoon. She'd even offered them some of her furniture!

Her new home was going to be better than anything she'd ever known in her life. When she'd been growing up in Bostock Street she'd envied Sandra Lewis because her mother had been so house-proud. They'd never had wall-to-wall carpets on the floor, though, or a bathroom! She'd loved the cosiness of Maggie Ryan's place, but there hadn't been any of the comforts there that she would have from now on.

She wouldn't have to put up with any more cursing, shouting, drunken brawls or raging rows. There would be no more bullying from Billy or rejection from Ellen Martin. There would be no more lies or deception.

Never again would she have to comb nits out of her hair, or check her bed to see there were no cockroaches or fleas in it before she got into it at night. Nor would she ever again have to use the public baths.

She was looking forward so much to putting her own unhappy experiences behind her, and erasing the memories of all the tragedies that had taken place as well.

In the past year there had been so many of these, as well as devastating revelations about the past. Sandra dying, the baby being Peter's not Sam's, and then the baby's death followed by Peter committing suicide. All still haunted her.

On top of that, she had felt almost bereaved by the fact that Sam had been so brokenhearted that he had gone to sea.

When Abbie finally summoned up the courage to go back to Bostock Street to ask Michael Ryan, since he was her dad, to give his permission for her to get married, she found that the Ryans were no longer there.

'They've all gone back to Ireland, and bloody good riddance to the whole bunch of them,' Billy snarled.

'I'm surprised they went on living here as long as they did,' Abbie commented.

His shifty eyes narrowed. 'They couldn't leave, could they, their consciences wouldn't let them. Her bloody husband wouldn't let her bring you up, even though their Michael was your dad, but Paddy Ryan was determined she would see you every day of her life. It was his way of punishing her and Michael, making them watch you grow up in muck and misery,' he sneered.

'They could have afforded to leave here years ago but he was a sadistic bastard,' Ellen added. 'Bloody skinflints, the pair of them. She said he always kept her short so she could never afford to hand over a penny-piece to help with your keep.'

'She was kind to me,' Abbie argued.

'Only when it suited her. Half the time she only did it to rile me,' Ellen replied, scowling. 'Anyway, they've cleared off. He's given up the sea. The old bugger saved up enough to buy himself a farm in County Kerry and Michael's gone with them.'

'So who is going to sign this document so that I can get married?' Abbie asked worriedly.

'I'm not bloody signing no form that has

anything to do with scuffers. You must be out of your sodding mind to marry one of those buggers!' Billy told her.

'That's her affair! As long as she gets off our backs she can marry who the hell she likes, so you shut your great gob,' Ellen told him. 'Since there's no one outside of Bostock Street what knows any difference I'll sign the bloody paper.'

'You mean as my mother? Will it be legal when you're really my grandmother?' Abbie asked in alarm.

'Who the hell cares. No one's given a damn all these years, so who's going to worry about it now?'

Abbie handed her the form and watched with mixed feelings as Ellen laboriously scrawled her name.

As Ellen pushed it back across the table towards her, Abbie felt an overwhelming sense of relief. It was over. The past really was behind her.

As she stood up to leave she looked round the untidy room, at the table piled with dirty crockery, the grate with its ashes spilling out on to the hearth, and felt a surge of sheer happiness knowing that it would be the last time she would ever be there. Impulsively, she put her arm around Ellen's shoulders and kissed her on the cheek.

'Geroff, you smarmy little bitch!' Ellen slapped her hand and pushed her away. 'You've got what you came for, so bugger off.'

When Ellen had rebuffed her in the past, Abbie had been brokenhearted. Now she felt indifferent and found herself smiling complacently. She'd been afraid that Ellen might show a display of affection and want her to stay, or even expect to be invited to the wedding. As it was, she could now walk away from Bostock Street and all its memories without even a backward glance.

If you enjoyed *Looking For Love* why not try
further Rosie Harris titles . . .

ONE STEP FORWARD

**Ever since she was eight years old, Katie Roberts
has dreamed of getting away from the Cardiff
slums where she lives.**

When she is only a girl, her handsome but wicked
father, Lewis, is imprisoned for theft leaving Katie
and her mother homeless and penniless. Life is
hard for Katie – not only because of their poverty
but also because of the stigma of her father's
shame.

When Lewis is released years later, it seems that
life must improve. But to Katie's horror, it
becomes worse than she has ever known it. When
she and her father are left alone together, Katie
seeks happiness and love elsewhere but, as she
struggles to make a new life for herself, there is
difficulty and danger at every turn . . .

PATSY OF PARADISE PLACE

After years of neglect by her mother, when her father comes home from sea and sets up as a carrier at the Liverpool Docks, Patsy dreams of having a proper family again.

But when her father is killed in an accident and her mother returns to her errant ways, Patsy must keep the business going with the help of Billy Grant, the boy who worked with him.

Billy is deeply in love with Patsy, but she has fallen for the charismatic charms of fairground showman Bruno Alvarez and believes that he is going to marry her. One fateful night she brings him home to meet her mother who seduces him. Heartbroken but still in love with Bruno, Patsy discovers she is pregnant. Bruno has disappeared and even her own mother disowns her.

Only loyal Billy stands by here in her troubles, but when he is badly injured at work Patsy is left friendless and without a home. Will she and baby Liam ever be part of a family again?

TROUBLED WATERS

When fourteen-year-old Sara Jenkins rescues her baby sister, Myfanwy, from the fire which kills their mother, little does she realise the burden of responsibility she is taking on.

Her father, Ifor, is perceived as strict and moral by everyone in the village. But as Sara struggles to look after Myfanwy and their home she discovers the depths of cruelty he is capable of. Then Ifor remarries, and Sara's new stepmother is a hard taskmaster who considers everything Sara does inadequate or wicked.

When Sara meets Rhys Edwards, nephew of the owner of the bakery where she works, she falls in love for the first time. Finally, she believes, she has a way to escape her father. Rhys and Sara plan to make a life together in Cardiff – but Sara finds herself alone there, pregnant and destitute.

She has to face the hardest times of her life and fight for herself, Myfanwy, and her unborn child, before happiness is finally within her reach . . .

TURN OF THE TIDE

When Lucy Patterson promises her dying mother that she'll leave the comfortable home they've shared with her mother's employer, Stanley Jones, to go and live with her Aunt Flo on the other side of the Mersey, she has no idea of the terribly consequences.

Life with the Flanagans in the slums of Liverpool, and Lucy's new job in a factory, are totally different from the world she has known. Mocked by her cousins and the women she works alongside, and terrified by the brutality of her uncle and the unwelcome attentions of her cousin Frank, Lucy is desperately unhappy.

And then one day, the worst happens and Lucy finds herself homeless, friendless and destitute. It seems there's only one person in the world willing to help her. But can she break her promise to her mother? Or should she accept that there's only one place a girl in her situation can go . . . ?

TURN OF THE TIDE

When Lucy Patterson promises her dying mother that she'll leave the comfortable home they've shared with her mother's employer, Stanley Jones, to go and live with her Aunt Flo on the other side of the Mersey, she has no idea of the terribly consequences.

Life with the Flanagans in the slums of Liverpool, and Lucy's new job in a factory, are totally different from the world she has known. Mocked by her cousins and the women she works alongside, and terrified by the brutality of her uncle and the unwelcome attentions of her cousin Frank, Lucy is desperately unhappy.

And then one day, the worst happens and Lucy finds herself homeless, friendless and destitute. It seems there's only one person in the world willing to help her. But can she break her promise to her mother? Or should she accept that there's only one place a girl in her situation can go . . . ?

Order further *Rosie Harris* titles from your local
bookshop, or have them delivered direct
to your door by Bookpost

FREE POST AND PACKING
Overseas customers allow £2 per paperback

PHONE: 01624 677237

POST: Random House Books
c/o Bookpost, PO Box 29, Douglas,
Isle of Man, IM99 1BQ

FAX: 01624 670923

EMAIL: bookshop@enterprise.net

Cheques (payable to Bookpost) and credit cards accept

Prices and availability subject to change without notice
Allow 28 days for delivery
When placing your order, please state if you do not wish to receive
additional information

www.randomhouse.co.uk

Acknowledgements

My sincere thanks to Caroline Sheldon, Georgina Hawtrey-Woore, Justine Taylor, Sara Walsh and everyone else at Random House who have been so helpful and supportive.

Acknowledgements

My sincere thanks to Caroline Sheldon, Georgina Hawtrey-Woore, Justine Taylor, Sara Walsh and everyone else at Random House who have been so helpful and supportive.